SYSTEM OVERLOAD

DIVORCED MEN'S CLUB
BOOK 5

SAXON JAMES

ABOUT THIS BOOK

Keller:

Banging my son's bestie was a total accident that will never, ever happen again. I'm sure of it.

While he might be gorgeous and caught me in a weak moment, when it comes right down to it, my son has been my entire life for the last twenty-six years. I don't know how to be anything other than his dad.

But with Molly heading off to Seattle, he leaves me with a parting gift: Will.

His best friend.

And my new roommate.

Still, I'm determined to focus on my plan of finding someone to settle down with and to start living for me.

Then Molly hits me with another gift: he's asked Will to help find me the perfect partner.

Will:

Molly leaving me to run away across the country made one thing very obvious. I crave stability. I crave a life where I get to control what happens to me, without the constant threat of having to move home to my homophobic family.

All I need to focus on is work and making enough money for the downpayment on my own place.

Except now I'm living in the spare bedroom of the man I've been in love with for years.

The same bedroom where we had one very messy, very quick, accidental frot sesh.

Now I'm cooking for him every night, and we're working out together every morning. It's all feeling very domestic and my heart can't separate reality from the fantasies in my head.

I know I'm going to get hurt.

It's only a matter of time.

But when it comes to Keller, it's impossible for me to walk away.

Copyright ©

SYSTEM OVERLOAD - 2023 Saxon James

All rights reserved.

First published in Australia by May Books 2023

Newcastle, NSW, Australia

Cover design by Story Styling Cover Designs

Image supplied by Wander Aguiar

Illustrations by Tal Lewin @caravaggia13

Edited by Sandra Dee at One Love Editing and proofread by Lori Parks

No parts of this publication may be reproduced, stored in a retrieval system, or transmitted in any form or by any means, electronic, mechanical, photocopying, recording, or otherwise, without the prior written permission of the copyright owner.

This book is sold subject to the condition that it shall not, by way of trade or otherwise, be lent, resold, hired out, or otherwise circulated without the publisher's prior consent in any form of binding or cover other than that in which it is published and without a similar condition including this condition being imposed on the subsequent purchaser. Under no circumstances may any part of this book be photocopied for resale.

This is a work of fiction. Any similarity between the characters and situations within its pages and places or persons, living or dead, is unintentional and co-incidental.

PROLOGUE
TWENTY-SIX YEARS AGO

KELLER

THEY'VE ALL DEFINITELY FORGOTTEN ABOUT ME. CAN'T blame them, really. I'm just the scrawny kid in the corner, watching on as Michelle goes through the most horrific thing I've ever seen.

Having our kid.

I thought this was something I should be here for. Could feel it in my bones. But from the second I walked into this room, her parents have done just about everything to make me feel like a turd under their shoe.

Fuck them.

It's my daughter.

Umm ... coming out of *their* daughter.

I haven't even been able to get close enough to Michelle to see if she needs anything. We might only be sixteen, but I love her more than anyone or anything, and I know her parents think we're mad for going through with this, but we've done okay getting to this point.

Michelle screams, and the sound curls in my gut. Makes me cringe away from the scene slightly. My thumbnail stings from where I keep gnawing at it, and my oversized hoodie feels like it's strangling me.

Her mom is on one side, and her dad is on the other, and I'm just curled up in this hard plastic chair, feeling helpless and left out. Which is stupid. Because this moment isn't about me.

Michelle's mom kisses her hand and whispers something I can't hear before glaring daggers my way. This definitely isn't the way I'd always pictured meeting them, but they were both adamant they never wanted that to happen.

The noise calms down for a second, and I pick at the frayed edge of my jeans, wondering if I should text Mom to come and get me. Once Molly's out, they'll probably hand her off to Michelle, and I'll still be left here, craning my neck to try and catch a look at the little flesh monkey.

"Okay," Jennifer, our midwife, says, looking up from where she's positioned between Michelle's legs. "I think we're ready to go. Next contraction, I want you to push, okay?"

Whatever else is said next drains away as the room closes in around me. This is it. We're ready.

I am really, really not ready.

My gaze finds Michelle's, her brown mop of hair plastered to her face with sweat, fear in her eyes, but when I get up and take a step closer, the next contraction hits, and her dad hisses, "We've got this, Keller."

I back up into my corner, the backs of my legs bumping the chair I was curled in. My heart is pounding, and with every scream and every push, the feeling of being completely fucking overwhelmed blankets me. How did we think we could do this? How the fuck is *Michelle* doing this? She has a goddamn alien coming out of her body.

The first glimpse of hair—a *lot* of hair—makes my knees almost buckle.

"That's ... that's ... baby. *Baby*."

But of course, I'm paid exactly zero attention because Jennifer says, "That's it, almost there," and I think I might puke.

My hands are fisted in my hair, whole body leaning closer, both wanting and not wanting to see, and after what feels like the longest time in the world, there's a weird kind of *whoosh* sound, and she's out. All flailing limbs and ... not looking right. A blotchy sort of reddish purple. She's not crying either. I go cold all over before Jennifer cuts the cord and tucks Molly in close to her body.

She's smiling when she looks up. Then she says three words that change my life forever.

"Congratulations. He's beautiful."

... *he*?

I'm not completely sure I've heard Jennifer around the pounding in my ears, but Michelle's eyes fly open, and she jerks upright.

"*She*."

Jennifer shakes her head, but before she can say anything, Michelle cuts her off.

"I'm having a daughter. A girl. Molly. Where's my Molly?"

"I'm sorry if you were told differently. The scans aren't always accurate, and this wouldn't be the first mistake I've see—"

"*No.*"

I jump back at Michelle's shout.

"Get me my fucking daughter!"

Michelle's parents hurry to calm her, but it doesn't work. She breaks into tears, huge racking sobs that I can't do anything about, and just keeps calling out.

"Maybe if you hold him, that will help," her mom suggests, but fuck you, woman, she's not getting my kid like this.

Thankfully, I don't have to jump in because Michelle shrieks.

"Get it away from me. I don't want it. That's not my baby." I can feel her sobs in my chest. "I want my baby."

All I can do is stare. Shocked at what I'm seeing as the girl I love with my whole heart completely loses control. I don't even notice Jennifer take Molly over to a table and be replaced by another midwife until Michelle's father approaches them.

"I'll take the child," he says.

But Jennifer turns and looks at me. "Would Dad like a hold?"

Dad. That's *me*. Fuck.

My nod is slow but gets faster. "Yeah, please."

I'm shaking as I hold out my hands, and Jennifer helps me position my arms right.

"S-should he be that color?" I ask, even though he's a lot pinker now.

"Totally normal."

"Isn't he supposed to cry or something?"

"Not always."

The baby—my *son*, fuck—lets out this warbled little noise like he's trying to cry but doesn't know how.

Michelle's still sobbing hard in the background, but the second I see his face, no one else in the world exists anymore. He's got two fingers curled out of the blanket Jennifer wrapped him in, and, heart in my throat, I reach up to stroke them.

Tears immediately prick at my eyes.

He weighs nothing. Looks like a red blob. Has a squishy face. And my heart explodes. I'm crying before I know it, huge, stupid, dumb tears that I try to muffle into my shoulder while Jennifer rubs the other one.

I settle enough to gasp out, "Is he supposed to be this small? Is something wrong with him?"

Jennifer laughs, but it sounds kind. Like maybe she's had that question a lot of times. "No, honey. Nothing's wrong. He's early, so he's on the smaller side, but six pound one is perfectly normal."

I release a shaky breath. "Thank you."

"Of course." She glances over her shoulder at Michelle and her parents. "I'm going to give you all some privacy and have someone come and talk to your girlfriend. If they give you any trouble, hit the call button, and I'll be right in."

"Thanks."

"Congratulations, Dad."

"Shit. That's so weird."

"I bet." She casts her eyes over me, but at least *she* doesn't seem to be judging me. "I know he wasn't what you were expecting, but did you talk about boy names?"

"No. As soon as Michelle found out it was a girl, she already had the name."

"It kinda sounds like you get to pick his, then."

I can barely pull my eyes away from his face. The tiny

nose. The fat cheeks. I go through a list of boy's names in my head, but none of them feel right.

When I look at him, all I see is Molly.

That's who he's been to me for the past few months, and while I'd thought I'd be holding a daughter right now, it doesn't make any difference to me. But the name is what I've always called him, what he's heard my voice murmuring to him. Changing it doesn't sit right, and ... well, maybe if we keep the name, it'll make it easier on Michelle to come around.

"His name's Molly," I finally say.

She's clearly surprised but doesn't fight me on it. "Okay. I'll be back shortly. Bye, Molly."

I collapse back into my chair, Molly held close, smelling like whatever the fuck it is babies smell like—blood and guts, I guess.

The other midwife helps Michelle get out the placenta, but I hardly notice. It's not until she goes that I remember there are other people in the room with me. So I clear my throat and do the very last thing I want to do.

"Does anyone want to hold him?"

"Not now," Michelle's dad snaps.

That's fine by me.

Now I have Molly, no one's ever going to take him from me.

Ever.

1

KELLER

ONE THING I'D NEVER EXPECTED ABOUT BEING A DAD WAS not only being responsible for my son but all his friends too. Or, more specifically, his *best* friend. They're inseparable, which means he's as much a part of my life as my son is, and yet, I *still* didn't see this moment coming.

Will Freeman is wasted. I have no idea what prompted him to go out and get wrecked tonight, but I'm glad he picked the same club I was at. This way, I get to look after him.

He groans as I carry him upstairs, the house dark since I didn't stop to turn on the lights. He's heavy, all those bulky muscles making him a solid weight in my arms, but he just keeps snuggling into me like a cat.

I almost want to snap a pic of him for Molly. Will's been my son's best friend since college and a constant in my life since then. He's a fun guy, and I'm so glad they have each other, but even on nights the two of them have gone out together, I've never seen Will like this.

I shoulder open the door to my spare room, sending it banging against the doorstop as I stumble inside and almost drop him onto the bed. Will doesn't let go of me though, and I follow, crushing him to the mattress.

"Shit, sorry," I laugh, trying to pull away, but he holds on tighter, arms wrapping around my shoulders and keeping my body an inch from his.

"So snuggly ..." Will mutters, low and drunk. Then his tongue slips out and drags over my bare chest.

Fuck. A flash of heat shoots through me that I definitely shouldn't be feeling, and this time, I manage to pry Will's arms from around me.

"Okay, okay," I relent, climbing over him and avoiding his grasping hands. "You're drunk. You just need to sleep it off."

"Need to sleep you off."

I flick on the lamp beside the bed in case he needs it later. "If you knew what you were saying ..."

Will's a sweetheart. Easily embarrassed, low-key flirty, and hot as fuck.

But since he's Molly's, it puts him firmly out of bounds, even if his brain wasn't swimming in vodka. The hand reaching for me drops as he lets out a monstrous snore.

I'd gone out tonight to find a hookup and found him instead, but the really shocking part is that I'm not all that disappointed. Something's changing with me. It started when I turned forty and has been getting worse the closer I get to Molly moving across the country. Even when he was away at college, I always knew he'd be back, for visits home and then after graduation. It was never a question.

This time, he's moving, and it might be for good.

I have no idea if Will is planning to go with him. And with the two of them gone ... fuck. I'll still have my friends, but they're different. Molly's my whole family, and Will is ... *Will*. I've gotten used to having him around.

With them gone, I have no one.

That thought is pretty fucking lonely.

"Kel ..."

I spring toward Will like he's got me under a spell, and this time, I crouch next to him. He's sweaty, blond hair sticking out all over the place, and I reach up to brush it back from his forehead.

"I got you," I tell him.

A shadow of a smile crosses his lips as he leans into my touch. "Stay with me."

"Will ..."

"Please. I don't feel so good."

"I'm not surprised. Why did you drink so much?"

He grumbles incoherently. "'M'a lightweight."

"I'll say." I stand to kick off my shoes, flick off the lamp again, and climb onto the bed beside him. Almost as soon as I've lain down, he rolls toward me and passes out again.

The next thing I know is the bed shifting, and I jerk awake.

Will's climbing back in.

"You okay?" I croak.

"Yeah ..." He shifts closer. "Embarrassed though."

I laugh and roll onto my side, blinking away the sleepy fog trying to pull me back under. "What's embarrassing about licking my chest?"

"I fucking what?"

I grab him before he can sit up again. "Relax. You sound a lot better now."

"I've gotta admit, I wish I wasn't."

He's so fucking cute sometimes. "So why did you get like that? It's not normal for you."

"I, uh ..." His deep voice crosses the darkness between us. "Was feeling a bit down."

"Shit, Will. Why?"

"Just hurting over something."

I hate that. Hate that Will could hurt over anything. He's the kind of guy who was made to be happy. Always. I have my theories on what could be wrong: his shitty family being top of that list and Molly moving being another contender. "I'm so sorry."

"Yeah ... okay."

"Hey." I reach out, finding his arm and giving it a comforting squeeze. "Whatever it is, you'll figure it out. And I'm here."

"Are you though?"

"Of course." I frown at the bitterness in his tone. He might have started as Molly's friend, but Will's around a lot, and I'd like to think we've built our own relationship outside of my son. I press up onto my elbow, even though I can't actually see him, and lean closer, wanting him to know I'm serious. "I care about you, and I'll always be in your corner."

His exhale is loud. "You care about me?"

"Isn't that obvious?"

He shifts closer, and then he surprises the shit out of me when his fingers trail over my chest. "Thank you."

His words are as strangled as my lungs feel. I know I'm supposed to say something, but I can't move on from where he's still touching me. Pulses of heat are spreading from his fingertips, lighting up my gut and traveling south.

My body doesn't care that it's Will next to me. All I'm aware of is that it's dark and it's late and a man is touching me in a completely unfamiliar way.

I'm used to sexually charged hookups. Not ... this. Not *gentle*.

He props himself up beside me, so close his breath puffs over my lips.

"Will ..."

I hear him swallow as his fingers move lower. Through my chest hair to my abs. A spear of lust shoots from my gut to my balls, and my cock thickens the closer he gets.

"What are you doing?" I whisper.

"Do you want me to stop?"

Yes. That's the only right answer here. But I'm hard, and he's so close, and I'd be lying if I said I wasn't attracted to him. "You're drunk" is what I try for instead.

His nose bumps mine. "Not anymore."

"We ... we ..."

His fingers reach the waistband of my shorts. Skim the hair covering my lower abs and then pop the top button.

My cock throbs.

Will's shaky breath shivers over my skin. Then he says one word that completely smashes my resolve to pieces. *"Please."*

How do I deny him after that? I roll on top of him, crushing his body beneath me. His hard length slots against mine, and even through our clothes, it feels indescribable. I barely know what I'm doing as I rut against him, caught up in the high, in the drive, the need. Will grips my ass, moving against me, and even though I want to pause to strip off our clothes, I'm scared to stop. For reality to hit.

All I know is his hard body, his deep groans, and the way he's lighting up every nerve in my body. My moan mixes with his heavy pants. Everything is broken and distorted. Just sound and heat propelling us along. It doesn't feel real. I can't stop. My cock is painfully hard, loving the friction, but it's nowhere near enough. I need him naked. Need to feel his skin under my lips.

But I can't stop from driving my hips into his. Harder, faster. Loving how his strong legs grip me. How he rasps my name. How he smells so familiar, and even though this is hot as fuck, there's something comforting swelling in my chest.

"I'm ... I'm close," he gasps.

Fuck. I want that. I want it so much. Want us both to reach that point and tumble over the edge together, but then it will be over, and I can't tell if I want this to last forever or if I want relief more.

My balls are aching. Each pass of his hard dick pressed against mine is incredible. Then Will leans up and tugs my nipple between his teeth. It sparks a roll of desire that sweeps from my head all the way to my toes, and my fingers curl into the sheets.

"Will ..." I drop my face to his neck, drowning in the smell of his skin as I can't hold back anymore. I shudder against him, balls finally releasing their load into my boxers as Will's grip on my ass tightens.

"Yes ... fuck, yes." He arches upward, pressing us together, holding on for dear life.

A shudder passes through him, all the way out to his limbs, and then he slumps back against the bed, and I follow him. I'm boneless, unable to think, let alone process what the hell just happened.

I fall into a haze of relaxation, maybe even drift off at one point, but his voice brings me back to a very harsh reality.

"Keller ..."

The familiarity in his tone has me jerking back. "Will."

"That ... was that okay?"

I hate that he sounds so vulnerable. I reach over him to switch on the lamp, and the light flooding the room is a mistake. His hair's a mess, eyes bloodshot but focused, tan skin flushed red. It's a glimpse of Will, raw and sated, and I hate how much I like it. But this was a giant fucking mistake, and as hot as that was, it can't happen again.

The longer I don't say anything though, the more disappointment sets over his features.

It kills me to see him look like that.

"Hey ..." I tilt his face back toward me. "That was amazing. Unexpected, but ... wow."

He almost smiles. "Really?"

I laugh. "I don't know if you know this, but you're hot as fuck."

"Umm, thanks. You too."

I'm old is what I am, but I'm not about to bring that up. Especially since what I'm about to ask of him is goddamn shitty of me. "But ..."

His face falls again. "You regret it?"

"No. Definitely not. I want that to be super clear. You're Molly's friend though, and—"

"Fuck."

"Yeah."

"*Fuck.*"

I laugh again. "So, you agree? We weren't thinking. It happened. It was amazing, but it can't happen again."

"Yeah." Will looks away. "Not again."

"And we *can't* tell him."

"Of course not."

There's something off about his tone. "Tell me I didn't fuck up here?"

His eyes fly wide, and he rolls toward me, already shaking his head. "No way. I wanted that. I *started* that. You were perfect."

"Perfect seems excessive," I say, relief flooding through me. "But thanks for the ego boost."

He sighs, and I can't help reaching out, cupping his jaw, thumbs stroking his cheek. "I'd hate myself if this changes things between us."

"No." Will covers my hand with his. "It won't. I promise. It'll be like it never happened."

2

WILL

I WILL NEVER RECOVER. I WILL NEVER FORGET.

Last night ... it happened. Actually happened. No matter what I told Keller, this changes so much because I will never get the sound of his raw, needy grunts out of my head.

He makes me breakfast to soak up the alcohol, but I feel better than I ever have in my life. No hangover, just the dull buzz of a phenomenal orgasm and the chance to spend an hour with him one-on-one. I've never had this before, and I crave it.

His black hair is pulled into a messy bun on his head, scruff dark and thick, bronzed skin gleaming in the morning sunlight filling his kitchen. It's all wood cabinetry and dark granite countertops, and something about this space has always felt homely. Like him. Keller moves around the room, telling me about his week at work, dishcloth tucked into his faded jeans, and just acting exactly like he always has.

It's like it never happened.

We both know it did.

Only hours ago, he was rubbing that impressive body against mine, unknowingly making years of fantasies come to life.

After breakfast, Keller gives me a lift home. He pulls up to the curb out the front of where I live with Molly and glances across the center console at me.

"You okay?"

I have the feeling he means more than about the hangover.

I give him the most convincing smile I can manage. "Yeah. Absolutely no complaints from me."

He laughs before he can stop himself, but when I go to climb out, his hand lands on my thigh. "I know it's shitty of me to ask, but please, please don't tell him."

"Molly?" I shake my head, cheeks getting all hot. "I don't want him mad at me either. I get it. It happened, it won't again, and we'll never even bring it up."

Keller lets go, but even through his sunglasses, I can feel him studying me. "Yeah, okay ..."

"I'll catch you later."

"See you."

I'm out of the car before he can stew on it anymore. The thing is, Keller's a really fucking good guy—it's one of the reasons I'm so head over heels in love with him, and what happened between us last night is more than I ever dared to hope for. Molly's his priority, and the fact that slipped, even for such a short time, means everything to me. I know it's not on the cards for us again, but I'll carry that moment with me forever.

Because I'm not in a hurry to hurt my best friend either.

It's why I've kept my crush to myself. Why I've smothered it down for years. It's hurt, been painful sometimes, hence me drinking too much last night, but Molly is as good as family to me. We bonded quickly in college, and on that first break, when he'd suggested I come back to Kilborough with him instead of heading home to my homophobic family, I knew I'd do anything for him.

And that anything doesn't involve his dad.

"Where the hell have you been?" he asks the second I walk inside.

Considering I thought he'd still be asleep, he catches me off guard. "Got embarrassingly wasted last night to the point your dad had to rescue me."

Molly's mouth drops, and he blinks big eyes up at me. "Umm ... what?"

I fall onto the couch. "Let me die of shame without reliving it, thanks."

But I know him better than that. He leaves the kitchen and jumps on the couch beside me. His floppy brown hair is flat on one side, like he's only just gotten out of bed. "You got *drunk*? You?"

"I know."

"Wow. Wish I'd seen that." He gives me a lopsided grin, and I roll my eyes at him.

"I hated every second, thanks."

"I bet. I can't believe *my dad* saved you."

"Least he didn't make me feel like more of an idiot than I already did."

Molly hums and looks me over, something *off* filling his gaze. "He's good like that."

"You're so lucky to have him."

"Yeah. I know." Molly jumps up like he's suddenly done with the conversation. "Come help me pack?"

"That'll only remind me that you're leaving."

He gives me a small smile, almost looking like he used to before he fell into this funk he's going through. "I'm leaving either way."

"You make me sad."

His gaze drops to the ground. "Lots of things make me sad. But I'm hoping Seattle changes that."

"And ..." I know I shouldn't ask the question because his answer hurts every time. "You really don't need me to come?"

He sags like he was waiting for me to ask. "I need to do this on my own."

I remind myself that I have to respect that decision, even if it puts me in an awkward place. Without him here, I can't afford our rent, and unless something affordable miraculously shows up, I'm going to be moving back home. With my parents.

"Hey," he says, injecting some life back into his voice. "At least you get to keep everything we bought together. When you find your own place, you won't need to buy a thing."

"It's just finding my own place that's going to be the issue."

"I'm telling you, you should move in with Dad. You can keep each other company, and he has the space."

And even though my answer is still a no, after last night, I know there's no way in hell Keller would want that either. "And I've told *you*: if he offers himself, I'll think about it."

Thank god I'll never have to though.

"I LEAVE IN TWO WEEKS," MOLLY HISSES ACROSS THE TABLE at me.

I glance around the busy restaurant, trying to avoid his eye. "And?"

"You haven't worked out anything."

"Sure I have. My parents said there's room there for me." Reluctantly. And I wouldn't at all be surprised if the room is a tin shack they've put together in the backyard.

"We both know it'll be a nightmare."

"Well, I don't have much—"

"Hey, guys," comes a deep, familiar voice from behind me. "Sorry, I got caught up with work."

Keller takes the third seat at the table, and all my annoyance funnels away as a rushing sound fills my ears. I've been avoiding him since I spent the night at his place, and I was hoping I could leave Kilborough completely without having to set eyes on him again.

Because holy fuck, he looks good. His knee is hovering right by mine under the table, and I have no idea how I can be so hyperaware of something that means sweet fuck all to him. He hardly even glances my way before directing a smile at Molly.

"You already miss me, don't you?" he teases.

I want to answer with a solid yes, but I keep my jaw clamped tight. Just being in his presence is reminding me of how much I do miss him, how bad it's going to be when I move, and the ache building in my chest is something I could have done without today.

Molly conveniently didn't tell me that Keller was gonna

be here, which has me on guard. He's never hidden Keller joining us before.

"I will," Molly pouts. "I'm going to miss you both."

"Aww, but we'll visit you," I tell him.

Molly snorts. "Good luck getting Dad on a plane."

"Hey, I could do it," Keller says defiantly. "Probably."

I laugh, and the gorgeous bastard sends me a cheeky wink. It reaches deep into my gut and knocks me off center, making me want to ask him to do it again and again.

"I'm so worried you're going to be lonely without me, Papa Bear," Molly says.

Keller gives him a bemused look. "Who's the parent here?"

"Speaking of parents ..." Molly flicks me a look, and I'm suddenly all too aware of what's about to happen.

"Ah, Molly—"

"Will's moving back in with his! It's going to be horrible, Dad. They don't love him like we do."

Oh.

Holy.

Fuck.

No.

Keller's head snaps around toward me. "You're *moving*?"

"Surprise?"

"I thought you were trying to find somewhere to stay here?"

"I was, and I failed."

"So you're *both* leaving me?"

It's hard to meet his eyes. "It's not like I wanna go."

"So stay."

"And be homeless?"

"Fuck." Keller shifts back from the table, and at least seeing him look annoyed about the situation helps feed that stupid lovesick part of my brain.

"Dad has a spare room," Molly says softly.

He's staring at his water glass, but there's no way he could be unaware that his words have brought me and Keller to a standstill.

"No, I couldn't ..." Even if I really, really wanted to.

Molly shrugs and looks up at his dad. "You don't want him to go, and I don't want him to go, so ..."

Keller thinks it over for way too long to be comfortable. I try to brush it off again, but he shakes his head, and when those dark eyes meet mine, my brain goes offline.

"The room's yours if you want it." His lips twitch. "I'm okay with it ... if you are."

He doesn't need to clarify. Even saying that much with Molly *right there* is a risk. But I'm following. If I'm okay to go on pretending like nothing happened between us, then so is he.

"Are you sure?" I don't even want to ask it. Wanna just tell him no and head home and pretend like I'm totally fine with that outcome. But home is the last place I wanna be, and even though living with Keller is my idea of a goddamn nightmare, I'll do it if it means I get to stay in Kilborough.

Keller grins. "Been a while since I had a roommate. Good idea, Mols."

Molly looks from his dad to me, but his smile doesn't reach all the way into his eyes. "Hey, with each other for company, you might even forget to miss me."

"There's no way."

"What he said." Keller nods my way. "I could never forget you, bub."

Molly hurries to pick up his menu. "Ready to order?"

I get the feeling that's not what he wants to say at all, but when I glance over at Keller to see if he's picked up on anything, I find him looking my way, expression soft.

The butterflies in my gut are out of control.

I'm finding it impossible to believe this might actually be happening.

And terrified for the day that it does.

3

KELLER

"I OFFICIALLY HATE TODAY," MOLLY WHINES, DROPPING A box into the spare bedroom of my house. It's a room I pretend doesn't exist since Molly left for college and then cleared it out when he got a place of his own. It's still the same blue color I painted it when we moved in here all those years ago, only faded. And now that I've done things with Will I refuse to think about in here, it's hard for me to be standing across from my son right by where it happened.

"At least that's the last of it," Will says, following Molly into his now bedroom. Nerves skitter across my gut at the sight of him in my house. This room. Knowing that he's staying and not disappearing again in an hour. I don't regret what happened between us, but it had been a whole lot easier to ignore when we didn't see each other.

And now we'll be seeing more of each other than ever because Molly somehow got me to offer Will my spare room.

The idea had been easy enough, especially if it meant keeping Will in town and not back with his parents. Faced with it actually happening now, though, has me questioning what the hell I was thinking. And not only because of what happened between us—I don't know how to live with someone. Molly left for college eight years ago, and other than the few holidays and breaks when he was at home, I've been running things solo.

I'm going to do everything I can to hide it though. The last thing I want is for Will to feel like a pity invite—even if he sort of was—because there's nothing worse than bouncing from place to place, worried about when you're going to have to pack everything up again. I had enough of that when I was younger and raising Molly, and Will's at the age where he should be building his life. I want that for him.

Those first few years of raising Molly on my own were a struggle. Michelle disappeared on us, and my parents couldn't afford to support me and my baby, so I left school and got a job. A shitty job. But I worked my ass off, and as soon as I could afford it, I went back to study and jumped through all the hoops in front of me to get into the police force.

It would have been so much easier to do all that with a place to call my own, so I refuse to let what happened prevent me from giving Will a chance at stability.

"Who would have thought you had so much stuff?" I tease Will, looking around at all the boxes.

"Those two big ones are my computers," he says. "And I've got some office stuff over there. I thought I'd set up in the corner—"

"In your bedroom?" That's not ideal. "There's a room next door not being used. Turn that into an office."

"I don't wanna take over your whole house." His voice gets louder the more indignant he is, and his Southern accent gets stronger. It's adorable, but I refuse to linger on that.

"I've already told you it's your place too. None of this *your* house business."

"But—"

"*Will.*" I laugh because he's too polite. From a glance, you'd pick him for this obnoxious frat boy, but he's only ever been a total sweetheart around here. "The room is empty. It's been empty for years. What's the point in not using it?"

His uncertain gaze flies to Molly, who shrugs.

"I won't be living here."

Will's tan cheeks darken, and his gaze drops to the timber floor. "Okay. Thanks."

"Good." I bring my hands together. "Now, let's eat." I'm fucking starving because skipping lunch will do that to you. Between moving Will into the house, putting Molly's stuff on the back of a truck, and then dropping everything he's not taking into Goodwill, we haven't stopped.

"I might head out," Molly says.

My head snaps toward him. "What? I thought you were leaving in the morning."

"Plans change, Dad." He looks up at me with an unimpressed pout on his face. "Besides, you'll both be fine without me."

I step forward and yank him into a hug. His head tucks neatly under mine, and I miss this. Having him here. "We might be fine, but that doesn't mean it won't be hard having you so far away."

"Please, you'll barely notice I'm gone."

"I raised you to be smarter than that."

He gives a skeptical hum, and it breaks my heart. Over the last few months, Molly's been pulling away. Closing off. I hate that the always happy kid I raised has turned into someone so deeply unhappy.

"Promise me one thing," I say, stepping back and holding his shoulders. His mop of brown hair falls over his forehead like Michelle's used to. "Promise this move will be good for you, that you'll take advantage of this new start. Stop worrying about boys, and focus on yourself for a bit."

"I promise."

I'm not sure I believe him.

Will cuts in and tackles Molly in a hug. "I'm going to miss you so much. You have to call every few days, at minimum. I want to hear everything about Seattle, and maybe when you're settled in, I can come and visit."

"That sounds good."

But again, the enthusiasm isn't there, and I hate that.

"Sure you won't stay for dinner?" I'm not above begging, but it won't get me anywhere.

Which is confirmed when Molly says, "It's okay, I'll get something on the way to the hotel."

"Hotel?"

"I booked the one by the airport earlier so I can get up and shower, then go. Madden's meeting me at Sea-Tac, so I don't want to risk missing my flight."

Wow. Okay. This is it, then. It's not like Molly's never left before, but every time, we've known when we'll see each other again. If he got into trouble, home was only a couple of hours away. Now ... Seattle could be permanent, and while I'll accept that if it's good for him, it doesn't make me worry any less.

"You all right, kid?"

His gaze flicks to Will and away again. "I'm fine." He's not fine, but he smiles anyway. "I'm glad you'll both have each other while I'm gone. Look after him, Will."

"Hey," I say, pretending to take offense. "Shouldn't it be the other way around?"

"Nah, you'll definitely miss me more."

"I dunno," Will says. "I'm gonna miss you a whole lot."

The way he doesn't hold back thoughts like that is one of the reasons I like Will. It's also one of the reasons I thought he and Molly were dating when I first met him, but thank *fuck* that wasn't the case. They're too ... mismatched for each other.

It's ten minutes later that Molly's car arrives, and he pulls his backpack on. I get one last hug, an "I'll call you when I get there," and then ... he's gone.

I'm left standing on my front porch, staring at the road, worry for him burning in my bones.

When Will touches my shoulder, I jump.

"Shit, sorry," he says.

I wave him off. "I thought I had until the morning."

"Me too. I'm gonna miss him so much."

"You and me both. We just have to remember he's trying. Hopefully, this move will bring his spark back." There's nothing worse than seeing your kid struggling and not being able to fix it for them.

Will's lips turn down. "Are you sure he doesn't care about me moving in?"

"He's the one who suggested it." I continue before Will does his whole charity-case act again. "And it was a brilliant idea that I don't regret."

"Good. Because if I ever get annoying, you've gotta tell

me. I'd be so embarrassed to find out one day that you'd been wanting me gone for weeks."

"I promise that won't happen." Because while I might not be sure about how to do the considerate roommate thing, I do know that I'll never reach a point where I'm dying for him to get lost.

"I've, uh ... Joey mentioned he'd have a room in August. So just a few months before I'm gone anyway."

"What?"

Will messes with the ball cap he's wearing. "I just thought ... you know, since ... well, after what happened, I thought it was probably smart."

"Hey." I wait for him to look at me. "No more of that. We agreed it didn't change anything, and it doesn't. Nothing's changed on my end, and I told you the room is yours for as long as you want it—I wasn't bullshitting you."

Will's smile is infectious. "Want dinner?"

I nod and follow him inside.

"Just grab a seat and leave it to me," he says. "This can be my thank-you for letting me move in. What's your favorite dish?"

"My favorite?"

Will cocks his head, fridge door half-open, and waits.

I laugh. "Anything I don't have to cook is my favorite."

"Well, in that case, dinner's on me most nights. I like cooking."

"Even better because I usually work too late to be bothered."

Will's face falls. "Dinner's too important to skip, Kel."

The nickname catches me off guard, my gut swimming as it brings back inappropriate memories of him begging me to stay with him.

"Don't worry, I've got you. We'll make sure you're good and fed every day of the week. You're *so* lucky to have me."

Even though he's joking, it's true. If he wasn't here, I'd probably have spent my night sulking. Dinner and company is a huge step up from that.

And when he bends over to grab some dishes from the cupboard, I'm not complaining about the eye candy either.

DMC GROUP CHAT

Keller: *I'm officially roommate-d.*
Orson: *Congratulations!*
Art: *IS this a 'congratulations' moment?*
Keller: *Jury is still out on that*
Orson: *Well I'm choosing to be positive about it.*
Griff: *That's because you're positive about everything. Regular sex makes people happy.*
Art: *Except when it's you and it just makes you more horny.*
Griff: *What can I say? Heath keeps up with me.*
Keller: *As always, this conversation has been fun.*
Orson: *You should know by now that this isn't the place for an existential crisis.*
Art: *Existential crisis? I thought we were talking about his roommate's D?*
Keller: *Is anyone's D off the table for you?*
Art: *You offering?*

4

WILL

My cheeks feel slapped raw as I jog up the front stairs and kick off my boots. It's been a great start to spring, but this wind has kicked up out of nowhere, and it isn't playing nice, which is what prompted the late drive to Joey's to help him board up a window that a branch blew into.

And while cleaning up glass isn't my favorite way to spend an evening, it was better than sitting around this big house, trying not to remember what happened between me and Keller.

In theory, moving in with my best friend's dad to save on rent and utilities sounded like a dream. It also got me out of having to move back home where my family are ... religious. They've never outright condemned me, but after I came out, things changed. Whenever I visit, the tension is so thick it's suffocating.

Living there would probably kill me.

Though I'm not so sure living here will be any better.

Because while my bank balance will thank me, my heart will not.

Serves me right for going and falling for Molly's dad.

When he invited me to come and stay with him, I'd been picturing nights in front of the TV, shirtless yard work, and running into him in only a towel in the hall. The reality has been so much different and kinda makes me think I should watch less roommate porn.

In August, my friend Joey's sister will be leaving for college, and I'll be able to move in with him, and while I'd love to stay living here indefinitely, I know by the time I finally leave, I'll be walking outta here heartbroken.

The only thing worse than loving Keller from afar will be loving him up close and having to give it up again.

I walk inside, straining my ears for any hint of life, but the house is dark and still. I think for a moment that Keller must be out—and try not to obsess over what he's out doing—but after kicking off my shoes and approaching the living area, I find a soft glow coming from inside.

Keller's on the couch, feet propped on the coffee table, short glass half-full of a dark liquid in one hand and pen in the other. He's also blindingly, incredibly shirtless.

"You're home," he says. His deep rumble is low, almost swallowed by the wind rattling the windows.

"Just helping Joey with something." I know I should take the spare couch across from him, but, nerves almost sickening, I flop down into the soft leather beside him instead. My heart is hammering like a motherfucker, but Keller shoots me a grin and tilts his crossword my way.

"Stuck on four down."

"What is it?"

"Software menu option. Like, what does that even mean? I'm not a computer expert."

I try not to laugh, but the lines over his forehead are adorable. "You know how you open a program on your computer, and it has those options across the top? That's the menu toolbar. Software's just a fancy name for program."

Understanding fills his face. "Okay, now I feel stupid. I'm sure I knew that."

"Still haven't got the answer though, have you?"

"Nope." He takes a sip of his drink. "Brain won't brain."

I eye what's probably scotch and reach over to take the crossword from him. "Wonder why."

"Hey! You did not just take another man's crossword puzzle."

I pluck the pen from his grip, too, and jot down *H-E-L-P*.

When I look up, he's staring at me. "I can't believe you just did that."

I snigger. "I can't believe you're sitting here at night, alone, and doing a crossword."

He nudges me. "Not alone now."

"You know what I mean." I toss the booklet on the table, and Keller picks it back up again.

"What's the alternative? Sitting here by myself doing nothing?"

"Most people watch TV."

"Ah. So if it was a TV and not a book, it'd be acceptable?"

"If it was literally anything other than an old-person hobby, it'd be acceptable."

Keller groans and flops back against the couch, dramatically reaching for the ceiling. "What's the world come to that I can't even enjoy downtime in my own home?"

Even though I know he's joking, he's got a point. Maybe my teasing was too much. This *is* his home, after all. "Sorry."

He looks over at me, easy smile settled on his face. "For?"

"Making you uncomfortable. Of course you can do whatever you want. It's your home. I didn't mean—"

"Jesus, Will." He whacks my thigh with the booklet. "I don't give a shit. You think a little teasing is going to make me all insecure about a fucking crossword?"

I shift, suddenly very aware of how close we're sitting. "Sorry. Just still, you know, trying not to overstep. I don't want to be a pain."

"A *pain*?"

"I'm being mindful that this is your place, and I don't wanna come in here and mess everything up."

This time, Keller drops the crossword booklet onto the table and turns to face me, one knee propped on the couch and resting close to my thigh. "But that's exactly what I want you to do. When I told you this is your home now, I wasn't kidding. I don't want you to feel like a guest here. That room is yours as long as you want it." His expression softens, and I'm a puddle at what that does to me. Keller's voice comes out all low and scratchy. "It's sort of nice to have someone living here again."

"It is?" It's sad and pathetic how much I perk up at hearing that.

"Yeah. Don't tell Molly, but I've been getting lonely. Seeing my friends start to settle down and with Molly off living his life in Seattle, it's ..." He huffs a laugh, scraping a hand down his face. "It's making me feel old."

I almost fall off the couch. "*Old?*"

"I'm forty-two now. Mols is all grown up, and I'm looking at the second half of my life and going *what next?*" He waves my concern—and honestly, shock—away. "You're still young. You'll understand one day."

"I might be young, but I'm not stupid. You're not old. You're cool and fit and successful." And *hot*. "Old is the last word I'd think to call you."

"You *really* are good for my ego."

I'd be good for his ego anytime he wanted.

"No more old talk," I say instead. Then I bite down on my tongue, trying to keep my questions to myself, but I'm far too nosy for that. "So what *is* next?"

Keller scrapes back his messy hair. "I think ... I think I want to start dating."

All the happy, sweet, wonderful nerves plummet at that. "Dating. Wow. I don't think you've been on a date in all the time I've known you."

"Yeah, I've always kept things casual. Never had that itch for someone permanent and to settle down." And like he's just remembered what happened between us, he adds, "Is it okay that we're talking about this?"

"Of course." Because it might hurt, but I want Keller to be able to talk to me about anything. "I hear roommates are supposed to do deep and meaningfuls at 10:00 p.m. while the wind is attempting a break and enter."

"Yeah, it's getting loud out there."

"So ..." I swallow, both wanting and not wanting to get back to the conversation. "What's your type?"

"Don't have one. I just need that vibe, you know. The feeling that when we talk and hang out, things are easy. We click. Attraction is important, obviously, but even the hottest person can be a solid no for me if they're a complete asshole." Then he completely surprises me by asking the same question. "What's your type?"

You. Obviously I'm not gonna tell him that, but since I met him, I haven't looked twice at another man. I've had empty hookups that have only left me feeling frustrated and down afterward, because whether he wants it or not, Keller owns my heart.

There are some days I wish I could ask for it back.

There are others where the pain is the greatest feeling I've ever experienced.

"I'll let you know if I ever find him," I say.

Then Keller's dark eyes flick up to meet mine, and for a whole second, I swear he *knows*. Just looks at me and reads it straight from my brain. He's the most sexy man I've ever met, but when Keller looks at me, with complete, one hundred percent attention, it's not even about appearance.

It's just him.

And the way he doesn't even realize he's my whole world.

5

KELLER

"Make it a double shot," I tell the barista before tapping my card and moving aside to let the person behind me order.

It's a busy day for the Killer Brew cafe, and the morning sun is weak but promising. People are sitting at the outdoor chairs and tables, while beyond them, others jog or ride bikes or walk in groups along the boardwalk. It might actually be a warm spring day. Which I'll be spending cooped up in my office.

As a private investigator, I assumed my workload in a small town would be minimal, but in the last few years, it's really started to ramp up. I've built a name for myself, and while I try to keep the majority of the jobs I accept close to home, the occasional case will pull me out to Springfield or even all the way to Boston if I'm interested enough.

I've seen some pretty shitty things done by some pretty

shitty people, but I know I'm making a difference. It helps me sleep at night, and those cases tend to be few and far between. Insurance jobs and background checks tend to be my most common contracts, along with the semiregular requests by Nevele Ounces. Working for myself also comes with a thousand percent less stress than when I was working in the police force.

Someone nudges me from the side, and I glance over to find Orson watching me.

"Lost in thought?" he asks.

"Ehh, not much thoughts happening pre-coffee."

He laughs, hazel eyes creasing at the corners. "This will already be my second. Ford woke me for, uh—well, when he was leaving for work, so I went into the shop early and set up."

Could he be any less subtle about the fact he had sex this morning? Some days, it feels like everyone is out there living their best lives except me. The restlessness is getting stronger, and I don't know what it is I'm looking for, but there's a deep drive in my gut telling me to keep moving, keep looking until that click I told Will about happens. So far, he's the only person I've even spoken to about that—yet another point in the lucky-to-have-him column.

I knew in my gut that him moving in was the right move, and I've learned to always listen to that feeling.

"How's the roommate going?"

"Truthfully, I've been working a lot, so we don't cross paths often, but he's neat, and if I work late, there's always dinner waiting." I smile at the memory of hanging out last night. "It's sort of nice to know someone else is existing in that space. It was starting to feel too big."

"I can understand that. Will seems like a good kid."

I snort. "He's twenty-seven. He stopped being a kid a good ten years ago." A fact I'm way too aware of.

"Wow, okay, I'm suddenly feeling my age."

Him and me both. I've never looked at myself and thought I was old; I don't feel any different to how I did ten, twenty years ago. But I can't deny that being in my forties has changed my perspective on things, and given the average life expectancy, my time is half-up. I've done a lot of things I'm proud of, my son being the biggest and best of them all, but ... what if that's it? What if the next forty years are just me working and gardening and hanging out at Killer Brew with my friends, week on week, right up until I die? It's not a terrible life, but I'm craving more. I'm craving someone to share it with.

"Do you and Ford have ... plans?" I ask.

"What do you mean?"

"Well, you're living together now. What next?"

"Personally, I'm just hoping for happiness. After losing Tara, I've had all the excitement I can take in life. We might go traveling at some point, but my only concrete plans are making him happy, and I'm pretty sure he feels the same way about me."

"That's cool. What about kids?"

"Not for us. But also, we're looking at opening a second mechanics shop," he drops like it's nothing. "They're too busy to meet demand, and Taylor's really stepped up. Ford's thinking about asking them to run it for him."

"Wow. Congrats."

"Early stages, but we'll see."

It's still something to look forward to. Something they're doing together, getting excited about and planning for. Most of what I've always done has revolved around Molly. How to provide for him. How to give him what he needs. How to get him safely through high school and into a good college. I loved that time of my life. I miss it.

Now, I have to think of *me*, and me doesn't know what the fuck is going on. I'm a real adult.

My order is called, and I grab it, then say bye to Orson and head out. The majority of Kilborough is clustered around the boardwalk and main street. It might be a small town, but with winter behind us, the tourists are starting to appear, and business will grow steadily until October, when we get hit hard. Ghost tours and sleepovers in the large prison Kilborough is built around are apparently too tempting when it's the spooky season and everyone is looking to be scared out of their wits. The hard-core enthusiasts stay in the haunted houses around Kill Pen, and you couldn't pay me enough money to do it.

I might be too old to believe in ghosts, but the aged buildings are spooky as fuck.

If it wasn't for the prison, Kilborough would just be another forgotten town in America.

Kilborough is my home, Molly's home, and while he might move across the country, or even the world, I want him to do that knowing full well he has somewhere to come back to if he needs it. That's what true freedom is.

I unlock my office since I'm in before Valerie and leave the almond croissant I bought her on the sleek, white reception desk. Then, I step into my small office that barely fits my desk, open the thin, wooden blinds, and breathe in the familiar smell of pizza from the restaurant next door. It might not be fancy, but it's all mine.

Being busy and self-employed is a blessing, and it'll feel so much better when I have someone to share it with.

6

WILL

MY LEAVE FROM WORK IS RAPIDLY WINDING DOWN, AND with only the weekend off, I need to get started on setting up my office. When I worked my butt off for an IT degree in college, I never would have thought that I'd end up working as basic tech support for a travel company, but it suits me just fine.

I don't need a lot of things. I don't have big dreams; I don't have unattainable goals. The only thing driving my life right now is finding a place where I can be settled and not always relying on other people. After the upheaval of Molly leaving, it made me realize, very quickly, just how alone and untethered I am in this world.

Facing the very real possibility of heading home to my parents has scared some sense into me, and while Keller and then Joey have both offered me a lifesaver, I need to be able to provide that for myself.

That's the reason I'm going through all this torture.

Renting won't do. I need permanence. I need roots. Maybe somewhere to start a family someday, I don't even know.

I hum out an off-tune song as I pull my computer screens out of the box I stored them in. They're wrapped in so much bubble wrap this stuff is going to end up all over the room, but when I bought these babies, I funneled a lot of money into them, and I'm not willing to risk them getting fucked-up.

Once I've made sure my pride and joys are safe, I sit down and screw the metal stand back onto my desk and make sure the up and down mechanics are working properly. Everything I need for work is on my computers, so I don't have an elaborate setup outside of my desk, the screens, and my big, comfy chair, but it's comforting to have it all together again. Like a tiny chunk of home that can wrap me in familiarity.

I fan out my tank top when I'm done, overly aware of how stifling the room has gotten. The weather keeps doing cartwheels on me this week, and even shoving the large window open doesn't let in much of a breeze. My hair is damp under my hat, but the view outside is all Kilborough, which helps. Keller lives on a small street with family-sized homes and a view of the mountain beyond them. The magnolias are still in full bloom, and I remember once when we visited and I saw them, petals all over the ground, and thought, *yep, this is the place I wanna be.*

The first time I came home with Molly for the holidays, I fell in love with the small town. After that, I tagged along with him every time, and when he was talking about moving back here and worried about leaving me, I packed up my life and moved with him.

It's both the best and worst decision I ever made.

Because I fell in love with Keller too, and now my best friend is across the country, and I have no one here to keep me in check.

I'm still not exactly sure when it started. My physical attraction to him was immediate but easy to ignore. He's always been friendly, welcoming, a little bit flirty, and with every moment I've spent with Keller, I've left more and more of my heart behind.

I toy with my phone, the familiar ache kicking in at the thought of Molly. I miss him. He hasn't even been gone long, and knowing I can't just head out with him or meet up to grab dinner is hitting hard. Joey's cool, but he's all loved up with his boyfriend and studying hard, so it leaves him limited free time. Without the two of them, I have no one.

Maybe that's why I'm clinging so hard to the pockets of time I get with Keller.

I mentally roll my eyes because that's the dumbest shit I've ever heard. Companionship isn't even in the top three things I think of when I picture him. Especially now that I know what he sounds like when he comes.

On a whim, and because maybe I'm feeling guilty about the graphic images of his dad that are playing through my mind, I open Molly's number and call him. For the first time in over a week, it doesn't ring out.

"Good morning," he says happily. "What are you doing?"

"Setting up my office. You?"

He laughs. "Literally the exact same thing."

"Great minds and all that."

"Yep. I'm splitting the room with one of my roommates though, so it'll be interesting to see how much of a distraction that is."

"Eh, just put some headphones on."

"Yeah ..." He's quiet for a moment, and it reminds me that things haven't felt right between us for a while now. "How are you guys?" he finally asks.

"Good. Back to work Monday, so it'll help keep me busy. I've been bored since you left."

"Yeah, sorry about that."

"Nah, I get it. It's fine." I mean it, too, because Molly was all lovesick over a guy who didn't deserve it and then tried to break up the guy's relationship. The feelings he had made him do shit I never would have thought my best friend would do, and I'm glad he woke up and realized his fixation wasn't healthy. I'm *not* glad he had to move across the country to work on himself, and I gotta keep reminding myself that it's what's best for him.

"So why have you been bored? I would have thought you and Dad would be having the best time living together."

Not for the first time, he's got me questioning whether he knows about my crush. He hasn't yelled at me about it yet, so I don't think so, but the way he phrases things kinda makes me wonder. "I haven't seen a whole lot of him until the other night."

"Why?"

"He's been working a lot. Does a lot of late nights."

Molly sighs. "I really, really worry about him."

I understand why, I do, but after the other night, I don't think Molly has much to worry about. And this is a problem I never realized I was gonna face with living here: how much do I tell him? I don't wanna betray Keller's confidence, but I tell Molly everything. Well, *almost* everything. I'm already feeling guilty enough keeping the hookup from him, even though it's for his own good, and Keller never said him looking to date was a secret ... "Pretty sure your dad's gonna start dating."

"What? Why?"

It doesn't feel right giving the whole reason, so I settle for a half-truth. "Just said it was time."

Molly lets out a shaky exhale. "Do you think it's because he's missing me?"

"Could be." I shrug even though he can't see it. "I mean, we were both always gonna miss you."

"And I miss you too."

"But we know why you left, and we're cool with it."

"Doesn't mean that I feel good about it."

That makes me laugh because there's the Molly I know. The one who wants to make everyone happy. The guy who's sweetness in a bottle and not running around kissing taken guys.

"Oh my god," he says suddenly. "This is perfect."

"What is?" I pull off my hat to fan it out and switch my phone to the other ear.

"If Dad's open to dating, he might actually find someone. They'll keep him company when I'm not there, and he'll be happy."

I frown, not liking this idea at all. "Not everyone needs a relationship to be happy, Mols." Despite what he might think.

"I know, but he clearly wants one. Will ..." Uh-oh, I know that tone, and I've got a feeling I'm not gonna like what comes next. "Please help him."

"Excuse me?"

"Help him find someone. You know, give him a gentle nudge. Put in a good word around town about how easy he is to live with, and how he's so clean and cooks and—"

"I'm not messing with your dad's love life," I choke out.

Because fuck that. Making sure Keller is happy might be something Molly and I both want, but we have very different ideas on how to go about that. Telling Molly *hey, why don't I date him?* will go down about as well as a helium balloon, and the only other goal I have in mind is to make sure none of these dates eventuate into something serious. At least not for the next few months while I'm living here.

"*Please*, Will?" Molly begs. "He deserves this. And you two are close—you can totally help him weed out the disasters."

"I dunno where you keep getting this 'close' idea from, but that sounds awkward as fuck for me."

Molly lets out a skeptical noise. "Yeah, right. If you offer him help, he'll take it. He likes you."

"As his kid's friend." *Wow*, did that sound bitter.

He huffs. "Why are you being difficult?"

"I'm not."

"So you don't think Dad deserves this? Even though he treated you like you were his own kid all these years? Let you move in there so you didn't have to go home? You can't do this one small thing for him?"

I let my eyes fall closed. Molly's right. I need to get my head out of my ass because Keller is that amazing and more. It hurts so damn much to think about anyone else with him, but this isn't about me.

So I unstick my jaw and say the words I know I gotta. "I'll help."

"Thank you."

I can tell he means it. Can feel the genuine relief in his voice. Molly feels guilty about leaving us here, and he probably thinks he can let go of that if his dad has his somebody.

Maybe if Keller has someone, I'll be able to let this thing go too. To actually try and move on from him.

My head's laughing at me because even *it* knows it's hopeless.

7

KELLER

I pause outside the bedroom Will set up for his office, where there are boxes and bubble wrap all over the place. He's sitting on the floor under the window, the steady *pop* of the plastic in his fingers breaking up his terrible humming. His permanent cap is on the ground beside him, blond hair a damp, spikey mess, and his head is tilted back against the wall, eyes closed, in his own little world.

My gaze snags on the damp collar of his tank top, taking in the long curve of his collarbones.

"Hot in here?"

I underestimated how zoned out he was because he startles so hard he headbutts the wall. It's impossible to hold in my laughter.

He groans and rubs his head, sending a glare my way. "That's an odd kinda sympathy," he complains.

"Sorry, but how did you headbutt a wall that was *behind* you?"

"Pure talent." He looks up at me, boy-next-door smile in place. "And I wasn't expecting you to jump out at me."

I snort and drop down to sit on the floor too. My hand immediately finds a square of bubble wrap that I start to play with. "Office looks good."

"It will once I've cleaned up. Sorry about all the mess."

I shake my head. "It's your office. Do what you've got to do."

"Yeah, but it's *your* house."

I pin him with a look. "How many times are we going to have this conversation?"

He shifts awkwardly. "I love that you want me to be comfortable here, but it's still your place, and I don't think that'll ever change."

"Well, why don't you try giving it more than two weeks?" That's the thing about Will. He's polite to a fault. Wants to do good by people and was always looking out for Molly, but now Molly's gone, I can't help but get the feeling he's lost.

"Just spoke with Molly," he says.

That perks me right up. "How is he?"

"Good, I think." He tilts his head. "Actually, we didn't talk about him much, but he sounded good."

Relief flows through me. "I really hope this helps him."

"Me too."

The fact Will understands, that he loves Molly as much as I do, is something I'll never be able to thank him enough for. It means a lot to me that Molly has people in his corner. He might be a grown adult, but he'll always be my kid, and nothing will ever be as important to me as him.

"So what did you guys talk about if it wasn't him?"

Will sends a cheeky look my way, face flushing darker. "Uh ... you."

"Me?"

"I maybe, mighta told Mols about how you're gonna start dating."

Ah, fuck me. "I didn't want him to know."

"I'm sorry. I know I shouldn't have, but I hate keeping things from him, and we're already not telling him about—" Will's mouth snaps closed.

"So much for never bringing it up again," I tease, refusing to let myself sink back into those memories.

Will scrunches his face up. "Sorry. For both things. I get why we're not sharing that, but why don't you want him to know about you dating?"

"Because I don't know if anything will come from it. And you know Molly. He walks around with hearts in his eyes, thinks everyone needs to find their Prince or Princess Charming. It's way too early to know if I'm after all that."

"Can ... can I ask ..."

"Yeah?"

"Why now? I know you said all that *old* shit, but Molly's been moving for months now, and you were always living alone before ...?"

I rub my jaw, nails scraping my short beard. "I get these feelings in my gut sometimes. Things that feel right. I've learned over the years to listen because it usually steers me to where I'm supposed to be."

"And you need to date?"

"That's what it's telling me. So we'll see."

"That's cool. Like your own gut-dian angel?"

I laugh. "Aren't I the one who's supposed to be making dad jokes?"

"Nah, you're way too cool for that."

"Hey, if the youth of today think I'm cool, I must be doing something right."

Will throws his hat at me. "Stop acting like you're so old."

I grin and pull his hat backward over my head. "'Sup dog."

"Okay, *now* you sound old." But even though he means it to be a joke, it's halfhearted. He's giving me that look I sometimes catch, the one that reminds me in a very raw and real way exactly what happened between us. I'm attracted to him, and it seems stupid to think it doesn't go both ways.

But I've got to say, a guy like *Will* finding me attractive? Hard to wrap my head around. Guys like him—blond, tan, sporty, fratty types—weren't even interested in me when I was their age, let alone fifteen years older. And yes, I've done the math.

"Didn't take you long to change your mind," I say, taking off his cap and flicking it back his way.

He scrambles for it and tucks it into his arms.

"What did Molly say?" I'm interested in the answer, but I mostly just want to get us back from … whatever that look was doing to me.

Will's whole face falls. "He …"

"Yeah?"

His exhale comes in a long rush. "He asked me to help you date. I told him no, but …"

"Molly's persistent?"

"Yeah. So if we can just tell him I did when I didn't, that would be great."

"At this point, I'm beginning to think I need the help," I

confess, turning my attention back to the bubble wrap. I'm not someone who opens up all that much because talking about problems doesn't make them go away, when there's usually a simple reason why they exist. But for some reason, I *want* to talk to Will.

Over the years, I've gotten comfortable around him, and I'd almost consider him a friend if he wasn't actually my *son's* friend. It's a weird and unfamiliar line, and never once did I think I'd end up here, but there's something about Will that settles me.

"You know exactly what you're doing. Trust me," he mutters.

This time, I throw the bubble wrap at him. It doesn't go far. "Twice in one conversation?"

His face goes red. "Oops?"

He's adorable. "I'm not talking about sex. I'm talking about dating. Honestly ... no one I've chatted with so far has that ... whatever it is that I'm looking for."

"Maybe it's because you don't know what you're looking for."

"It could be, but I don't think so. I figure when I find my person, I'll know it. They'll get me on a level no one else does."

Will nods. "It must be nice to trust yourself that much."

"Eh, you're still young. It just takes time."

"I'm not *that* young, you know."

"Compared to me, you are."

"There's only fifteen years between us. That's nothing."

Huh. Turns out Will has done the math too. Something about that warms the intuitive side of me, and we hold eyes a beat too long to be appropriate.

"Right." I push to my feet. "I'm heading out."

"Where are you going?"

"Art's putting on a lunch at Killer Brew for a few of us. Maybe I'll go and bug them with my worries."

"You're allowed to bug me."

"Am I?"

He pushes to his feet. "Of course. We're roomies now. I told you that."

That almost makes me laugh again. "Yeah, but you're also my kid's friend. I think that borders on creepy."

For some reason, that pisses Will off. His scowl is heavy as he stalks closer. "Can you maybe, now that we're living together, try to see me as my own person?"

"What?"

"You've always seen me as Will, Molly's friend. Well, maybe that's not all I am. Maybe I'm just Will, and it'd be kinda nice if you acted like it. Especially since we shared an orgasm."

He's a foot away, and we're eye to eye, almost the same height. I'm so used to looking down at Molly, so used to him being smaller, that I struggle to see him like the adult he is sometimes.

That's never been a problem when it comes to Will. He might be slightly naive and sheltered, but he's a grown man, and he's right. He deserves to be treated that way.

It's also way too sexy seeing him stand up for himself and talk about what happened without blushing.

"That's three times." The anger drains from his face, and before he can apologize *again*, I jump in. "But good point. I'll do better. I'm so used to Molly always being around that it's hard to separate you two, but since you're helping me with my love life and all ..."

Will winces, but at least he doesn't look angry anymore.

"I'll take that as a yes. Excellent."

"Can't wait," he deadpans.

"You're obviously super excited to get started on this, but we're going to have to take a rain check. Maybe later tonight?"

"Sounds good." His face falls.

"Everything okay?"

"Yeah, I ... it's weird. Without Molly here. And Joey's working today, so ..."

"No one to hang out with?"

"Exactly."

"Come with me."

Will looks at me like I've grown a head. "I wasn't out for the pity invite."

"It's not a pity invite if I want you to come. I would have invited you to start with, but I didn't think you'd want to hang out with a bunch of old dudes like us."

"Are you kidding?" I get one of his cheeky smiles. "Old dudes are hot."

I drop my head back and laugh. Loudly. I'd forgotten about that. How Molly said that Will has a thing for older guys, but how old is *old* to him? Thirties? *Forties*? Or is he less of a Daddy man and more of a Granddaddy man?

None of these thoughts are ones I should be having, though, because it's none of my goddamn business.

"Sorry, most of them are taken."

"That's okay. I can enjoy the eye candy."

Huh. Forties it is, then. And that's ... interesting. Just interesting. I refuse to think too deeply about what that means for us and what happened.

I clear my throat and wave toward the door. "Come on. Can't stand between you and your man candy."

"Trust me. You never do."

Well, *damn*. I shove him toward the door. "Save the thirst for my friends. They won't know what hit them."

DMC GROUP CHAT

Keller: *I'm bringing Will. Be nice.*
    Griff: *What kind of nice?*
    Keller: *The kind that won't make Heath murder you.*
    Art: *I'm offended you'd even say that. I'm always nice.*

Orson: *Remind me who it was that got jealous Will was flirting with his man and made a ridiculous show of pissing on his territory?*
    Griff: *I know the answer.*
    Keller: *Everyone knows the answer.*
    Art: *Who?*
    Payne: *JFC I'm worried he's for real.*

Art: *I know you can't mean me because I've never been ridiculous in my life.*
    Keller: *Can't help notice no one agreed to be nice.*
    Orson: *I like Will. It'll be fine.*
    Griff: *Oh yeah, me too. Wink wink.*

8

WILL

SEEING KELLER WITH HIS FRIENDS ALWAYS MAKES ME HAPPY. He's less rowdy than the others, doesn't like to make a fuss, but there's something soft in how relaxed he gets around his people.

It makes me want to find my people.

I watch him laugh at something Art says. He's sitting on a couch in front of a large window that has a view up the mountain toward Kilborough Penitentiary, knees spread wide with the perfect gap between his legs for me to kneel between them.

Kill me now.

Art de Almeida is the owner of the Killer Brew, the largest and most popular bar in town, and every now and then, he'll throw some get-together on the mezzanine level above the main bar area for his group that he calls the Divorced Men's Club. I'm not real sure on Keller's story when it comes to the group, just know Molly's mom left when he was still little, but I get more than a bit curious every time I try to imagine Keller getting married to someone. He doesn't seem like the type to wanna do the whole get-down-on-one-knee thing, right before having a big day with all the attention on you.

Maybe I'm wrong. Maybe he used to be different back then.

I only know Keller as he is now, and the him he is right now has me obsessed.

"You're so not subtle, Will," Joey says from behind the bar. He's working for this party, but now that he and Art are out as a couple, he's given his notice. I'm happy for him to have gotten the attention of the man he's got feelings for; I only wish I could have the same luck.

"Shut up," I grumble.

"Would you prefer that I didn't point out when you're being all lovesick and staring his way?"

"Urg, no. I'd just kind of prefer not to do that in the first place." I swing my whole body around so I'm facing the bar and the room is behind me, then press my palms to my eyes. "How many days now until Hannah's moving out?" I ask. It's phrased like a joke, but I'm kinda serious.

"Soon enough. You've barely got three months to get through."

"Yeah, well, it'll probably fly, considering he's never home."

"Where is he?"

"Work? Balls-deep in a date? Who knows?"

Joey tsks. "So the whole thing sounds like it's going super well, then."

"I think I've only seen him shirtless once."

He slides a beer across the shiny wooden counter toward me. "My commiserations."

"It's the middle of the day."

"And?"

I slide the beer back toward him. "Somehow, I don't think that'll help. Besides, I don't want Art yelling at me again over you buying me a drink." Once was more than enough for me.

"He only did that because of jealousy." Joey looks way too happy about that. "He's got me now, so he has nothing to get jealous over. Besides, I never said I was paying." He pushes the glass back my way.

I'm about to argue with him again when the familiar scent of vanilla clothes detergent washes over me, and Keller's large body takes the place by my side.

"Drinking already? Go easy. I don't want to have to carry you out of here."

I immediately flush at the memory of Keller carrying me shirtless when I'd been too drunk to walk myself.

"I didn't even order it," I say.

"Well, in that case …" Keller swipes the glass and has a long sip. "Delicious."

"Too bad if I wanted to drink that," I say, turning toward him.

"You took too long. The poor thing looked lonely—you weren't paying it any attention."

I almost laugh. "I'm sure the beer was very offended."

Keller leans in. "Now, I could be wrong, but sitting over here isn't exactly giving you the best view of checking out my friends, is it?"

With him standing this close? *Little do you know*.

"I'm good."

"They like you," he says. "You can come over there—no one will bite. Well, Art might have." He waves toward Joey, where there are visible hickeys along his arms and neck. "But that was before he got all loved up."

"True …"

"I'll give you your drink back if you come with me." He lifts the beer between us, and I reach out to take it.

My hand wraps around the glass, fingers grazing Keller's wrist and making my skin burn. He doesn't let go, dark gaze meeting mine. Then he smiles.

Butterflies let loose in my gut.

"*Yoink.*"

The glass disappears, and I'm left staring at the empty space in front of me. "Hey!"

"Get your own drink, then get your butt over here," he throws back over his shoulder as he walks away.

Joey slides up beside me, drink already in hand. "There's that subtlety again."

"*Shut up.*" I take the drink and slip off the stool, heading toward the couches in front of the enormous mullioned window.

I'd be lying if I said I wasn't nervous. I've been to these sorta things before with Keller, but Molly was always with me, and I wasn't facing the guy whose relationship my best friend had tried to ruin. He'd kissed Keller's friend Ford at the Halloween party last year, and while I'd been pissed at Ford before that for leading Molly on, after Molly told me what happened and how great Ford's boyfriend had been about it all, I couldn't exactly hold it against him. Mols was the one in the wrong, which isn't easy for me to process.

"Hiding, were you?" Art asks as soon as I join them. Because of course he couldn't let me sneak in unnoticed.

"Just chatting with Joey."

His eyes narrow just the slightest bit, and Keller tugs me down to sit next to him. We're not as close as I'd like, but my wrist tingles at the brief touch.

"Simmer down, Art. I was wrong."

"I know you were wrong."

I look back and forth between them. "Wrong about what?"

Keller turns to me, a sheepish look on his striking face. "I might have thought you had a thing for Joey."

"Which you don't." Art grins, eyes sliding from me to Keller. "Do you, Willy-boy?"

"We're not calling me that," I say as he laughs. And I have to admit, it's slightly borderline amusing that Keller would think I have a crush on *Joey* when he's the only one I've been properly interested in for years. Yet somehow, he has no goddamn clue how I feel, and I'm so fucking grateful for that.

"How's Molly?" Ford's boyfriend, Orson, asks. "Settled in okay?"

Keller shrugs. "I haven't heard from him. He texted when he got there, and that's it."

"Really?" My neck twinges I turn to look at him so fast. "Nothing?"

Keller tries to look like he doesn't care, even though I know how much that must hurt him. "He needs a bit of space, so I'm giving him it."

The urge to hug him is strong, but I hold back. We don't need his friends looking into the contact, and also, I'm starting to feel a bit guilty that I got to talk to Molly a few hours ago.

"I hope it helps," Orson says. "I've been worried about him."

Ford sighs. "Yeah, me too."

"Don't be." As much as I appreciate their concern, when it comes to them, they'll always be why Molly skipped out of town. While I *know* it's not their fault at all, they're tied into that illogical grudge and are part of the reason I've lost my best friend. "We'll make sure he's okay."

"Spill, Will," Joey says as he approaches and drops into Art's lap. "What's it like living with Keller? He an asshole? He snore? Does he turn the TV up too loud or leave towels all over the bathroom floor?"

"He has his own bathroom, so I wouldn't know." That damn en suite will be the bane of my existence.

Joey groans. "I want the gossip."

"No gossip here." Keller slings an arm around my shoulders, and I go stiff from my calves to my neck. "Will's the best roomie I ever had."

"I'm the *only* roomie you ever had."

"Not true. I spent some time in a share house when I first had Mols."

I pretend to fist pump in triumph. "I'm one step up from a bunch of random, creepy people."

"Who said they were creepy?"

"I'm assuming to feel better about myself."

Keller knocks me, thankfully—and unfortunately—releasing my shoulders. "They were actually nice, considering I had a baby that kept them up all night. And it's just occurring to me that maybe I was the annoying, creepy roommate."

"What do you mean *was*?" I mutter.

"Hey!"

"You snore pretty loud," I say. "I can hear you from my room."

Keller turns to his friends, looking scandalized. "Will answered my crossword the other night."

"I *said* I was sorry!"

"Damage was done though." Keller folds his arms over his wide chest. "Got the whole thing messed up."

I splutter. "It was four letters."

"Four too many."

My mouth drops. "You were doing *a crossword*."

"I don't think I want any more of this conversation," Art says at the same time as Keller whispers from the corner of his mouth, "That was between you and me, Willy-boy."

"Aaand I'm out!"

Keller cracks up and pulls me back down when I try to stand. "Relax, I'm only teasing."

"I'm not sure I wanna help you later."

"Help with what?" Art asks, pumping his eyebrows.

Keller gives me a flat look before finally saying, "Pick out some dates."

"You're going on dates," Art says. "Why didn't I know about this?"

"Because we all agreed not to tell you."

His mouth drops. "Ex-fucking-cuse me? I'm a professional at this dating business." He slaps Joey's ass. "Tell 'em."

"Oh, yeah. Art's got all you losers beat."

Ford laughs. "And no one here trusts your judgment, considering you're the one tied down to all that. Someone who enters willingly into a relationship with Art? We're concerned."

"I'm hurt," Art exclaims. "You've all hurt me. Now, get out so Joey can kiss me better."

Keller leans back and kicks his feet up onto the coffee table. "You promised us lunch, so we'll go when you've fed us. And don't bother with the fire alarm. We all know you pulled it last time."

Art huffs, and Joey jumps up so Art can stand. "I'll feed you. I'll feed you all real good. You just want to hope I don't put a little something extra in there while I do it."

"Like *love*?" Orson teases.

Art flips him off and leaves while Keller shakes his head. "It's fun how much he pretends to hate us."

I eye where Art's just disappeared down the stairs. "I'm not so sure he was pretending."

"That's the fun with Art," Ford says, taking a sip of his drink. "You'll never really know."

KELLER

"So where do you want to do this?" I ask Will as we step inside the house and I toss my keys in the glass bowl by the door.

"I can't believe I agreed to spend my whole afternoon on you," he grumbles.

"It's because you're such a good roomie."

Will's scowl deepens, and it's about as effective as a puppy trying to growl. "You owe me."

"Deal."

"I wanted to work out this afternoon."

"Yet this is the first you've mentioned it," I say happily, taking his shoulders and steering him toward the door down the hall that leads to the basement. "We can date search for me down there."

"In the gym?"

"Yep. I'll hook my phone up to the TV, and we can scroll through profiles while we work up a sweat."

Will groans. "Kill me now."

"Wow. You want to get out of it that desperately?"

He goes to respond, then hesitates. "Nah, I'm just being dramatic."

"I'll say. Go change, and I'll meet you down there."

Will bounds away up the stairs, and I smile as I watch him go. He fills the house with life and staves off some of that suffocating loneliness.

It's not until a minute or so has passed that I realize I'm just standing there, listening to the sounds of him moving around above me.

I shake the moment off and head down to the basement to change into some clean shorts from the hamper in the laundry that hasn't made its way to my room yet, and then I link my phone to the TV. The whole basement has been filled with equipment over the years, with the TV being the most recent addition so I can listen to music while I work out. There's nothing worse than grunting and huffing with a silent, echoey room around you. It's blindingly white down here, windowless, with gym mats laid out on the floor, a workstation along the far wall, and storage racks in a back corner.

I'm tempted to get started flicking through the MyMatch profiles when what I'm about to do actually hits me. This is Molly's friend. A guy I've inappropriately rubbed myself all over, and I'm just going to what? Sit here and judge potential dates together like that's a totally normal thing to do?

I try to release my nerves on a long exhale and remind myself of what Will said earlier. He had a point too.

Will's a grown man, and we have a relationship outside of Molly, so why won't my brain drop the association? I'm getting as annoyed with myself as Will is at this point. So, new mission.

Yes, we're trying to find me a date, but I'm also going to do everything I can this afternoon to not think about Molly.

I'm going to do what I told Will I'd do and picture him as my roommate. That's it.

He thunders down the stairs, and when he comes into view, he's in loose gym shorts, trainers, his backward cap—and nothing else.

Roommate. He's just my roommate. My sexy, sexy roommate.

"Sorry I took so long," he says, throwing me one of the shakes he's holding. "Stopped to make us these."

I flip the top open and give it a sniff. "Banana."

"Yeah." Uncertainty crosses his face. "You like that one, right?"

"Sure do." I turn away before I can take the time to admire his muscular torso. The torso I'm way too overly aware of. "I'm going to warm up on the bike."

"Cool, I'll take the rower."

For a few minutes, there's nothing but the *whirl* of machines and the rhythmic flash of skin as we work side by side. I put my head down, push harder than I normally would, and focus all of my attention on the display right in front of my face.

And not on Will's heavy breathing, which is taking over the entire room. I curse myself for not putting on music because this is even worse than the grunting.

"Okay, I'm good," I say, suddenly pulling up. He doesn't stop, and without the riding to distract me, I glance over and am confronted with Will, large muscles rippling, face set in concentration, and blond tufts of hair sticking out from under his cap.

Fuck.

An uncomfortable flush passes through me as I jump from the bike to walk it off. It's just a physical reaction. Nothing I need to worry about. To distract myself, I grab my phone and bring the screen to life.

"I thought we could go through some profiles and work out our top three?"

He slows, and there's the clatter of the handles hitting the machine. Will stands, stretching his arms out, and tilts his head to the side. "Sure, but ... I'm not gonna be much help to you when it comes to women."

"That's okay. It's a queer dating site. Plenty of men for us to drool over as well." I give him what I'm hoping is a friendly wink and not something that will creep him out.

"Well, this just got interesting."

"Want to create an account for you too?"

"Fuck, no." He grins my way, all white teeth and shining eyes. "I don't need an app to find my guy."

My eyes almost jump from my face. "You have a boyfriend?"

"No. I ..." He opens and closes his mouth a few times. "Just don't."

I take that to mean that he doesn't want to talk about it with me, and fair enough. We might be about to deep dive into my relationship, but that doesn't mean he has to give me the same. This is probably overstepping enough as it is, but thankfully, Will isn't as hesitant as he was earlier.

"Not her," he says, moving close beside me and reaching over to swipe away from the profile I had it on.

The sudden rejection takes me by surprise. "Why's that?"

"You're young at heart." He glances at me and away again. "You need someone younger than you."

When it comes to age, I'm not hung up on the number, but I meant it when I said I can't put into words what I'm looking for, so I'm happy to let him take over and see if that gets me any better results.

"Oh, he's hot," Will says suddenly.

I glance up to find a guy my age with inky curls and neat stubble. "Hard pass." I snort, swiping away myself this time.

"I'd do him."

Like I want to know that. "He's a friend. And so is his ex-husband, who I'm pretty sure is still in love with him."

"Ouch."

"Yep."

"Unrequited love sucks."

The way his voice dips catches my attention. It wasn't just a statement; there was emotion behind it, and I wonder if he's talking about himself. If he is, whoever the guy is clearly thinks highly of himself if he can turn someone like Will down. Who the hell wouldn't want someone as sweet and hot as him?

"Come on, let's deadlift a set while we search," I say.

Anything to get him to stop thinking about whatever it is making him look all wistful and sad.

While Will does his reps, I read the profiles out loud, and he gives his opinions: "The guy has a fishing photo as his display. Immediate red flag," and when it's my turn to lift, we switch.

"She's pretty," I say, nodding to the screen.

Will stares for a moment before scrolling down to the bio. "Three young kids. You don't want to be tied down to all *that*."

It's hard to laugh and hold the bar, so I set it down with a thud. "Kids don't scare me. Raising Molly was the best."

"Yeah, but do you want to do that *three* more times?"

"It's not something I feel passionately about either way, so it isn't a deal breaker for me." I take my phone and mark her to message later.

"Still think she should have been a no," he complains, heading for the dumbbells. "Bet your gut thinks the same."

Unfortunately, he's right about that. Just like with most of the people on here, I'm not overly excited about the thought of meeting her. With a sigh, I remove the mark on *Ashley* and then walk over to sit on the bench by Will.

"Maybe I'm trying too hard."

"Maybe," he agrees, starting on his bicep curls.

I watch for too long as he lifts the dumbbell to his shoulder and lowers it to his side again. Over and over, he's got a vein that stands out on the back of his left hand, and my gaze catches on it every time that hand comes up again. It matches the veins that run over both his biceps, each one standing out with the strain of the weights he's holding.

My gaze runs over his round shoulders, to the depression between his collarbones, before dropping to his pecs. The tan nipples. The lightest sprinkle of blond hair that runs down the center of his chest to his incredibly defined eight-pack. Will is all tight muscle and slim waist, making me overly aware of the differences between us. I'm not exactly self-conscious, but it's impossible to ignore that while I'm still muscular, I'm a lot bulkier. Less cut, broader, definitely hairier.

It takes me too long to realize Will has stopped, his breathing heavier than before.

"Did you wanna turn?" he almost whispers, and when I meet his eyes, they're a stormy shade of gray.

Oh, fuck. That's exactly the kind of look that could get me in trouble.

"Just what I was thinking," I say, playing off my silence. The weights are lighter than I'd normally use, but I'm not about to tell him that. He hands them over, and I can't help noticing how careful he is not to touch me in the process.

Which means I've gone and made him uncomfortable. Fucking hell.

"I got lost in thought," I hurry to explain to him. "You don't need to worry—I wasn't checking you out."

"Oh."

"I used to look like you, you know."

"What do you mean?"

"Body of a god. Seeing you just made me realize I'll never have that again."

Will blinks at me, and then his gaze drops very obviously to my torso. Where I feel it. I tell myself that the urge to shift away is because I'm self-conscious and nothing else, but I'd be lying. It feels good. Too good. Him looking at me with that spark of appreciation in his eyes makes me want to flex, show off, drive that attraction deeper.

"And yet, here's me wishing I could look like you," he says weakly.

"You need better taste." I'm under no illusions that I've aged, that I'm not peak anything right now, but hearing that someone like Will doesn't think I'm a total lost cause does wonders for my confidence.

It's easy to tell myself that what happened between us was because it was dark. Because I was there. It was easy. We were horny.

But the simple fact is that if Will wanted to hook up again, I don't know that I'd turn him down. But even aside from Molly, being roommates makes things murky because his place here will always feel conditional, no matter what I say.

Another mind-blowing orgasm isn't worth making him feel like that.

We spend the next hour working out and going through the profiles, thankfully without any more awkward staring by me. And when we finish up, I check my account and ...

"Wow. This must be a new record."

"For what?" he asks, slinging my spare gym towel around his neck.

"Dates. We ended up with a grand total of—are you ready?"

He lifts his sandy eyebrows.

"Zero. All that, and we didn't find a single person."

He laughs as I set my phone down and pull my hair out of its knot. Surprisingly, I'm not disappointed by that result when any other time I've spent an hour looking through people, I've gotten so frustrated with the process that I've just clicked on anyone. Apparently, the cure to frustration is to make this a team sport.

I shake my hair out, but it's damp with sweat, so I don't bother putting it back up until I shower. It's past my shoulders and gets annoying sometimes, but every time I've decided to cut it off, I haven't been able to go through with it. It's just a part of who I am now.

When I go to tell Will that we'll try again another day, he's gaping.

"You okay?"

"I just … I don't …" He swallows, face flushed from the workout. "You don't take your hair out much."

"Usually gets knotty. It's just easier to tie it back."

"I like it."

My gaze catches his, and that needy warmth hits me again. I shake it away. "Just full of compliments today, aren't you? How do we get you to stay here permanently? You're quickly becoming my ego's best friend."

His flush is sort of adorable as he whips the towel from around his neck and snaps me on the ass with it.

I grunt as he chuckles.

"Now you're just trying to embarrass me."

And as much as I'd like to embarrass him some more, I keep my mouth shut. I'm still feeling things out between us, and I haven't worked out where the lines are yet. With any of my friends, I'd be fine teasing them until they left, but I want to get it right with Will. I'm oddly protective of him—even from myself.

It's not until we head back upstairs that I realize I did it. Got through a whole few hours with Will without thinking about Molly once.

And it was easier than I thought it'd be.

10

WILL

I FIND JOEY AT HOME, TEXTBOOKS SPILLED OVER HIS TWO-seater dining table and pen caught between his teeth. He glances up when I let myself in, but instead of asking what the hell I'm doing just stomping into his house, he kicks out the chair opposite and gestures for me to sit down.

My body is wanting to keep pacing, but I take the offered seat anyway.

"I'm in hell," I say. "I'm in my own personal hell."

"What now?"

"Last weekend, Keller and I did the trying to find him a date thing together, and we did it while working out. Now, he's been waking me at six every morning to work out with him, and of course, we're both shirtless, and he smells like sexy man-sweat and vanilla, and then at the end, he takes out his hair, and I swear he's only doing it to tease me."

"Tease you?"

"I told him I liked it." I face-palm. "I know he's not

trying to tease me because why the hell would he? But fuck, I have to bolt out of there every time to stop him from catching on to what it does to me."

"You pop a boner?"

"Major, major bone over that man."

Joey makes a real show of pulling his chin-length hair from the knot at the back of his head. Then he pouts. "This do it for you?"

"Not even a little bit."

His eyes crease with amusement. "Want a custard tart?"

I glance up at him. "What?"

Joey stands up, crossing to his cupboard. The kitchen is '70s-style wood and laminate. "Art makes them. They're the best. And they always help when I'm trying to think." He carries over a container and offers me one that I take because what the hell else am I gonna do? Luckily, it's not bad, even if it's a bit sweet for me.

"Maybe you need to start saying no to the working out?"

"Umm ... did you miss the part where I said he does it shirtless?"

"Did you miss the part where you called it hell?"

"I'm a dumbass. I know it. It kills me to be around him, but it also kills me not to be around him, so I'd rather suffer and get his company, if you know what I mean."

"Sure do. I was the same with Art."

"How the hell did you make that happen?"

Joey rubs a hand over his jaw as he thinks. "Flirted nonstop. Made sure to get in his face all the time. Cockblocked him whenever I could."

"Yeah, well, I got the cockblocking down to an art form by this point."

"What do you mean?"

I take another bite of the tart, feeling the tiniest hint of guilt. "I may have been a bit catty about some of the people we saw on the dating site. In my defense, he told me to help him find someone I think he should date, and I don't think he should date any of them. Even the hot, perfectly nice, probably super well-adjusted ones. Maybe I should make a profile, and when it pops up, be like *him, that's the one!*"

Joey's eyeing me like he's concerned for my mental health.

I wave the look away. "I'm fine."

"I'm not judging. We both know that I'm not above desperate moves to get what I want, but at the same time, I could sense interest from Art. He flirted back. He was frustrating as fuck about it, but I had a chance. Has Keller ever given you a sign like that?"

I slump. A sign like dry humping me into a bone-melting frenzy? Can't exactly tell Joey that, can I?

"Still think he only sees you as his son's friend?"

That's one thing I'm sure has changed. "I talked to him about that, actually. Well, more like yelled at him over it. I think it must have gotten through because I can tell he's relaxed a lot and doesn't handle me with kid gloves."

"In what ways?"

"Well, he's always been good about keeping things surface level, even the unfortunately very platonic teasing, but like, the other day, he told me he liked my body."

"He what?"

"Nothing like that. Just said he wished he still looked like I did. He never would have said that before."

Joey rolls his lips in like he's trying not to laugh. "You know, when I was growing up, there were plenty of guys I wished I looked like too. Turns out, I didn't want to *be* those guys. I wanted to be *in* those guys."

"If only that's what was happening here."

"Well, why couldn't it be?"

I take another bite to buy me time. I know exactly what he's saying, but I'm trying to figure out how to nicely say it's the stupidest thing I've ever heard. I got one time. A time when all the planets aligned or some shit and things just happened. Who gets those moments twice in a lifetime? "Because Keller doesn't feel like that about me."

"It's been a week or two since your whole dynamic has changed, yeah?"

"A week."

"Then, fuck. Give the guy time. The way I see it, you're in the perfect position. You have complete access to him. Start off small. Light touches, some subtle flirting, and see if he picks up on it."

"I don't know how to flirt, let alone make it subtle." Fuck, I have enough of a hard time just trying not to blush around the guy.

"Then use the chance to show him how good of a boyfriend you'd be."

"I dunno if I even would be."

"Of course you would be." Joey tucks his loose hair behind his ear. "You're already cooking for him when he works late. Find more things like that."

At my doubtful look, he throws up his hands.

"Find common ground? Something to bond over? Watch a movie and do the old yawn and stretch."

"The what?"

Joey groans. "Why don't you just say, 'Hey, Keller, I want your dick,' and then see where it goes, huh?"

"Because I'd like to be able to look him in the eye again." This is hopeless. I made the first move last time because I'm ninety percent sure I still had a buzz, but I can't just go around being drunk every time I want to touch him. "Besides, I want more than his dick. I mean, I definitely want that too, don't get me wrong. But this isn't just some physical attraction for me that's gonna blow over. He hurts my heart, and he doesn't even know he's doing anything more than existing."

"Man ... I'm so sorry."

"Yeah. It's my own fault, but he's just incredible, you know?"

Joey leans forward, looking serious, which isn't something he is often. "I know it's hard, but I think you should try. Keller *wants* you to help him find someone good for him: *you're* good for him, Will."

I give a rueful smile and voice the thing that always nags at me when I give the illusion of me and Keller a minute to exist. "What about Molly?"

"What about him?"

"You think—even if I stood a chance—that he'd be cool with me shacking up with his dad?"

"Sorry, but that's a him problem. And if you guys are as close as you say you are, maybe you should give him more credit and consider he might actually be happy if you're happy."

It's a nice thought, but not something I can see happening. Maybe before Molly fell into his funk, he might have been open to it, but now?

That's not a conversation I ever want to have. "Oh hey, Mols. I know you're all desperate to fall in love or whatever and that your dad is the only person you've ever had in your life, but I'm in love with him, and we're settling down together. That's cool with you, right?"

Urg. I'd rather take a bullet.

"None of it matters anyway because Keller doesn't feel the same."

"Then it's time you got him to. Since you're kind of hopeless—no offense—we're going to come up with a plan together. And you're jumping into the big leagues, my friend. No warming up for you. You've beelined straight for dad territory, so we need to bring out the big guns."

"Like what?"

Joey thinks for a moment. "I know you don't share a bathroom, but are your rooms close?"

"Right next to each other."

"Okay, two options. First, leave your bedroom door open and one of your sex toys lying on your bed—it'll put you and sex in the same context for him."

"I don't have any sex toys."

Joey gives me a pitying look. "We'll fix that. But the second option is that you jerk off just loud enough for him to hear it through the wall. Hearing you turned on will get him all turned on—"

"Or ridiculously uncomfortable."

Joey throws up his hands. "I seduced a man who constantly has sex on his mind. All my methods come from that."

While Art and Keller are nothing alike, Joey *was* successful and is now in a loving relationship. Unlike me. Would following his lead really be the worst thing?

"I guess ... I guess I could try the toy thing?"

"Perfect." Joey picks up his phone and types. "Are you a Fleshlight or dildo man?"

"Am I supposed to know that?"

Joey's mouth drops open. "Fucking hell, Will. I'm ordering you one of everything, and so help me, god, even if this plan fails, you need to use them all. Every one of them." Joey's eyebrows are pulled into a severe frown as he taps his phone screen harder than he needs to. "A sexually active man with no sex toys. What is the world coming to?"

"My hand works just fine."

"Let me guess, you're still doing it in the shower?"

"Well, I don't want Keller to hear me!"

Joey cracks up laughing. "If only he was into the innocent thing. You two would be fucking like bunnies by now."

I drop my head forward onto the table. "It's cruel to even put that image in my brain."

"Gimme your card," Joey says. "I'm ordering these for you. I'm not paying too."

I slide my debit card over to him and watch as he completes the purchase. "Do I wanna know what I just paid for?"

"Probably not. But you can thank me once they're here."

11

KELLER

It's late when I get home, and I rub the tiredness from my eyes as I shoulder open my front door. Whoever it is, I'll get the bastard. I always do.

I'm about to drop my keys in the hallway bowl when I pause at a noise from deeper in the house. It sounded like it came from the kitchen, but all the lights are off, and usually, Will is fast asleep by this time.

I set my keys down as quietly as I can and creep forward, avoiding the wooden boards I know will creak. The crime rate in Kilborough is low, but in my line of work, this wouldn't be the first time I've had someone sniffing around my place. Just the first time they've ever stepped inside of it.

There's another sound—a grunt, maybe?—and I glance around for anything I can use as a weapon. Turns out my place is surprisingly low on blunt instruments, so I'm going to have to hope all those hours in the gym pay off.

I'm not hopeful.

The only thing stopping me from heading back outside and calling the cops is that Will's probably upstairs sleeping, and no way am I letting anything happen to him.

My fists tighten as I approach the kitchen door, only when I reach it, there's another grunt and ... humming. Off-key. A familiar tune I can't place, but I know that hum.

"*Will?*"

I turn to the corner to find him standing in the middle of the kitchen, chugging from the milk bottle in total darkness.

"You couldn't turn a light on? I thought someone broke in."

He doesn't answer me.

"Will?" I take a step forward, but even that doesn't catch his notice.

The milk spilling all down his front catches mine though. When the bottle's finally empty, he drops his arm, and the carton clatters to the floor. He starts up humming again, but the stiff way he moves for the cupboard ...

Holy fuck, is he sleepwalking?

I have never in my life seen someone do that for real. The closest I've ever come was when Molly was super small and would wake up in the middle of the night, garble gibberish at me, and then pass right back out again.

The old advice never to wake someone sleepwalking rings in my ears, but what the fuck am I supposed to do here? Just let him go?

He tears open a bag of chips, half of them scattering over the floor, and, with the coordination of a two-year-old, shoves them in the general vicinity of his mouth. It's the weirdest fucking thing I've ever seen.

Torn between worried and creeped out, I grab my phone and search for what the hell I'm supposed to do in this situation. Like I thought, waking him is a no go, and so is trying to restrain him. My options look like they're sticking around and watching the show or trying to guide him back to bed.

I pull out a stool, hoping Will's sleep-hunger doesn't last for long, and while I'm waiting, I type out a text to Molly.

Couldn't have given me the head's up that your old roommate and my new one, oh, what was it again? ... fucking sleep walks?

The whole situation is completely unexpected, and I'm struggling to hold back a laugh. Not at Will—I get this isn't something he can control—but just ... just that this is even happening at all. Why didn't he say something?

A simple "hey, sometimes I might get hungry and eat while I'm asleep, but it's fine, just leave me" would have at least prepared me for—well, that he's now moved on from the chips and is pouring salted nuts straight into his mouth.

Yep, he's definitely going to choke.

I jump up and cross to him, grabbing his arm tight enough that I can wrestle the bag of nuts from his grip. He jerks in my hold, grunting and muttering nothing that sounds like actual words, and when I yank the bag from his hand, Will throws himself off-balance, slips on the milk on the floorboards, and almost goes headfirst into the countertop.

Fuck. My arms close around his waist just in time to catch him and pull him back against me. He thrashes in my hold, letting out muffled screams for a second before he goes limp in my arms.

For one panicked moment, I think he really has choked on something until he snorts.

Nope. The bastard has just fallen back asleep.

His full body weight leans into me, steadily growing heavier as his legs refuse to do their job. His shirtless body is sticky with dried milk, and I'd imagine the rest of him is in a similar state.

I shake him a little. "Will?"

He whines and turns to bury his face into my neck. His heavy exhale tingles along my flesh and makes me overly aware of the fact I have an almost naked, incredibly attractive man pressed against me.

And once again, it's up to me to carry his ass to bed. Not in a fun way.

I stoop as best I can under his weight until I get one arm behind his thighs and can heft him up into my arms. He still doesn't wake, just cuddles in closer, but at least his arms wrapping around my neck make it easier for me to move with him.

The whole way upstairs, I'm trying not to think of what it led to the last time I did this.

I'm panting by the time I get him up to his room and lay him on his bed. Then it's like some expert-level mind puzzle, trying to extract myself from his groping limbs.

Not only does Will sleepwalk, but he's cuddly as fuck when he does it.

When I'm free, I stand there and watch him while I steady my breath. He looks out of it and hasn't made a move to get back up again, but how do I know he's going to stay put?

Does *Will* even know that's something he does?

I need to head downstairs and clean up his mess, but what about him? Do I leave him to wake up feeling disgusting? Or do I get a washcloth and clean him?

Dear god, I can only imagine his reaction to waking up and finding me lathering up his body while he's sleeping. It'd be funny if it wasn't so creepy.

Come to think of it, standing here and staring while he sleeps probably wouldn't be the best thing for him to wake up to either.

Fuck it. Will can shower in the morning.

I back out of the room and return to the kitchen to clean before heading up to bed. Normally Will and I wake early to work out, but I don't think either of us is going to be in any state for that tomorrow.

A loud yawn rips through me as I reach my bedroom and strip down. That might have been strange and unexpected, but since no one got hurt and he's safely back in bed, I'm able to breathe again.

I flop face-first onto my sheets, expecting to drift straight off, but I'm too tense. My whole body is tuned in to Will's room and any sounds that could be coming from it because the last thing I want to do is risk him going for another midnight stroll.

It's around three in the morning when I give in and grab my phone instead. Maybe this is a one-off, or maybe it's a common thing he does, but I want to be prepared for it if there's a next time.

I search for more information, doing a deep dive that, instead of making me feel better about the situation and ready to handle it, only fills me with the kind of apprehension bad news in the dead of the night can bring.

Articles about people leaving the house, driving their cars, doing seriously dangerous shit that has them wind up dead. And sure, a lot of those events are linked to certain antidepressants and how they react differently with people, but that fact doesn't make me any less wary.

If Will is capable enough to get up, walk down the stairs,

then help himself to the kitchen, there's no reason why he couldn't go outside and jump in his car.

Based on his coordination skills, I doubt he'd make it far, but that's beside the point.

I need it to be morning already. There are way too many questions I need answered.

And there's no way in hell I'm falling asleep after reading about all the things that could happen to him.

Not on my watch.

12

WILL

Something stinks, and I'm pretty sure it's me. I'm also sticky as hell and have that feeling like I've been chewing on trash all night. I smack my lips a couple of times to try and make it go away, but no dice.

What gives? It's not as though I went out last night. All I know is that I need to shower before Keller sees me like this.

"Keller's already seen it all."

My eyes snap open at the voice. "Ah … was I talking out loud?"

"Sure were, but at least I could understand you this time."

I turn toward where he's standing in my doorway, arms folded, big shoulder leaning against the jamb. I try for a grin, but judging by Keller's expression, I don't manage to pull it off.

"What do you mean this time?"

He smiles, the type of smile that makes him look like he's trying to eat a laugh. "Figured you might need this?"

He holds up a washcloth, making me acutely aware of how disgusting I am.

"How did you know?"

"Let's just say we've got some talking to do."

Well, that doesn't sound good. What ... oh no. Tell me I didn't hit on him in my sleep. "Is this ... is it ... cum?"

Keller makes a choking noise, then throws the washcloth my way. It lands on my chest with a wet *thump*.

"No, it's milk, you twit."

"Milk?" No wonder it smells so nasty. Then, through my early morning confusion, reality catches up with me. "Fuck. I sleepwalked, didn't I?"

"Well, that answers my question on whether you knew about it."

I groan and drop back, not bothering to clean myself. I don't deserve it. I'm such an idiot. Then—I jerk upright.

"Fuck, did you see me?"

"Sure did," he replies happily. "At first, I thought someone broke in, and I was getting ready to defend my household. But nope. Just my roommate raiding the kitchen."

"No ..."

And maybe he picks up that I'm well and truly mortified enough because his amusement softens. "Why didn't you tell me?"

"It's only ever happened a handful of times. A few nights here and there through college, and then a stint when Molly and I moved here. It's been so long I'd just forgotten about it."

"So why again now?"

I grab the washcloth, getting to work with scrubbing the grossness from me. "It usually happens when I'm stressed. Maybe the move is what did it?"

"Definitely could have been."

He doesn't say anything else, and when I look over, his eyes are trained on where I'm cleaning myself. Heat sweeps through me, and my hand slows. I'm more deliberate as I rub circles over my chest, finding it hard to breathe with Keller watching me.

"So how can I help?" he finally asks, voice so steady it makes me wonder if he was even watching me at all. It'd be just my luck that he was spaced out rather than turned on, though it would make a hell of a lot more sense.

"There's not much that can be done other than keep your fingers crossed that it was a one-off."

"You nearly fell and hit your head. Hopes and prayers aren't something I'm putting my faith in."

"Ooops?" I say, because what the hell else am I supposed to manage? The guy I'm in love with—the cool, fun, sexy guy—witnessed me wandering around the house, completely out of it. I don't even want to know what I was doing. I don't even want to know what he thinks of me now. All I know is that I'm embarrassed as hell, and while Keller might not want to rely on hopes, they're all I have.

"The tune you were humming has been in my head all night, but I can't place it. It's super familiar though."

"I was humming?"

"Badly. But it's how I knew it was you."

"And now I'm never humming again."

"We'll see. I don't think you even know you're doing it half the time."

He's right about that. Unfortunately. But if I catch

myself, I'm sure as hell gonna stop. I don't want to be the humming guy or the sleepwalking guy. I *want* to be the guy who brings Keller to his knees. How is it fair that I can't even trust myself while I'm asleep?

My cheeks are *burning* over all the possible scenarios that might have taken place last night.

"Wait, I think I've got it. It's ..." He hums over something, and just when it seems to click into place for him, I realize exactly what I was humming.

"It's that ... that Romeo and Juliet song. You know the one ..."

I cover my eyes. "'Love Story' by Taylor Swift."

Keller pitches forward with laughter. "That's the one!"

"I hate me."

"Nah, you're fucking great."

Well, I'm not gonna argue with that assessment, am I?

"Guess I better go clean up my mess," I say, throwing my legs off the bed. My briefs are crusty with milk too, and once I've cleaned up, I'll be drowning myself in the shower.

"I've already done it. You can pay me back by cooking dinner."

"Like I wasn't already gonna do that."

Keller shrugs. "How would I know? Take the deal, Will."

"Easiest deal ever." And while getting real words out around him is hard, I'm so grateful he hasn't turned this into a big thing. I wish I could let him know that I appreciate it, but I'll have to show him by cooking the best food he ever put in his mouth. Sure, most of what I fix is the heavy dishes my momma taught me, but he hasn't complained yet.

Good thing he has a gym though, or I'd be kissing all my hard work goodbye.

When I make it downstairs, the smell of disinfectant is

heavy on the air, but there's no other sign of what the hell I could have gotten up to last night. I'm still torn on whether that's a good thing or not. In some ways, I hope my imagination is overshooting it on the embarrassment, but if it's not, do I wanna know? Probably not.

I've got a full day of work ahead today, so hopefully, that'll help take my mind off it, but I don't know what I'll do about tonight. Maybe I'll duck down to the store before I start on dinner and grab some duct tape to strap myself down. I don't even know if it'd work to keep me in bed, but I've gotta try something.

Not only to prevent further feelings of wanting to crawl into a hole and die, but also, Keller shouldn't have to deal with me like that. Knowing he thought someone broke into his home doesn't make me feel good about myself.

It's another stinker, and after I shower, I change into some loose clothes to try and combat the heat. I'm lucky to not have to wear a uniform, but if this is what spring has in store, I'm dreading working during the summer.

Maybe I should have set my workspace up in the basement, where there's less sun heating things up.

With a coffee full of ice in one hand and my laptop in the other, I shoulder open the door to my office and ... *where in the heck did that come from*?

An enormous industrial-sized fan has been set up in the corner, with a tiny remote resting on my desk. I hit the On button, and the fan roars to life, gust so strong the notebook on my desk flies open as the papers flick through. I snatch it up and quickly turn down the speed until the fan reaches a mode that's cool but not about to start a tornado in Keller's house.

My day just got one thousand percent better because there's only one person who could have put that there.

I pick up my phone and, nerves in my damn throat, type out a message.

Me:
You bought a fan! I could kiss you!

I read the message over way too many times, trying to figure out if it's overly obvious or just a casual statement. People use that expression all the time, right? It's totally normal. Nothing weird here. I bite down into my lip and hit Send, then stare at my phone like the whole thing might explode.

It doesn't.

But Keller does text back.

Keller:
If that made you happy, you should see what I'm picking up for tonight ;)

Now, I know he's not meaning to flirt, but my brain is *determined* to turn that sentence sexual. I fight imagining Keller walking in with some kind of sex toy and warn myself to be good. I might push things by getting flirty with him, but I have to remember boundaries.

Me:
Do I get a hint?

Keller:
shush face emoji

I guess that's my answer.

It's painful to set my phone down and get to work, wondering over and over what he's got planned and constantly having to remind myself that whatever it is, it's not *that*.

The day drags by like it's determined to punish me, and

the second I hear the front door open that afternoon, I change my work status to break and charge downstairs.

"What did you get?" It almost comes out like one word, but Keller obviously catches on because he produces a large square box from behind his back, like *tada!*

"A ... baby gate?"

"Yep. I'm going to set it up at the top of the stars, and hopefully, it'll stop you from roaming. I also picked up a bell I can attach, so if you do get it open, I'll wake up right away."

Fuck my life.

Any chance I thought I had of him seeing me as an adult is gurgling down the drain. This is the exact opposite of what I'd been hoping to achieve. Instead of seeing me as an adult or a kid, he *sees me as a baby.*

He bought me a fucking baby gate, for fuck's sake.

Kill me now.

"You don't look thrilled," Keller says, and I both love and hate that he's amused.

"It might just be me, but this feels condescending."

He makes his way toward the stairs. "I'll condescend you all day long if it keeps you safe."

"And while I'm appreciative of that, I still hate it."

His warm, rich laugh gets me right in the chest. "I'll remind you of that tomorrow morning when you don't wake up smelling like milk."

I fold my arms and glare at him.

My death glare apparently isn't as scary as I think it is. "You can go back to work, Willy-boy. This is a one-man job."

"So is cutting your hair off while you sleep. Remember that."

THE SORRY SUCKAS GROUP CHAT

Keller: *sends photo*

Mack: *Who gave you the shiner?*

Art: *Sex injury.*

Carlton: *I love that he has a dangerous job and that's your first thought.*

Art: *I said what I said.*

Keller: *It was Will.*

Art: *See? I was right!*

Mack: *Did you two have a fight?*

Keller: *He was sleep walking and hit me when I tried to stop him.*

Carlton: *I didn't think you were supposed to touch someone while they're sleep walking.*

Art: *No, you're thinking of stripping.*

Mack: *Will was stripping?*

Keller: *Sleep walking. Like I said. The mark's already going down though.*

Art: *Hate to say I told you so but the roommate thing was never a good idea.*

Keller: *I don't know. It has its benefits.*

Art: *Sex benefits?*

Keller: *Yes, art. Sex. Lots and lots and lots of sex.*

Art: *I don't like this role reversal. I don't know whether you're fucking with me or not.*

13

KELLER

The baby gate is a dud. After wrestling with Will to stop him from climbing onto the banister to get around it, I end up with an errant backhand to the face before he slumps in my arms, and I once again have to carry him to bed. It's not the worst thing. He might be heavy, but it's been so long since I've had someone cuddled up against me that I'm probably not as fast as I should be.

I'm back in his doorway when he wakes with a face-twisting yawn.

"Morning, Sleeping Beauty."

He scowls, and if he thinks he looks mean doing that, he needs to think again. "Tell me I didn't."

"You did. Also tried to swan dive off the top of the stairs." I point at my cheek. "Got a solid slap for saving your life, too."

"Fuck. I'm so sorry."

I chuckle at how horrified he looks. "Don't worry about it. Your hand was flailing first. I just got in the way."

He lets out a long groan and pulls the blanket up over his head. "Please leave me to die here."

"Even if I did, we can't be sure you won't sleepwalk out of there tonight anyway."

"How are you not creeped out by this?"

"It's kind of amusing."

"Molly used to hate it."

He mentioned that when he wrote back yesterday. I'm going to have to call him today and figure out how the hell he managed to stop Will from killing himself. Before I can bring that up though, Will stretches, kicking off his blankets in the process and revealing miles and miles of muscular, tan body.

All the awareness of his body funnels into one spot between my legs.

Fuck. I drag my eyes away from those incredible abs and focus on the boring beige wall instead.

"Wanna work out?" he asks, and in this moment, I hate that I started that with him. It'd been a good idea to have a workout partner, but knowing he'll only be wearing a pair of loose gym shorts right after my body had a ridiculously inappropriate reaction to him doesn't seem like a smart move to me.

I scrub my jaw, trying to do the sex math on when my last hookup was, and it's actually a struggle. It was definitely before he moved in ... by like a week? Two? Fuck, maybe even closer to a month? No wonder I'm getting all boned up over him.

"Actually, I'm heading in to work early," I say on a whim. "I've got a date tonight, so I want to make sure I'm finished early enough." Date, hookup, whatever. I'm not in a position to be picky, and at this point, I'll take what I can get.

I have a problem, and there's a very easy solution. Even if that solution isn't the man standing in front of me wearing the most revealing pair of briefs ever made. My gaze flicks down for a look, and I immediately regret it because while he's not hard, he isn't exactly soft either, and that cotton isn't shy about showing off the ridge around his head.

I quickly back up from his doorway, deciding these morning wake-ups are way too inappropriate. Crossing lines.

He used to call me Mr. Gibson, for fuck's sake, and it took a solid year or two for him to break that habit, and now I'm getting spontaneous hard-ons over him. I don't want him to feel like he *has* to sleep with me to stop from ending up on the streets, because that would be sickening, so I just have to be content to remember the one time I got to experience what that impressive body felt like against mine.

No, meeting up with someone to fuck tonight is definitely the way to go.

"A date?" Will echoes, voice soft.

I was so lost in my own head that I didn't notice the frown settle over his face. "Sorry, we'll be back to working out tomorrow."

"I didn't think we picked anyone."

"We didn't."

"Then—"

"It's not technically a date I'm after. I'll be using a different type of app." Which is far too much information to be giving him anyway.

"Oh." He picks up his hat and shoves it on, but the movement looks awkward, like he's only doing it for something to do. The brim sits low, cutting off half of my view of his face. "Will you want dinner?"

"You know you don't have to cook for me, right?"

"Obviously. I want to."

I chuckle. "Okay, snappy. I'll be home in time." Knowing how much Will loves to cook, I'll have to make it happen.

Unfortunately, it doesn't make him less scowly, and I really don't like that look on his face.

I sigh, figuring I know what's wrong. "You don't need to worry about the sleepwalking thing. We'll figure it out. I don't care."

He eyes me before nodding. "Yeah. I'm gonna go shower. Have fun getting your dick wet, I guess."

"Thank you?" It comes out as a question because I'm not sure what that tone was or why he stomps past me and slams the bathroom door behind him. If it is embarrassment, he needs to let that go because sleepwalking isn't something he can help.

The sound of the shower fills the hall, and my mind flashes to Will kicking off those briefs and stepping under the water, trails of it flowing over his sculpted back.

My cock does more than twitch this time; the bastard gets all the way hard.

I turn and thump my forehead on the wall, trying to clear the delicious images from my mind. Will is sexy. I get it. Nothing I haven't noticed before. Also nothing I can do a damn thing about.

While I'm getting ready, I open Grindr to an account I've met up with a few times. No idea the guy's name, only that he lives near Springfield somewhere and can suck a cock as good as any other. I check that he's free to meet up this afternoon and get a thumbs-up straight back.

Easy as that.

I'm not as excited as I'd usually be, though, because while it's something I need, I'm also getting bored with the hookup scene. I've been doing it for the majority of my adult life, and while it's been fun, that need to settle down is only getting stronger.

I refuse to do it with just anyone though. Been there, done that. After the mess with Michelle, it really turned me off relationships.

There isn't a single part of me that can understand why she did what she did. I tried. A lot. But gender isn't something that's ever meant a thing to me, and sure, it took a day or two to adjust to Molly being a boy and not a girl, but it wasn't hard. Just had to break the habit.

I assumed there was something twisted in her head, and I was mostly right. Postpartum depression kicked in hard with her, which is why, when Molly was two and Michelle wanted another chance, I gave it to her. I'd thought I had it made.

Molly got attached to her quickly, we got engaged, she was talking about trying for a second baby, and while I wanted that badly, I was still scarred from what happened the first time.

I got her to agree to wait until after the wedding, and it's lucky I did because six months later after that, she woke up, decided being a mother wasn't for her, and disappeared on us both. The only connection I ever had with her again was the divorce papers showing up in the mail.

I'm not going through that again. And Molly might be an adult now, but I know he's always wondered what he did wrong, and there's no way I'm going to bring just anyone into our lives and risk opening up those old wounds.

It's impossible to tell at the start of a relationship if it's going to be forever, but I'm not settling for something that doesn't feel right. If I'd trusted my gut with Michelle the second time, she never would have had that chance to break Molly's little heart. And mine. I'll never understand people who are reckless with another person's emotions.

It's not until lunchtime, when I've just finished typing up a report for a case, that Molly finally calls. My heart fills with love just at seeing his name, and I know my grin is dumb as shit when I answer the phone.

"Hey, bub. How's Seattle?"

"Will's sleepwalking?" is his answer. He sounds like he's holding back laughter.

"Yep. Well, he has the last two nights, at least."

"Good luck with that."

"How long did it go on while you were there?"

"Maybe a week or two? I found him in the front garden totally naked and decided I needed to put a stop to it."

My face screws up because there's no way I can risk that happening. Carrying him to bed in next to nothing is bad enough. Totally naked? I don't deserve that torture.

"I will do literally anything to make sure that doesn't happen. How did you get it to stop?"

"We tried a few ideas, but the only thing that worked was sleeping next to him."

"Wait. Like in the same bed?"

Molly giggles. "Are you five, Dad? Obviously. For whatever reason, that helped, and after a few nights, it broke whatever was causing it."

"He thinks it's stress related. Surely, if that's the case, we can just get rid of whatever is stressing him."

"If you know what it is, that's worth a try. But if it's from moving ..."

"Shit." I pull my hair out and scuff my hands through it in frustration. "Any other ideas?"

"No, but *do not* handcuff him to the bed. We tried, and he tore the skin all around his wrists trying to get out of it."

"Ouch."

"Yep."

This conversation is not at all what I was after because there's no way I can sleep in the same bed as Will, even if it's as platonic as Molly's making it out to be. While I'm having these thoughts about him, it'll always feel too inappropriate.

"Seriously, just have a few sleepovers. It's not a big deal," Molly says. "Do yourselves both a favor before Will ends up getting hurt."

"It's feeling borderline creepy to me."

"Why? It's a big bed. It's not like you'll be touching or anything, right?"

I don't like the suspicion in his tone. "I don't want Will to feel uncomfortable while he's settling in."

"Eh, don't worry about that. He's a cuddly guy. He'll probably appreciate the company."

"Really?" I ask skeptically.

"Yep. I think he's lonely. I know I told him to help you with all the dating stuff, but maybe you could help him make some friends or something? I just feel bad for leaving you both and—"

"Never feel bad about putting yourself first," I remind

him. "Now, stop worrying about us. We'll nip the sleep-walking in the bud, and then everything will be fine."

"I hope so."

"Give me some credit, Mols. I raised a whole person; I think I can look out for myself."

"Yeah, I guess. Love you, Dad."

"You too."

We hang up, and it takes me way too long to realize that he didn't say anything about Seattle. My paternal worry kicks in, which only adds to everything else filling my brain.

14

WILL

I CLOCK OUT OF WORK EARLY BECAUSE I FEEL TERRIBLE, BUT it's a dumb idea because I only end up feeling terribler. All day, the only thing I've been able to concentrate on is that Keller's meeting up with someone this afternoon. Every time the thought flashes through my mind, my gut clenches, and I worry I might be physically sick. Working out doesn't help, pacing doesn't help, cooking dinner doesn't help.

Fuck, even crying does sweet fuck all but make me feel like an idiot for caring so much about a man who doesn't feel the same.

The thing is, none of this is Keller's fault. I asked, he answered. Now, I'm dealing with the repercussions of my inappropriate feelings. The pain is so bad it almost makes me want to tell him, if for no other reason than to make sure I don't have to go through this again. Knowing where he is, knowing what he's doing, it's got me green with jealousy, and my stomach hasn't unknotted all day.

Me:
How did you do this with Art? Knowing he was with someone else and there wasn't anything you could do about it?

Joey:
When he was still sleeping around, I didn't know what my feelings were. He stopped before we ever got together so I didn't have to go through that. I'm sorry. It must suck.

Me:
Suck doesn't even cover it. I feel like I'm losing my brain.

My phone rings, and I answer, only because I know Joey will keep trying.

"Don't wanna talk," I say thickly.

"Fuck. Do you want me to come over? Want to come here?"

"No."

"Will, I—"

"I want to be here when he gets home."

It's like I can hear Joey's cringe. "That doesn't sound healthy."

"I don't think any part of this is what you'd call healthy, but I'm doing it anyway."

"I can come there and wait with you if you like?"

There's a muffled complaint in the background, and I smile. "Tell Art to relax, I ain't gonna take you away."

"He can deal. If you need me, I'll be there. He'd do the same for any of his friends."

I find that hard to believe. Art, putting friends before getting laid? I might not know him that well, but I do know that he has a reputation—one that's confirmed by Joey being constantly covered in fresh love bites.

"I want what you have," I admit softly. "Someone who wants my company like that."

The phone switches over to speaker, and Art's voice fills the line. "You talking about Keller?"

"What? Who? Nooo. What do you mean?"

He laughs like he doesn't believe me.

"*Thanks*, Joey," I snarl.

"He didn't tell me." Art sounds smug. "You're very obvious about it."

"Can't be that obvious if he hasn't picked up on it. You won't tell him, will you?"

"Nope, but I can do recon."

That perks me up. "What do you mean?"

"When Payne moved in with Beau, Griff used to talk about how hot he was all the time. Now they're together. I'll do the same with you. We've got a group chat, and I'm not above teasing him over how he hasn't banged his roommate yet."

My cheeks flush hot. "You're both regular little matchmakers, aren't you?" I ask weakly.

Art snorts. "What matchmaking has Joey done?"

"I sent him sex toys. Might have put them under Keller's name so he'll be the one to open them."

"You did *what*?"

They both snigger, but fuck. I definitely need to intercept that box first. "And now I suddenly don't feel bad over your boyfriend's offer to talk about how hot I am."

"Yeah, that only happens if Joey gives the go-ahead," Art says.

Joey sniggers. "Permission granted. As long as I can pretend to be you and help too."

"What have I done?" I whine.

"Relax, we won't embarrass you too much."

At this point, it's not possible to be any more embarrassed around Keller.

"I'm sending the first one now," Art says, sounding like an overeager puppy and not the millionaire owner of the town's biggest brewery.

"Read it out to me first."

"I wrote: man, I have no idea what you're doing out with some stranger when you have that hottie at home," Art reads.

There's some jostling in the background, then Joey's voice. "You've been living together for a month now, and you haven't slept together? I'm beginning to doubt either of your intelligence."

"Yes, that's good," Art says, but I'm only shaking my head.

"He's going to see right through this."

"No way."

"Hey, he's writing back," Joey points out.

My breath is caught in my throat as I wait.

"Oh." Joey exhales loudly. "Just heart hands. He's going to be harder to ruffle than I thought."

Don't I know it?

Art bursts with laughter. "He just suggested Joey and I should open to a third if I want your dick that much."

And that response only makes me want to cry again. "Good to know he's happy to see me passed around like that, I guess." I swallow thickly. "Stop messaging him."

"Will—"

"This feels wrong. Just … just don't. I don't know how many times Keller has to show he's not interested, but I'm getting pathetic at this point. I think I need to leave the poor man alone."

"I probably shouldn't say this," Art begins.

"Then you definitely have to," Joey cuts in.

"Keller's protective of you. There's no way in hell he means that message. He's just trying to show that I won't get a rise out of him. I'm known for shit stirring, and Keller is good at ignoring me. Don't give up hope."

"What am I supposed to do instead? Cook him dinner while I wait around for him to finish getting off with his plaything?"

"You're cooking him dinner?"

I should have known Joey would pick up on the fact that's exactly what I'm doing. He switches the phone off speaker, and his sigh comes down the line.

"As much as I do think you two would be amazing together, you can't put your life on hold. You should be going out too. Hooking up and having fun until you brave up enough to tell him how you feel. Otherwise, he's going to blindside you one day with someone he really likes, and you'll have missed your chance."

"How am I supposed to say actual words with actual emotions to my best friend's dad?"

"You do what you yelled at him to. Take Molly out of the equation. He's not your best friend's dad—he's the guy you're living with who you've got some pretty strong feelings for. Maybe that will make it easier."

"Maybe."

The front door opens, and I almost drop my phone. "He's here," I hiss. "Gotta go."

Then I hang up on Joey before he can say bye. And while I still feel like shit the second I remember where Keller's been, the conversation with them helped, at least.

I'm at least able to fake a smile when Keller walks into

the kitchen.

"I'm ravenous," he groans, dropping his phone on the counter. "What did you cook? It smells amazing."

My teeth grit. "Fried chicken, mac and cheese, and some greens. I figured you'd be working up an appetite."

He laughs. "I've been thinking about your food all day."

"No way my food is better than a hookup."

"Eh. Close call."

My energy is at rock bottom. My whole face is hot, and I'm not blushing this time. No, my gut is curdling with jealousy, and I wish I could make it all go away, but the longer he moves around the kitchen, acting like this is all normal and fine and getting us drinks, the more I wanna doink him over the head with the fry pan.

I rein in the urge, though, and go about serving out our food and trying not to cry.

"Want to watch something with me tonight?" he asks.

Even though being around him is painful, saying no isn't something I can do. "Like what?"

"Something hilariously stupid that we can make fun of the whole time."

I nod, and that'll have to be good enough for him.

Keller tells me about a case while we're eating, but I'm not paying attention. The whole time I'm looking at him, all I can think about is whether he kissed someone tonight. Fucked them. Did he have a cock or pussy in that same mouth he's putting the food I cooked him?

I know my thoughts are messed up. I know they're not fair. If he knew the way I'm hurting, he'd feel horrible, even though it's not on him.

"You okay?" His low, concerned tone catches my attention, and when I look over, his eyes melt me.

I hate feeling this way. Hate the way I've made him worry and can barely pull a smile together for his benefit.

"Just, uh, worrying about tonight."

Something crosses his face too fast for me to catch, and he straightens in his chair. "I actually spoke to Molly about that today."

"You did?"

Keller rubs his scruffy jaw in the way he does when he's thinking. He's got big hands, strong arms, intense eyes. Every single little thing about him, from the vein that runs along his thumb, to his chipped tooth, to the way he commands all of my attention, turns me on. I couldn't look away from him if I wanted to.

"Molly had an idea that worked for the two of you."

It takes a moment for what he's saying to sink in. "But … he slept in my bed with me."

"I don't want to make you uncomfortable, obviously, but—"

"Yes."

He blinks, clearly thrown off.

I hurry to clear my throat and force confidence into my voice. "That worked last time. It sounds like a great plan."

"Okay. Well … If you're cool with it. Then—"

"I am."

"And no, uh … what happened between us—"

"Now look who's bringing it up." But he's safe. I'm not about to hit on him knowing I'd be getting someone else's sloppy seconds.

"Then let's try it. Can't hurt, right?"

Oh, it will definitely hurt. He has no idea how much.

But there is absolutely no way I'm passing up this chance, even if I'll hate myself after.

15

KELLER

THE MOVIE IS EVERY BIT AS RIDICULOUS AS I WAS HOPING IT would be, and even though the slasher is probably supposed to be scary, my abs hurt from laughing. Will's beside me, clutching his ribs, face stretched into the kind of smile that could warm anyone. Including me.

All day, I'd been so ready to go out and hook up, but the closer the time got, the less right it felt. I'd made up an excuse about needing to work and then forced myself to stay back and do it, all the while distracted thinking about Will and his backward cap and whatever he was cooking.

As far as roommates go, he's a keeper. Never noisy, never messy, fills the house with amazing food, and I genuinely like hanging out with him. Molly wanted me to help Will make friends, but he doesn't need the help. He's full of all this pure energy that anyone would want to be friends with him.

Including me.

Maybe that's not what Molly meant, but he's just going to have to deal with it.

"The way ... the way ..." He gasps. Will shakes his fist up and down.

"I didn't see any jerking off in the movie." I shrug. "Probably would have made it better."

He chokes and thumps my shoulder, then does the motion again. "Stabbing. The stabbing and the—" He blows a raspberry, and I just can't with him.

"Anyone ever told you that you're great with words?"

"It was *so* dumb!"

"It was incredible."

His eyes widen like he can't tell if I'm serious. "Her eyeballs exploded. Why? For what reason?"

"Entertainment."

"I don't think I've ever watched a movie that made less sense in my life."

"And that's what I liked about it." I grin when he looks even more incredulous than before. "Seriously, why do you watch movies?"

"I dunno ..." Will frowns. "For ... fun? To relax?"

"And you're telling me that wasn't fun?"

"Ah ... well ..."

"You laughed the entire time. Look, it's not winning any awards, and it was obviously stupid as shit, but I watch to be entertained, and that did the job. Things don't have to be deep and meaningful to have value."

"Huh. Never thought of it that way."

"I am *incredibly* wise."

"Or full of shit." He gives me his lazy, crooked smile. "Still not sure which yet."

"I'll have to keep you guessing." A loud yawn rips

through me. "Ready for bed?"

Will sucks in a sharp breath, reflexively reaching for his cap. He lifts it, puts it back on again, radiating nerves, and damn, I feel the same.

This is purely to help him. Nothing else.

Yet for the first time in a long time, I wish I didn't listen to my stupid gut and went out instead. I would have gotten off already, and then I'd be a whole lot less tempted by the hard, warm body beside me.

"Yeah, just … gotta get changed." His voice deepens, running through me like syrup.

"If this is too weird for you, just say. We'll figure something else out."

"No, it's fine. All good. Just two grown men sharing a bed. There's nothing wrong with that."

I eye him, debating whether I believe his words. I'm torn because I do need to stop the midnight strolls, but on the other hand, I hate the way I'm almost excited by this. The way I can't picture sleeping next to him without my cock making its presence known. It doesn't make me feel good about myself. I might not act on those thoughts, but I'd be lying if I said I didn't want to.

"Okay, I'll get changed and meet you in there."

Will heads upstairs while I hang back, switching everything off. It's not the first time I've had to sleep next to someone before, and I doubt it'll be the last, but while my gut is telling me this is the right thing to do, I can't stop the extra *something* swimming through me.

I've been trying to pinpoint the feeling all day. The way I simultaneously want and don't want to do this. The way I'm almost craving it, but it feels … wrong. In the best way.

And when I finally change—wearing a T-shirt where I

wouldn't usually—and walk into the room to find Will spread out in a bed that suddenly feels too small, that something clicks into place.

Need.

Will's young, gorgeous, sweet, but while he's asked me to forget the next part, it's almost impossible: he was Molly's friend first, and that's how I've known him for years. I can't imagine my son being happy about the thoughts I'm having about the near naked man stretched out in the bed.

But I'm having them anyway.

My cock thickens as I force an easy smile, switch off the light, and cross the room to climb in next to him.

"Budge up, Willy-boy. Make some room."

"I'm hugging the wall over here."

I pull back the covers before slipping under them. Thankfully, the shadows hide my hardness the whole time.

"Should we put pillows between us?" he asks.

It'd probably be the safest option, but like hell am I going to say that. "Do you want pillows between us?"

"I dunno, I just ... I don't want you to feel uncomfortable. Having to share a bed with a dumb kid and all."

That almost makes me laugh. And wince. "That's definitely not how I see you. Trust me." And trust my very hard dick.

"Okay ..." His voice deepens. "Well, I'm good without one if you are?"

I'm definitely going to hell because instead of insisting it makes sense, what I actually say is, "The more room we have to spread out, the better. Are you sure this isn't a double bed?"

"I'm positive. My feet reach the edge in a double."

I guess I've never shared a bed with someone Will's size

who I was putting all my energy into not touching. "Good point."

We both lie on our backs, staring at the ceiling until the awkwardness kicks in enough to make my dick settle down.

"Are you sure you're okay with this?"

"I was just thinking the same about you," he croaks. "Do you always sleep like you're dead?"

"Do you?"

Will lets out a huff. "Fine. Maybe this is a bit weird. But not because I'm uncomfortable or anything, but more …"

"I keep thinking about last time."

"Exactly!"

Thank fuck he feels the same way. I roll onto my side and prop up on my elbow. In the darkness, I can just make out Will's eyes blinking my way.

"Wanna talk about something that will help us relax?" I ask.

"Sure, like what?"

That's a harder question to answer. Something to make us feel comfortable around each other has to be more than "what's your favorite color," and given Will's childhood, I'm not going to ask questions about that, am I?

"Is there anything you want to know about me?" I ask on a whim.

Will nods. "Lots."

"Then shoot."

He pauses for a second, and I can just make out him chewing on his bottom lip. "What was it like being a teen dad?"

"The fucking worst, but also the best."

"Molly said you don't talk about it much?"

"It's not that I don't want to talk about it, more that I've tried hard to move on since then. I was sixteen and a dumbass. Michelle was no better. My parents supported me through it all, but we didn't have the extra money for a baby, and when Mom suggested it might be better for Molly to be put up for adoption, I moved out." The darkness of those few years hits hard. "She wasn't trying to hurt me, but when you put your whole soul into something only to hear it's not enough ... that shit stings. Especially when you're a bone-headed teenager."

"Molly says you were the best dad ever."

I don't know what I did to deserve such a good kid. "I wasn't, but it means the world that he sees me that way. Michelle stopped all contact between us, and her parents wanted nothing to do with me, even though they tried to take Molly from me a few times—even going so far as to call child services. So I was on my own, and while people tell you that raising a baby is hard, it's nothing to the reality. But I loved Molly, so I was determined."

"That's kind of incredible."

"That's being a parent."

Will sighs, and I know I've said the wrong thing. "Tell that to my parents."

Even thinking about it makes me so fucking angry. I saw Molly when Michelle left. He was only four, but he couldn't wrap his little head around Mommy not being there. I can't imagine Will growing up his whole life with two parents who loved him ... until they didn't. "If I ever met your parents, you can bet your ass I would."

He rolls onto his side to face me. "What would you say?"

"That they should be ashamed of themselves."

"And?"

"And they can't claim to love their kid after suggesting

you don't live there anymore. And that if you want to visit, you need to let them know first so they can give your siblings the heads-up. Like you've got some kind of fucking disease." My anger ticks up a notch. "They don't deserve you. And that's not me speaking as a parent but as a person. You're an incredibly sweet and kind man, Will, and if they think there's something wrong with that, I'd be more than happy to tell them to go and fuck themselves."

He's quiet for a very long time, and I worry that I was too harsh. He might have a complicated relationship with his parents, but it's not really up to me to be the one to say all that. If he loves them, no matter what they've done, it's still hard to hear.

"Thank you," he whispers, voice heavy with the kind of emotion that makes me want to hug him. To remind him that shitty people don't make us who we are, and he's a perfect example of that. I hold myself back, though, because this conversation has done what it was supposed to. I'm more relaxed lying here now, but where before I was horny for the man, now there's something deeper flowing between us.

He suddenly props up on his elbow too, face closer to mine. "You know I can call them, and we can tell them all that right now."

I laugh, glad to feel the tension lessen. "Get them on the phone, and I won't hold back."

"That'd be a dream." His smile slips. "Did, umm ... was your *date* everything you hoped it would be tonight?"

"Actually, I canceled."

"You did?" His voice actually squeaks.

"Yeah, I wasn't feeling it."

"Was that another gut thing?"

It sounds ridiculous when he says it like that. "Actually,

yes."

"I'm sorry," he says, but his voice has more life in it than before, and his smile is back, wider than ever.

"Probably not appropriate to talk about."

"Of course it is. We're roommates. Roommates gossip about things like that."

"Oh, really? You want me to talk about getting my dick sucked, huh?"

Will chokes. "If you wanted to. But it's not like you did tonight, right?"

"Right." There's something in his tone that has me curious. "Why are you so interested?"

His breathing deepens, and then he says in a rasp, "Everything about you interests me."

I swear it's like my heart stops. The words burn through me, chipping into my consciousness, and I piece together what he means by that.

It could just be simple curiosity.

But I'm no idiot.

I've blown off any interest from him a few times for whatever reason—he was drunk, I'm too old, he could never see me as more than a convenient hookup—but ... but what if he did?

Is it completely out of the question? The fifteen years between us definitely makes it unlikely, but if Will likes older guys, why not me?

I lick my suddenly dry lips, trying to work out how I feel about that. Trying to put together words and wondering if I should lean into my suspicions or keep holding back. In the end, I give Will exactly as much as he's given me and hope like hell he takes it in whichever way he meant first.

"I think you're really interesting as well."

16

WILL

EVERYTHING ABOUT YOU INTERESTS ME.

My eyes snap open as I jolt upward, not able to believe I said those words last night. Fuck, fuck, what was I thinking? I might as well have just cut open my chest, pulled out my heart, and said, "Oh yeah, this kinda belongs to you."

The place he was sleeping last night is empty, and when I press my hand to the bed, there's no residual warmth, making me think he's been gone for a while.

There's no rule I gotta get out of bed this morning, is there? I groan, tempted to pull the covers over my head and go about my day like I didn't say things to Keller last night that I really, really meant.

My only hope at this stage is that he didn't think anything of it and just had to get up early for work. That'd make total logical sense.

I mean, he did say he finds me interesting too. Not the same thing, and definitely could be that I'm about as interesting as that horrible slasher movie we watched, but ... it's something.

I'm at the point where I'll take *anything*.

Instead of burrowing through the earth until I hit Australia, I get up and pull on some pants, prepared to act like everything is all totally the same and normal. If shit is weird, there's just under two months until I move out—surely I can avoid the man in that time.

I take my time choosing a shirt, the pressure mounting on my shoulders with every second I delay. It takes reminding myself that Keller isn't the type to be weird over a little crush to get my feet out the door and moving. Keller's endlessly understanding, and if he picked up on my crush and doesn't feel the same, he's not going to make me feel bad about it. Intentionally. He will be frank about his non-feelings though, which will definitely make me feel terrible to know that there's absolutely no hope between us.

I sniff, and I jog down the stairs, following the smell coming from the kitchen. It's rich and immediately makes my mouth water.

"Oops, you beat me," Keller says, transferring a hash brown from the pan and onto my plate. "I was going to cook this and then wake you up."

"I could have done it."

He smirks and shakes his head. "Breakfast is something I can do with my eyes closed." His long black hair is out and stylishly swept over one side. I'd be willing to bet he has no idea how sexy it makes him look. Especially shirtless with the dark hair across his wide chest.

My knees almost buckle.

"Catch." He slides the plate across the counter toward me, and I catch it before it slips off onto the floor.

"Thanks."

"What are your plans for today?" he asks, adding salt to his food before rounding the counter to join me.

But the second I open my mouth to answer him, Keller reaches over and snags the cap from my head. He scrapes his hair back with one hand and shoves it down over the top with the other.

"It suits me better."

My mouth is still hanging open when he reaches over and, with two fingers on my chin, closes it for me.

"You can have it back when I'm done eating." His deep voice sets my whole body alight.

What is happening?

Did I fall asleep and wake up in some alternate reality? I've gone into shock while Keller turns and starts on his food like nothing out of the ordinary is happening. And I guess, on the surface, it isn't.

Did I actually say what I thought I said last night? And if I did, Keller obviously hasn't taken it the way I meant. This is best-case scenario. Am I really that lucky?

"If you keep staring at me like that, I might need to steal this hat permanently."

"I'm not staring," I hurry to say.

Keller side-eyes me, lips twitching upward.

"I'm not."

"And yet you still haven't looked away."

I hurry to turn back to my food. It looks delicious, obviously, but it's not what's making my mouth water. Keller looks way too good in my hat. I've seen him in it before that one time in my office, but for some reason, it didn't hit the way it is this morning. Maybe it's the sharing a bed thing or the fact he took it right from my head? Maybe it's that he's acting a whole lot more comfortable around me than he has since I moved in.

"I'm surprised you haven't asked about last night yet," he says.

"Fuck, yeah." I spin back to him. "Did it work?"

"Mostly. There were a few times you woke up—once where you tried to climb over me, but I just guided you back to lie down, and you fell right back to sleep again."

I sag with relief. "That's good, right?"

"I think so. Is that how it was with Molly?"

"Yeah. It was only a couple of nights until I stopped waking up again."

"Well, that's one down."

"You'll be rid of me soon enough, and everything will be back to normal."

"Maybe." His eyes trail over my face. "It wasn't all bad though, was it?"

"Well, no …" I hold my breath, on edge over what he might be about to say.

"I thought so too. It was nice getting a chance to talk."

"We can talk anytime."

"I know, but there's something different about night." He takes a bite and chews for a moment. "Feels more honest."

My gut fucking cartwheels at the word. Does … does he mean … Did he pick up on … I'm definitely reading too much into this because if Keller knew I had a crush on him, there's no way he wouldn't bring it up with me and address it head-on.

I think.

"Want to work out after this?" he asks.

It's only then I notice the shorts he's wearing are his gym

ones. I'd been too busy checking out his naked half to worry about the rest of him.

"Sounds good."

"Let's see if you can catch me on the rower this time."

I huff, playing up my annoyance. "It's not my fault you've had years of practice on me."

"You'll get there one day, grasshopper."

"Gonna show me everything you know?"

"Nope. I'm gonna kick your ass until you're tired of losing."

I bark a laugh, not able to stop from picturing the many, many things I'd let him do to my ass. All he has to do is ask, and the answer will always be yes.

The thing about working out with Keller, though, is that it's not only testing my fitness but is an exercise in restraint as well. The whole hour, I'm watching him get steadily sweatier, bulky muscles swelling under the exertion, listening to the way he grunts as he lifts and trying not to transfer those sounds to the bedroom.

My compression shorts keep my dick under control, but it's a close one.

"What do you have on for the rest of the day?" I ask, upping the weight on my bar. For a Saturday, I should have more plans than just sitting around the house, but I didn't grow up in Kilborough. Molly was my only tie to this place, and while I've made friends with Joey, that's about as active as my social life gets. In college, I did so much more, and with Molly gone, it's made me remember just how much I love company. I'm an extrovert. People are my thing.

"I was going to see Barney, then I have a job on tonight."

My breath hitches for a second before I ask my next question. "No date?" I was blindingly happy last night to find out nothing happened, but it was temporary relief. That kind of thing is a given for Keller, and it's going to hurt just as much every time.

"Nope. The app isn't helping. I might have to go back to the old-fashioned way."

"And what's that?"

"Meeting someone and getting to know them, then asking them out if I'm interested."

"Pity there aren't that many people in Kilborough."

He looks over and catches my eyes. "There are enough."

Before I can ask what he means by that, Keller completes his reps of power cleans, then reracks the bar and picks up his towel. My gaze is stuck to his throat as he wipes off the back of his neck and follows the sweat down his chest. The sight is damn near pornographic.

All I need now is for him to pull out his hair and have all those damp strands in a chaotic mess around his head, but he doesn't, and I try not to pout over it. Ogling my best friend's dad isn't getting me anywhere in life.

Even if I really, really enjoy it.

"Need me to spot you on that?" he asks.

I blink down at the bar by my feet, almost having forgotten it was there. "Nope, I'm good."

Cheeks blazing, I complete my reps and then set everything back as well. Keller needs to come with one of those labels that drugs do, only instead of warning about drowsiness and operating heavy machinery, his should say, "WARNING: may cause intense stupidity. Do not attempt heavy lifts while under the influence."

And I'm definitely under the influence. My whole body is tuned in to his, and I even go heavier on the weights than I normally would because I want my muscles to stand out to him. I have no idea if that's what he's into, but if he is, I'll do everything I can to make sure he notices mine.

What Joey was saying about putting myself out there flitters through my head. I'm playing in the big leagues. Can't afford to stick to the safe plays.

I clear my throat, feeling like an idiot before I even say anything. "Actually, could you spot me on the bench press? I want to try for three hundred."

"What's your max?"

"Two seventy-five."

I'm a complete idiot for even wanting to try this, but with Keller on board, I'm not about to say no. Impressing him with my strength would be a bonus, but him being close, standing almost over my head, giving me an entirely inappropriate peek at the glimpse of thigh those shorts are covering … I remind myself to focus and not be distracted while I have three hundred pounds hovering over my chest. We build up to the weight, and even though it's at the end of a session, I manage it in one smooth movement. Unassisted. I'm grinning when he helps me steer the bar back onto the rack, and then I jump up and punch the air.

"Shit yes."

"Impressive." Keller holds his hand up for a high five that I gladly meet. My skin buzzes at the contact, and I'm an inch away from pulling him into a hug. I only just keep it together.

What was that I was saying about two months not being so bad?

It's only been a week of us spending proper time together, and I'm already desperate to put it all out there. How the hell am I going to get through the rest of this stay with any dignity left?

17

KELLER

I'M NOT PROUD OF MYSELF.

I'm not impressed by my lack of self-control.

If anything, I should be pissed that I give in so easily, but when I step under the shower post-workout, water beating down over my very hard, very sensitive cock, I have no restraint left.

That gym session was absolute torture.

I grip myself and jack off unashamedly. Even when Will's gorgeous body passes through my mind, I don't push it out again. Don't try to deny myself what I want. Instead, I melt into the image of those smooth, rounded shoulders, the deep grooves where they meet his collarbones, his eight-pack, and the perfect little belly button that I want to dip my tongue into.

The veins down his biceps stood out enticingly today, and only the threat of him dropping a very heavy weight on his very pretty face made me concentrate on his lift rather than him.

It's a close call though.

This is getting ridiculous.

I strangle my shaft, thinking of the way his mouth hung open at breakfast and even the feel of him pressed against me last night. I might have told Will that he tried to climb over me, but I left out the part where he dropped down and fell asleep on top of me as well.

Rolling him back onto the bed was the right thing to do—unlike what I'm doing right now—but that doesn't mean I didn't appreciate the few seconds I had him pressed against me.

And I'm reaping the full benefit of those few seconds right now.

My head hangs back, free hand pressed to the tile as I sink deeper into the fantasies. Into the thought of pulling Will in close, hands dipping to grip tight to his hips, abs pressed against mine, tongue licking into my mouth.

I shudder as my balls tighten and unleash, orgasm satisfying and frustrating all at once. When the high sucks away faster than usual, I aim the shower at the drain and watch my release disappear along with the water.

So.

I'm attracted to Will.

It hasn't taken me completely by surprise as I've always registered him as being *attractive*, but us hooking up had just been a spontaneous event. This wanting to consciously act on it is new. The idea of touching him is ever-present in my palms, this deep temptation, and knowing I can't do anything about it only makes it that much worse.

The thought of him being attracted to me, too, is a confidence boost, I'm not going to lie. It's more than possible I've imagined it all, but I'm happy to live in that delusion. Flirting with him this morning stretched muscles I haven't had to use in years, and seeing his reaction to me wearing his hat just about confirmed my theory. I won't believe it completely unless he says the words out loud, and given how flustered Will can get sometimes, I can't imagine that will ever happen.

Which leaves me in a dilemma.

Do I keep flirting and hope it leads to something? Or do I be the dad I've always been and leave my son's friend the hell alone?

Molly is the main variable here. I don't know how he'd react. If it was one of my friends with my dad, I know for sure that would ick me out. Forgetting the fact my dad is straight, he's *my dad*. That man and sex don't belong in the same sentence, and it's the same way with Molly. Thinking of one of my friends with *him*? Sure, he'd tried with Ford, and if it had worked out, I would have kept my mouth closed and let him be happy, but I would have been watching that man like a hawk. If he fucked up, I would have murdered him.

The last thing I want is to gross Molly out. To make him uncomfortable. And with the mood he's been in lately, I can't be sure he wouldn't turn his back on us, and that would fucking kill me. I'd like to think my son is better than that, and six months ago, I might have believed it, but after he got drunk and kissed Ford right in front of Orson, I don't know what to think anymore.

Will's his best friend.

Out of everyone in the world, why does my gut have to be pulling me toward him?

I talk a lot about trusting it, but can I be sure it's accurate in this situation and not just my dick jamming the signal?

No. There's no way I could risk my relationship with Molly for some fun sex. No fucking way.

My attraction will have to stay on the down-low. Flirting is fine; acting on it is not.

I get out of the shower and towel off, drying my hair until it isn't dripping water everywhere. While I might be trying to throttle this attraction, it doesn't mean I can't spend time with Will. He's lonely, I'm lonely, and the cure for loneliness is company, which is something I can give him.

I head downstairs to see if he wants to come with me today but redirect at the knock on the front door.

"Keller?" the delivery guy asks.

I nod, trying to remember if I ordered anything. He pushes a plain box into my hands.

"Have a good day."

"You too."

I kick the door closed behind me and carry the box through to the living room. It's from a company, but the business name doesn't look familiar, so I know I didn't order anything from them.

My suspicions immediately ping, and I set the box down on my coffee table before taking a step back.

What the hell could be in there? I've had shit delivered to work and been followed before by disgruntled cheaters, but my work is usually on the down-low, and my name is left off almost everything. Most people don't know what my job entails, but the ones who think I've screwed them over? Yeah, if they're morally bankrupt enough to do the wrong thing in the first place, I wouldn't put anything past them.

I know I'm being overly cautious and suspicious, but the

police force taught me to approach the unknown like it's the worst-case scenario, and then I'll be prepared for anything. Maybe Molly sent me a gift, or maybe it's a bloody horse head to send me a message. I won't know until I open it.

I retrieve a pair of scissors from the kitchen and drag the blades over the tape holding the top together. Then, I slip the scissors under the cardboard flaps and fold them open.

Lots of plastic packaging covers the top, and I slowly move it with the sharp end of the scissors, picking it up bit by bit, prepared to move back if I need to. But the more I remove, the more curious I become until—

"Is that ..."

I pick up the enormous green-and-purple tentacle dildo.

"Oh my fucking god, that's mine!"

The garbled shout from behind me takes a second for me to decipher, and when Will literally *dives* over the back of the couch for the box, it all clicks into place.

"You like tentacle porn?" I ask, mouth hanging open in shock. It's not even that it's a turnoff either, because the thought of using this on him is hotter than I'm expecting it to be. No, it's that in a thousand years, I never would have guessed that Will was down for anything kinky. And I'm usually a good judge of those things.

His face is a heated mess as he climbs up from where he landed on the floor, eyes locked on the tentacle I'm holding. "I'm going to fucking kill Joey."

I just stare at the toy. "What does Joey have to do with me being sent a box of *your* sex toys?"

His whole face falls. "Please don't make me explain."

I poke him in the cheek with the tentacle, which he immediately bats away. And I can't help it—laughter slips out as I drop onto the couch beside where he's sitting. "This is a story I'd be happy to wait all day to hear." I prop my ankle on my knee, arms spread along the back of the couch like I'm prepared to wait him out. And I am. Though the glare he's giving the abnormal phallus I'm holding is enough to make my entire day.

"I'm waiting," I sing, swimming the tentacle like a conductor's baton.

"What's that? I'm moving out today? Oh, well, if you insist. I'll just—" Will tries to stand, but I pull him down onto the couch beside me, so close that his thigh touches my thigh, and I inhale a whole noseful of his body spray.

"Don't make me poke you again."

"Why are you doing this to me?" He pouts.

"My own amusement."

"That's horrible, just so you know."

I shrug, running my fingers over the suckers. "Bet these feel good."

"Oh my god." He flops backward, hands covering his face. "I might have, umm … Joey might have found out that … that … *I've never tried a sex toy, so he wanted to rectify that situation.*"

Again with the thousand words in one, but this time, I hear him loud and clear. My lips twitch, gaze tracking shamelessly over his stretched-out body. Will has never tried a sex toy? Turns out my kink radar is still working in full effect.

I press my tongue into my cheek to stop from saying the words I really, really want to let out, because offering to help Will with learning how to use these doesn't fit into my plan of ignoring this attraction.

Still … I *did* say I could flirt a little.

"He thought he'd rectify it by ordering you a tentacle? He's certainly making sure you have a diverse range."

Will's face reappears as he peeks out from between his fingers. "I'm still torn on whether that makes him a good or a bad friend."

My gaze flicks to the box. "Well, let's see."

Will works out what I'm about to do just as I move. He goes for the box, but I jump up and grab it, yanking it just out of his reach. My hand dives inside as Will lets out a cry and—jumps on my fucking back. His legs close around my waist, one hand trying to pull my arm out while the other tugs at the box in my grip.

My hand closes over something, and as soon as I get a good hold on it, I stop fighting Will. He tears my hand from the box, fingers wrapped around my wrist while I brandish ... what the fuck is that?

A Fleshlight, but instead of being a recognizable body part, it looks like an alien flower surrounding the hole.

"What the fuck?" Will asks weakly before he drops his forehead to my shoulder. "I'm going to kill him."

I laugh as Will slides from my back. "I dunno, I'm interested."

"In *that*?"

I set it aside. "Willing to try anything once. And hey, since I'm struggling to find a date, it might come in handy."

Will stares up at me with wide eyes that slowly move from me to the toy. In my imagination, he's imagining me using it, and maybe it makes me a dick, but I use the distraction to upend the box on the table. A lot of lube, condoms, and tiny appendages fall out. There's also what looks like an egg inseminator, a regular-shaped cock vibrator, and a double-ended dildo that's as thick as my forearm.

I pick it up, and it droops over like a dying flower. "I'm not one to judge, but I have questions."

"Is your question how the hell anyone can fit that thing?" Will lifts the side I'm not holding and inspects it closer, then wraps his hands around the girth. "I'm clenching just looking at it."

Do not picture him clenching. Do not. "You'd be surprised what the body can fit."

Those wide eyes find mine again, and I can't stop myself from pumping my eyebrows his way.

"Anyone would think you've never seen fisting porn."

"Because I haven't!" His voice gets higher with each word, and it's so adorable the need to use one of these things on him builds even stronger.

"Well." I set the monster toy back on the table and look around at the assortment, trying not to laugh again. Art's a shit stirrer, and suddenly, his relationship is making a hell of a lot more sense because apparently, Joey is too. There's no way anything here is for a beginner, and half the stuff—like the candy G-string and sex dice—can't be used solo. Just what the hell was Joey thinking?

"For a beginner," I say, wanting to dim his embarrassment, "start here." I pick up the regular vibrating dildo and hand it over. "If bottoming isn't your thing though, there's always this." The green Fleshlight is a weird shape, but at least it's not alien-looking and isn't one of the ones that looks like an animal mouth.

He takes both toys from me and gapes at them. "I don't know …" When he looks up, those gorgeous gray eyes meet mine. "Do you want them?"

I grab the alien flower thing with a smirk. "I'm going to take this baby for a test drive."

His face is still insanely flushed when he runs a hand down it. "I can't believe we're having this conversation."

"Neither can I, but I don't hate it."

"You don't?"

I know I shouldn't say it. I try to make myself hold back. The words are insistent though, and with the way Will lit up, there's nothing stopping them from coming out. "Seeing what you're going to be playing with ..." I swallow, gaze dropping to the toys in his hand. "I'm never going to be able to look at you the same way again."

Instead of the horror I'm petrified I'll see, Will's gaze sharpens on me. A rare confidence flickers to life in the curl of his lips. "You're the one talking about letting an alien suck on your cock."

"Looking forward to it too."

His pupils flare wide, and when he speaks, his voice is a sexy rasp. "Is there anything else you want to try?"

I can't stop my eyes from falling to his lips. Tracing those full shapes. Imagining what he tastes like. I look him directly in the eye again when I say, "I can think of at least one more."

"Oh yeah?"

"Something so sexy I'm struggling to resist."

Will's exhale hits my chin. It's what alerts me to how close we've moved. Reminds me of the promises I made to myself. So, with all the willpower I possess, I give him a cheeky smile and lean forward to scoop up the ribbed anal beads.

"I'm gonna have some fun with these."

His next exhale falls out on a laugh, and he leans forward to pick up the monster again. "Why don't you give this a go while you're at it?"

"That's more of a two-person toy. And also, ouch." Then, before I can stop myself, I say, "But I'll let you know if I find someone who lets me use the tentacle on them. Because I think I just found a new fantasy."

He eyes the toy for a moment, then leans forward and packs everything into the box except the two things I handed him ... and the tentacle. That shouldn't make me grin as hard as it does.

Will shoves the box at me. "Anything in here is fair game for whichever of us gets to it first, on one condition."

"Oh, yeah?"

"They're for us only. No using my toys to play with anyone else."

Heat boils in my veins as I think about the implications of that. "What about the toys that need two people?"

He steps in closer so the box is crushed between us both. "You're a smart man, Keller. I'm sure you can think of a solution."

Then Will leaves me standing there, jaw on the ground, as he grabs the toys and leaves.

He might not have admitted it outright, but there's no confusing what Will was implying. If only two of us can use the toys, it means he wants to use them with *me*.

And fuck do I want that.

So badly it's overriding everything else.

Except Molly.

I will not hook up with Will. I will not hook up with Will.

Even I'm not so sure I believe the words.

18

WILL

ALL DAY, I'M FROZEN IN A STATE OF BEING BOTH HORRIFIED by what I said to Keller and proud as fuck I got the words out.

It helps that he'd definitely, probably been flirting with me over those sex toys, and then when I dropped my little suggestion, he didn't freak out or pull me up on overstepping. In fact, if I were a more confident person, I would have assumed that he was interested in my offer.

"Who's Barney?" I ask as we climb out of his car in the Kill Pen parking lot. We're right on the cusp of the summer break, so it's not crowded yet, but there's definitely an uptick in the usual crowd, even for the weekend.

Keller hits his key fob as we leave his Volvo behind and make our way into the tourist trap. To get into the ghost town and the prison, you need to buy a ticket, but the streets surrounding it are filled with retailers and people dressed up doing reenactments. We're higher up the Provin Mountain, and from certain streets, I catch glimpses of Kilborough just below.

"He's the one who started the Divorced Men's Club with Art. He runs a souvenir shop with his partner, Leif."

"Won't they be too busy to talk today?" I'd imagine a Saturday is prime business for them.

"Nah, around this time is when a lot of tours start, so they should be okay."

We reach a little shop that sells souvenirs, and I follow Keller inside. There's a bigger, blond man standing behind the register and ringing up a customer, while a darker-haired man restocks a middle shelf.

Keller greets the dark-haired man as Leif and then introduces me.

"You're the roommate, huh?" Leif says. "I've heard a lot about you."

Keller gives him a blank look. "Did Art put you up to that?"

"Up to what?" His tone is anything but innocent, and I get the feeling this is an extension of the Art and Joey nudging Keller in chats idea. Dear god. Does everyone on the planet know I have a thing for him? Where Joey's involved, I doubt this is a coincidence.

Keller doesn't answer Leif, and we're saved by Barney joining us. At least, that's what I think until—

"So *you're* the roommate?"

I want to face-palm.

Keller gives him a dry look. "Leif beat you to it."

"Gah, dammit."

"You done now?"

Leif laughs. "Look, Art might be a horndog, but even I can agree with him. Your roommate is hot."

My face burns. "I'm standing right here."

"And don't we all know it?"

Barney backhands his boyfriend, and Leif rounds on him.

"Is my sexy man jealous?"

I watch on as Leif pulls Barney possessively against him, biting his jaw as he palms Barney's meaty ass. No matter what Leif might have said to me, his attraction to Barney burns between them, and the longer Leif feels Barney up, the more wistfulness settles over me.

Do I want to be publicly and aggressively groped like that? Nope. Not for me. But having a man who wants me that much?

My gaze slips to Keller, who's already watching me.

"Sorry about them. They'll be done in a minute."

"Nothing to apologize for." Even if my cheeks are still hot. "It's kind of sweet."

"Yeah, well, they've still got their clothes on for now." Keller nudges Leif. "How do you two manage any work around here?"

"Barney doesn't usually have a reason to be jealous, and a jealous Barney is my weakness."

"Good to know. Done yet?"

Leif bites Barney's neck. "I dunno, we done yet, baby?"

Barney's bright red and so obviously turned on I have to look away. That's way too intimate for me. "No, come back later."

"Dude, keep it in your pants and get me a drink," Keller says. "Then you can go out the back and get off so I can get a straight conversation out of you."

The bell above the shop door sounds, and it brings Barney back to earth. He sighs as Leif releases him.

"I'll get that one. You stay and chat." Leif kisses him quickly before going to help the customer.

Barney leads us over to a small table and chairs near the counter and sinks into a seat, hands covering his face. "I'm so sorry. I hate myself, but when Leif touches me, I just lose it. Forget anything else exists."

Keller shrugs. "I'm used to it. You might have scarred Will for life though. He's a virgin."

Barney's jaw drops as I swing large eyes on Keller.

"No, I fucking am not!"

"Could have fooled me."

"Why, because I've never used a sex toy before? Sorry I like to have sex with men and not silicone."

He chuckles, gaze running over me in a way that makes me weak. And maybe I can sympathize with Barney because if Keller touched me here and now, I don't think I'd tell him to stop. "Let me know if that's still the case after you've played with that Fleshlight."

"Will do." Though I'm all talk because there's no way I'll be telling him about that. All I know is I'm torn on whether I want the sleepwalking to continue so Keller has to stay in my bed or to end so I can give those toys a go.

"Not that all this sex talk hasn't been enjoyable," Barney says, "but you're making it hard to think with my big head."

Leif finishes up serving, and when the customer leaves, he brings over three bottles of Coke and joins us. If I thought it would be weird that I'm here with him, it's not. Barney and Leif are easy to talk to, and after the initial teasing, they don't bring it up again.

While they talk, I pull out my phone and text Joey.

Me:

Did Art tell Barney and Leif that I have feelings for Keller?

Joey:
What are you talking about?

Me:
We're with them now, and they were acting super weird about me when we got here.

Joey:
I just asked him. Art definitely told them to rib Keller about you, but not that you have a crush.

Me:
You're both perfect for each other. And no, that's not a compliment.

Joey:
Hey, you let me use you to make Art jealous once and I told you I'd return the favor. This is me doing that.

Me:
I suppose I should thank you. We had a moment over the sex toys.

Joey:
A MOMENT?! Holy shit, I'm a genius. Yes, I'll be the best man at your wedding.

Me:
I said a moment, not a proposal, calm down.

Joey:
That's how it starts. Art and I had a "moment" as well. It ended with me bent over his office desk, being sent to the stars.

Me:
I'd be happy if Keller just took me to bed.

Joey:
Sometimes you make me sad for your sex life.

I wish I could dispute it, but know I can't.
Me:
Me too, Joey. Me too.

"So what are you doing with the rest of your day?" Barney asks.

"I have to work tonight. I've got a job on."

"Ohh ..." He leans forward excitedly. "Is it a good one? Stealth work? Disguises? Crawling through air ducts?"

Keller shoots a bewildered look Barney's way. "What exactly is it you think I do?"

"Mr. and Mrs. Smith stuff, right?"

Considering I agreed to go with Keller tonight, I certainly fucking hope not.

Keller's expression turns serious. "Exactly. So you should know that if I tell you, I'll have to kill you."

Leif leans forward, looking more intense than he has so far. "You kill Barney, and I burn this whole fucking town to the ground."

I choke on my awkward laugh. "Why don't we all agree just to play nice?"

"Bet Keller would like to play nice with you," Barney mutters.

I know I would.

"My job is way less fun than all that," Keller says, ignoring Barney completely.

And thank goodness for that. While stakeouts and government plots are fun in movies, it's not something I wanna experience in real life. That's one of the reasons I went into tech support. I had offers to join some promising start-ups fresh out of college, but while I might be an IT nerd, I'm also a practical guy. I'll take my cushy desk job and livable wage over the type of high-risk, high-reward road so many people from my classes went for. I know at least one guy whose gamble paid off, but the vast majority of them have gone silent on their ventures.

"We'll let you guys get back to work," Keller says, standing and nodding at me to do the same.

On the way back to the car, that worry line is still creasing his forehead.

"Everything okay?"

Keller slips his mirrored sunglasses on, looking every bit like a Viking rock god. "Yeah, just rethinking bringing you along tonight."

"Why?"

"My job isn't all that exciting, but I've had people I've caught out find me before. Thankfully, nothing's escalated. I'd just hate for something to happen while you're there."

I shouldn't feel so good about the fact he cares. "I'm not worried. Wanna know why?"

"Why?"

"Because you'll be there."

Keller's smile shadows the corners of his lips. "That's a lot of confidence you have in me."

"I said what I said."

"Now there's even more pressure." He bumps his knuckles on my jaw. "Wouldn't want to disappoint you, would I?"

"I don't think you ever could."

I can't make out his eyes behind his reflective lenses, but by the set of his face, I get the feeling he's studying me. And I look right back.

His hair is in a chaotic bun, tight tank top showing off his round shoulders, and torn jeans hugging his powerful thighs. I've always done my best not to openly check him out like this, to store my attraction away in the deepest, darkest parts of me, but it keeps sneaking out. Keeps wanting to be discovered. And when Keller drags his tongue over his big bottom lip, my heart damn near stops.

I want to feel that tongue on my skin. Even just once. Even if it means absolutely nothing but a chance to get off, I'm long past caring. Let Keller hurt me. Let him stomp my heart into the ground.

So long as I get to experience what it's like to be with him, I don't care about the rest.

DMC GROUP CHAT

Keller: *Barney and Leif were sufficiently obvious and embarrassing today, thank you.*

Payne: *It's really fun for me that now everyone is focused on you two, I get left alone.*

Griff: *Speaking of Beau ...*

Payne: *Do not.*

Keller: *There is no "us two". Theres a huuuuge age gap and son between us.*

Art: *You guys have a son already? 0/10. Do not recommend.*

Orson: *You're using Molly as an excuse.*

Keller: *You don't think I should consider my son's feelings?*

Griff: *Speaking as someone whose son found out the wrong way—if something does happen, he needs to hear it from you.*

Keller: *Just the threat of that conversation is enough to make sure nothing happens.*

Art: *Ahhhh ... but you want it to?*

Keller: *Don't "ahhhh" me like you've uncovered something amazing.*

Art: *You have feelings. That's kind of amazing.*

19

KELLER

I'M NERVOUS BRINGING WILL ALONG ON THIS JOB. I NEED TO be focused on what I'm being paid to do, not on him. The problem with Will, though, is that I didn't want to part so soon. And "soon" is fucking ridiculous, considering we've spent the whole day together already.

"Do you think he's cheating?" Will asks.

I glance over at him from the front seat of my car, where his face is half in shadow and half-lit from the streetlight down the block. "I'm not paid for my opinion. I'm paid for the facts," I explain. "So I try to be as impartial as possible."

His jaw ticks unhappily as he turns to face the empty street again. "He probably is."

"What makes you say that?"

"Well, you'd think most people in relationships aren't suspicious unless they're given a reason to be suspicious."

"That's a good theory."

He rubs his palms over his denim-covered thighs. "How many cases like this have you worked?"

"Suspected cheating? A lot."

"And how many of them are actually doing it?"

I cringe, not wanting to say. "More than the ones who aren't."

Will sags into his seat. "Why do people do it?"

"Cheat? Usually, because they're looking for something they feel like they're missing. Sometimes for the thrill. Sometimes they just don't give a fuck."

Will turns to me, propping his elbow on the center console and resting his chin in his hand so he's closer than he was before. His low voice softens. "You'd never do something like that, would you?"

I chuckle. "Nah, I know what it's like to be hurt. Not cheated on, but hurt is hurt. Besides." I think of Molly and how broken he was after his ex did that to him. "After what happened to Molly, I can't help but take it personally."

"Ha!" Will grins, a warm thing that clears the cobwebs clinging to my mind. "I knew you couldn't be totally impartial. You're such a protective papa bear."

"I am." I scan the street again, but we're still alone. "Protective of you too, you know."

Will blanches. "Please tell me you don't picture me as another son?"

My surprised laugh jumps from me before I can stop it. Considering my body's reaction to him the other day? Hell fucking no. "I already have a kid, and he's more than enough for me. You two might be similar in a lot of ways"—sensitive, caring, fun—"but I only need one son, and you're not him. Sorry."

I'm *not* sorry.

Will settles back closer again. "Don't apologize. That's probably the best answer you could have given me."

He sounds genuine, which helps me relax because the last thing I want is for Will to picture me as some kind of surrogate parent when I'm picturing him as a man. All man. A man I'm having way too many inappropriate thoughts about. Yet I can't stop myself from teasing. "So you *don't* want me to be your Daddy?"

Will smirks. "I don't think I used *those* words."

Nrg. I really need to learn that teasing Will only teases myself because now all I can think of is Will under me, large body totally naked, and moaning how he wants to make it good for Daddy. I might not be into the whole kink scene, but I love it when the person I'm with can just submit and let me play with them.

The image of Will's gray eyes on me while I explore his body is too much.

And not something I'll ever experience because sleeping with him is a fast way to complicate my life. There's no point doing that when I have so many other options for a fast hookup.

Will's gazing back out the windscreen. "I could never cheat," he says.

"I'd believe it."

"Imagine breaking someone's trust like that? Knowing they're sitting at home, assuming you're theirs, while you're balls-deep inside someone else? Makes me sick just thinking about it."

"Me too. That's kind of what happened to Payne."

"What do you mean?"

"Found out his husband had an OnlyFans and was

making money fucking a bunch of random men. Someone sent him the link."

Will sets his feet on the seat and wraps his arms around his knees. "That's horrible. What did he do?"

"Cut ties and moved back here. Shacked up with Beau, and now he's ridiculously happy." And saying it like that almost makes me believe in the theory of things happening for a reason. But then I remember Molly's ex and that my son's on the other side of the country, and the way Michelle walked out on us not once but twice, and the theory goes out the window again.

There are no reasons.

Just shitty people.

"Does it make you sad?" Will asks.

It's a question I don't have an immediate answer for, and the silence stretches out between us. When I finally have an answer, it's not something I'd say in front of just anyone, but I can talk to Will. It's not even my attraction to him that makes it easy; it's just ... him. I turn in my seat to face him, which puts us a few inches apart.

"The cheating does," I admit. "Obviously. But I also view it as though I'm setting their partners free. It's gotta hurt and be life-changing, but the alternative is staying with someone who doesn't respect you."

"Respect is a big thing for me."

"Me too. So is treating your partner right. Whoever it is. None of us deserve to be betrayed like that."

Will sighs. "There you go again, just proving what a good guy you are."

I laugh. "I don't think that should be the standard for a good guy. It should be the standard for *any* guy."

"True. But you're a good one anyway. You put everyone else to shame."

The fact that Will is pushing this amuses me. "How so?"

"There are a lot of reasons. You said one yourself before about how protective you are. You let me move into your place and won't take any rent. You raised Molly, who's one of the best people I know. You care about others and not because you're supposed to but because you want to. Those all seem like good things to me."

They do, and it'd be a lie to say I don't love Will seeing me that way. But I still need to set the record straight. "Good makes me sound like some kind of saint. Or martyr. I'm neither of those things. A lot of the jobs I take are on the side of huge insurance companies. I lie when I need to. I got pissy with Molly over kissing Ford when I should have had my kid's back. I let him get hurt. I let him move and didn't ask him to stay. I have an app full of people I can text for a hookup, and I've never once wondered if any of them have a person at home waiting for them."

Will snorts. "None of those things are going against my point. You work for a living, and I'd bet you're always fair in whether you find anything. Molly deserved a talking-to and wouldn't have wanted you to try and change his mind about moving because it would have worked. Those people you text also aren't for you to hold accountable. You still haven't said a single thing to change my mind."

There's one thing I could say. *Good guys don't dream about railing their son's best friend.* Luckily, I'm smart enough not to bring it up. "I know one place I'm not good," I mutter, and I'm not sure that answer is any better.

But Will hears me. "Oh, yeah, where's that?"

I give him a knowing look that sets his face on fire.

"Oh. Right. There."

"Exactly."

"Well, this is all very good information I should know in case your friends succeed in setting us up."

Urg, I was really hoping he wouldn't catch that. "They weren't exactly subtle, were they?"

"Nope. It was fun." Will side-eyes me. "Nice to know they think I'm hot, at least."

"I don't think there's a man alive who doesn't."

His head snaps toward me. "Even you?"

I roll my eyes and try to play off *how* hot I find him. "You're shirtless most of the time. Like I have a choice."

"Note to self: burn all my shirts."

"Then what would you wear when it gets cold?"

He shrugs and sends me a sly look. "Dunno. You?"

"*Will.*" I just stare at him, mouth hanging open at the blatant confidence I've never seen from him before.

He cracks up laughing. "Your face is priceless."

"Dude, I'm old. Give me a break—you almost gave me a heart attack."

"Because it was a shock ... or because you liked it so dang much?"

"I—" My words disappear when I glance out the window and see our guy heading down the street. I nod his way, and our flirting comes to a stop. "We're on."

20

WILL

AS MUCH AS I LOVED THE ONE-ON-ONE TIME WITH KELLER, I'm loving this even more. His large hand is burning up the blood pumping through my arm and pooling in my palm that's wrapped around his.

Cheater cheatface headed to a club in Springfield, and I had the most amazing, brilliant idea ever that we pretend to be a couple and follow him. The idea had nothing at all to do with Keller admitting he finds me hot, and I'm feeling a bit reckless with that information.

"Now, what are we not going to do?" he asks, lips by my ear and deep voice sliding through me like a drug.

"Get shitfaced and need to be carried home."

"Good boy," he says, amusement tinging his tone. "You're learning."

So that happened *one* time.

The way he cared for me the next morning made it hard to regret anything.

"It's not my fault I'm a lightweight."

"I'd argue it's exactly your fault."

I turn my head to look at him and am surprised to find those intense eyes soft. "You want me to drink more?"

"Not at all. I think it's awesome you never got into that."

"You can have just as much fun without it."

"That you can. And actually, considering it's better to be sober when you're hooking up, I think you can probably have *more* fun without it."

"You stay sober when you hook up?" That information probably shouldn't surprise me.

"Not always. If I'm just looking to get my dick sucked in a club, no." His lips tilt toward my ear again. "But if I take a person home, it's because I'm planning to discover every inch of their body that makes them feel good. Every touch, every caress, every little thing that makes them wet or hard. And it's way easier to do that with a clear head."

The rasp in his voice shivers down my neck, through my chest, and settles in my groin. I wonder if Keller knows he doesn't even need to touch me to make me hard. Him paying that kind of attention to me is such a turn-on; I can only imagine what he'd do with his hands, his mouth, his tongue if given a chance.

I'd give him all the chances. Anything to be the one he spent the night with.

What started out as an amazing idea is becoming the worst one I've ever had. I don't know if Keller is meaning to be an epic cocktease or not, but he's fucking succeeding, especially when he lets my hand go and wraps his arm tightly around my shoulders.

We're two people behind the man he's following, so by

the time we reach the bouncer and get let inside, the man has been swallowed by the crowds.

"What now?" I ask over the loud music.

"Bar."

"You're drinking?" I have to stop myself from drooling. His hair is out and flicked over to the side, leaving his thick, brown neck exposed. It's a fight to stop from burying my nose into it.

"Nope. Our guy will most likely be heading there," Keller explains. "Cheating's easier if you're blind drunk."

I let Keller pull me further into the club. The way he's able to look so casual while his sharp eyes never stop moving is something he must have spent years perfecting, and the way he's taking everything in only makes me fall for him that little bit more. This is his job; he's in his element, knows what he's doing, and while I'm tempted to help, I don't think standing on my tiptoes and scanning the club would fall under covert.

"There," he murmurs right into my ear. "By the bar, watching the dance floor. Let's dance not too far away, but I want you to keep your whole attention on me, okay? Don't look at him once. I'm pretty sure he doesn't know he's being followed, but we don't want to make him suspicious."

Keep all my attention on Keller? Oh, damn, no, however will I survive?

I fist my hand in the bottom of Keller's shirt and drag him onto the dance floor. He stops me when we get just inside the inner ring, and while I can't see the guy, I assume Keller can. He tugs me back against his body and says, "Right here. Now, close your eyes and dance against me."

Done and done. With Keller's arms wrapped around me and the pounding music and crushing bodies closing in on all sides, it's easy to forget why we're here and just relax into the music.

Keller keeps a frustrating amount of distance between us, and while I hate it and want nothing more than to feel him grinding against my ass, that probably wouldn't do anything to help my feelings for him.

Keeping some cock-to-ass distance is crucial for my sanity. Especially because his hands resting on my abs is enough temptation. The way they skim the waistband of my shorts. How his hair tickles my neck. His breath hot and heavy by my ear.

I smother my building moan.

Then we're knocked from the side, and I'm jolted out of bliss and into … fuck.

The man we followed offers me his hand, and while I want to tell him to fuck off, I take it instead. No need to act sus and raise the alarm.

Only when he helps me off the ground, he doesn't drop my hand, just uses it to yank me against him.

"What are you—"

"You're so fucking hot," he grunts into my ear, arms closing around me.

Unlike when Keller did it, this doesn't feel safe. It feels … My skin crawls under the contact.

But I guess this is exactly what we needed.

I grit my teeth through a smile, not that it matters, because the man just grabs my ass and grinds his cock into my hip. He's slobbering all over my neck, telling me over and over how hot I am, and I have to force the hands I have planted on his shoulders not to push him away.

Keller's glare is burning a hole in the back of the man's

head, but before he can interfere, I lift one hand and mime taking a photo.

Surprise flashes over Keller's face, and his gaze clashes with mine. The protectiveness he mentioned earlier is reflected back at me, and it almost takes my breath away, but then the man I'm dancing with snaps my focus back to him.

He cups my face and slams his mouth down over mine.

I stay stock-still, not returning the kiss and keeping my mouth pressed closed, even as his tongue runs over my lips, trying to find a way in. There are no words for how much I hate this man, both for taking what he wants when I'm clearly uncomfortable and for betraying his partner like this.

I want to shove him off me. Punch him. Maybe knee the bastard in the balls and cause some permanent damage. But I won't because I'm me.

The unwanted kiss feels like it stretches on for way too long, but it can only be a few seconds later that his mouth is gone and the grasping hands disappear.

Keller has the guy by the front of the shirt, and he looks menacing. I can't hear what he says over the music, but it's enough to send the guy running.

And I'm left standing there like an idiot.

Like an idiot who has disgusting spit drying on his lips.

I scrub at my mouth with the back of my hand, but it doesn't make that creepy-crawly feeling go away.

"Are you okay?" Keller asks, hands closing over my upper arms.

I want to sink into his grip, but now that he's asked the question, I'm not so sure I am.

"Did you get what you needed?"

His eyes search mine as he slowly nods.

"Good. Can we leave?" I turn before he can answer and push my way off the dance floor and through the club. There's a tiny part of me that's thrilled I got to help Keller. That I made his job easier. That we got the asshole and he's going to pay as soon as Keller shows those photos to whoever needs to see them.

But it fucking sucks to know that people like him exist, and someone is going to be hurt because of him.

I push through a side exit into an alleyway and gulp down the fresh night air.

Keller's right behind me. "Will, talk to me. Did I mess up?"

I whirl on him. "What?"

"Should I have stepped in sooner? *Fuck.* I should never have brought you."

The wild panic on his face calms me. "No. That's your job, Kel. As long as you got the photos you needed, it was all worth it."

His jaw tenses. "Not sure I agree with you."

I step closer, desperately wanting to take his hand but not daring to. "That wasn't your call."

"You shouldn't have had to do that."

"I didn't *have* to." But even reassuring him doesn't help him lose the deep frown settled between his eyebrows. "Why did you step in?"

"I ... I didn't like how you looked. You weren't enjoying it."

I shudder and scrub at my mouth again. "It was disgusting, and I can still feel him."

"I'm so sorry."

I give his shoulder a light whack. "You didn't do anything wrong. Now, stop it. I'm a big boy. I make my own choices."

Finally, the frown fades the tiniest amount. I only notice because I'm watching his face so closely. Just like he's watching me, those dark eyes drinking in my features from my eyes to my cheeks before resting on my mouth.

"I don't feel right about this," he says. "How do I pay you back for that?"

"There is one way," comes out before I can stop it.

"Anything."

I'm holding my breath as I make my suggestion. "Take the feel of him away."

Keller's lips part with surprise as his eyes meet mine again. I'm pretty sure he knows what I'm saying, but I'm trying really, really hard not to get my hopes up as I wait for the no I'm sure is coming.

But it doesn't.

When Keller's warm, large hands cup my face, he feels like he's holding glass. More gentle than I've ever known him to be, and I'm too afraid to move and wreck this.

I'm not breathing as he moves closer, and I don't think he is either. My brain is struggling to believe that even with all the flirting, I'm actually living this moment. This moment where Keller Gibson is inches away and closing the distance.

His eyes fall closed, and mine follow. Then it's just darkness and light hands and a buzz of awareness tightening my skin.

The second his lips make contact, my body flares to life. It's barely a kiss. Barely a touch. Featherlight, a whisper of skin brushing mine.

Once, twice, three times, he kisses me, getting slightly harder each time before he pulls away again. I didn't kiss him back, but I'm struggling to regret it because my whole head is dizzy with Keller and the lack of oxygen, and I'm not so sure this isn't a dream.

My eyes flutter open to find him watching me.

He's still holding my face, and his eyes don't break from mine for what feels like an eternity.

"I'll take a thanks like that any day," I say when I remember to breathe.

Keller's lips hitch up on one side. "Let's hope you're never in that position again."

As much as I want to kiss him, I have to agree. His lips have completely rid me of the cheating scum, but it's still not something I want to relive.

No.

If I want to kiss Keller, for real, I need to do it the old-fashioned way.

No more playing it safe. Joey's right. If I want to get a chance with Keller, I need to step it up. And not because he's my best friend's dad but because he's *him*.

Keller only deserves the best.

21

KELLER

Will and I are together all day, and it makes one thing overwhelmingly clear. I like spending time with him.

Will is cool. He doesn't bullshit like a lot of people, and I like seeing him go from self-conscious and almost shy to having the kind of confidence that makes my balls ache. As sexy as he is on the outside, I'm finding I'm equally as attracted to him on the inside. And that's a real problem.

That almost-kiss has rearranged my brain.

A lot of people don't understand what it means to be pansexual. It runs deeper for me than external attraction. Sure, I can meet someone and hook up no problem, but that way of doing things is transactional to me. It means nothing. Just a different way to get off that isn't my hand.

It's when I connect with who someone is on the inside that I'm in real trouble. That kind of attraction runs deep for me, which is why I'm so set on following my gut. I can pick up quickly the type of person who's going to reach me in that way. It doesn't mean it's going to be forever or even more than a few dates, but the potential is there.

And unfortunately, the potential is definitely there with Will.

We eat a late dinner and wind up watching another wonderfully horrible movie together. This time, he sits closer, gets more into it, pointing out the inaccuracies and sheer stupidity over his stir-fry, and that's when the niggle hits me. The comforting hope that blooms in my chest as I realize I can see this being a regular thing for us.

That I *want* this to be a regular thing for us.

I promised myself I wouldn't have sex with him just for something to do. But that promise is hard to hold on to as my affection for him deepens.

He asked me to kiss him. Could he feel the same?

No matter how many signs he gives me, that's something I can't wrap my head around. All I keep focusing on is how much older than him I am. Keep asking myself how Will could be attracted to me, let alone think anything more than that.

I disregard the swirling thoughts and remind myself that every problem has a simple solution. And right now, the solution I have is not to think about it too hard.

Simple.

"Ready for bed?" Will asks, and the question slithers through me.

It's past midnight, and I've been ready all day, but it doesn't make it any less awkward to walk up the stairs with him, knowing we're going to be lying side by side again, the darkness pressing us together and bringing us closer. I literally fucking kissed him, but lying beside him feels way more intimate.

I'm almost excited about the possibility of him trying to climb over me again, to feel his body sleepily relax onto mine. Maybe I should tell him all these thoughts, give him full disclosure so he knows exactly what he's sleeping next to.

But I'm worried he'll see me as some creepy old dude ... and I'm also worried he won't.

If I tell Will the thoughts I'm having about him and he invites me to act on them, there won't be an inch of his body I don't explore. I'm able to keep myself in check for now, but his encouragement will make it impossible.

Still, when I get changed for bed tonight, I don't pull on a T-shirt this time. If Will could sleep in only sleep shorts, why the hell shouldn't I? Which is not at all a thinly veiled excuse for wanting to feel his skin against mine should last night repeat itself.

I walk into his bedroom, and only the light beside his bed is on. He's already under the covers again, and the second he sees me, his eyes dip to my chest.

His gaze brings my skin alive, and even as I try to ignore it while I climb into his bed, the tension around us bubbles outward. It's a delicious, forbidden feeling. To be so close to him and not be able to touch. To hope he feels the need as deeply as I do.

"Planning on reading a book or something?" I ask, pointing to the light.

He stares at me, looking almost afraid, before he gives his head a quick shake.

"Is everything okay?"

"I ... Maybe?"

A sinking feeling hits me that maybe he's picked up on my attraction and I'm making him uncomfortable. Jesus. Did

I misread this whole thing? Where all that wonderful tension was before, a sickly feeling takes its place. "Have I done something?"

"No." The speed with which he says that helps ease the knot in my gut.

"Are you sure? Because you can tell me. I'd never, ever want you to feel uncomfortable."

"It's not you. It's ... I'm suddenly freaking out that I'm about to make *you* uncomfortable."

I cock my head and prop up onto my elbow. Will's eyes immediately drop to my chest again, and he draws a shaky inhale, and it's in that one sound that everything becomes clear.

Will isn't put off by me.

He's turned on.

Fuck. That sound unlocks something deep in my gut that I can't resist any longer.

My smile stretches wide. "What do you mean?"

"I don't think I want to say."

"I promise you won't make it weird. Whatever it is."

The obvious doubt in his gaze makes it clear he doesn't believe me.

"Will." His gaze clashes with mine. "Tell me."

"I ... can't."

I lean in, *right* in, until my face is hovering inches from his, crossing all kinds of personal boundaries, and while I know I'm being a goddamn idiot for getting myself into this kind of situation, I'm sure as hell not planning to stop.

I drop my voice. "What if I *really* wanted you to tell me?"

He swallows, still not dropping eye contact as he folds back the blanket and shows me what he's holding.

The fucking tentacle.

Want flashes through me, a wave of lust so heady my cock thickens in seconds.

I need to make sure I'm not misinterpreting him though. "You want me to go so you can ..."

"No, I ... I want you to stay."

Damn.

"I-I'm sorry," he says, hand lifting to cover his face, but unfortunately, he's still holding the tentacle, and it's taken over my entire focus.

I flick the blanket off us, getting his attention, and grab my cock through my pants. His eyes track the movement, surprise evident on his face. "You have nothing to be sorry for."

"I ... but ... Molly."

And goddamn Will, that's about the only thing he could have said to make me pull up in my tracks.

"Fuck."

"He'd kill me," Will whispers.

And he might be right. But my attention is on his body, all that skin, all that muscle, my brain not moving the way it normally would.

"Fuck, you're so sexy."

Will lets out a husky laugh. "Like you can talk. *Look* at you."

We take a moment just drinking each other in. Wanting, looking, needing. My teeth drag over my lower lip.

"We shouldn't ..." I say.

"Agreed."

"But ..."

"Yes?"

"Well, we're worried about what would happen if we had sex, right?"

"Right."

"So we won't have sex."

Will cocks his head. "I don't think that solves anything."

"No, I mean ... if I don't touch you, is it sex?"

He shivers. "You could instruct me instead."

A filthy smile crosses my face at this loophole. "Technically, you've never used one of those things before. What kind of man would I be if I left you unsupervised?"

He nods quickly, big, innocent eyes full of heat. "I don't know what I'm doing. Help me, Keller?"

I tighten my grip on my cock. "Your first step is taking off that underwear."

"And then?"

"And then you're going to come harder than you ever have in your life."

22

WILL

Keller's looking down at me like he wants to make a meal of my body, and I'm totally okay with that. That mouth, those hands, his teeth. His intense, dark eyes burning into my skin.

We might not be able to touch, but I don't think it matters all that much. Being here with him, getting intimate, this is sex, no matter how much we might try to deny it.

Either way, if Molly found out, I have to hope he'd understand. This isn't just fun for me. This is *Keller*. The man I went and fell in love with before I realized what was happening.

I set the toy beside me, borderline concerned about how that thing is going to happen, and hook my thumbs into the waistband of my briefs. My cock's already pushing to escape, but I take a second to steady myself before freeing my dick. I kick the underwear to the foot of the bed, then take a second before glancing up at him again.

Keller's gaze is glued to my cock, sending shivery feels all through my length and down into my balls. His eyes shine in the low light, and he must like what he sees because his tongue drags oh so slowly over his bottom lip.

His obvious want gives me confidence.

"Do I get to see you?" I croak.

"Do you want to?"

"Well, that thing doesn't go in my ass until I've got an eyeful of your dick."

Keller barks out a laugh, then kicks his sleep shorts off.

I actually whine a little bit. The fact I can't touch all that is criminal. He's hard and thick, black pubes trimmed at the base and dark purple head shiny with precum. I want to taste him. I want to circle his crown with my tongue and watch Keller's eyes roll back.

"That's one pretty cock," I breathe out.

Keller rolls his balls in his palm, drawing my attention to how nicely they'd fit in my mouth. "You took the exact words out of my head. Your cock matches the rest of you: perfect."

The compliment turns me on more than anything else so far.

It makes me crave more.

I grab the weird-looking dildo and hold it up between us. It might not be my kink exactly, but turning Keller on definitely is, so if I need to shove a tentacle up my ass to do it, so be it.

And like he can sense my hesitation, he chuckles. "You can use the regular one if that's more your thing."

"No." I turn it slightly to inspect it. "Why, out of all of them, did this one catch your eye though?"

"Something different. Also, I have a feeling those suckers on the side are going to feel incredible."

Okay, so maybe he has a point about that.

"Plus, full disclosure, I just really want to see you put something that fucked-up in your ass."

"Ha! Woooow."

"It feels kinda pervy and wrong. Which is just so goddamn hot to me."

My exhale feels heavy as I scramble for the lube. "Why does that turn me on?"

"Maybe you like pervy, older men?"

"They're basically my weakness."

Then again, everything about Keller is my weakness. I squeeze a large amount of lube over my fingers, then hold the tube up, ready for him. Keller reaches out, and when I fill his palm, he wraps his hand back around his cock and lets out a long sigh.

"So good."

"Watch me, okay? The whole time."

Keller's exhale shivers over my skin. "Like I want to miss a second."

Ignoring the way my cock is leaking, I reach behind my balls and rub the lube against my hole. I've never done this in front of anyone before, so I'm nervous as fuck, and maybe he can tell by my movements or my expression, I don't know, but Keller moves closer. We're still not touching, but just his presence is enough to get my skin crackling with awareness.

"Lift your leg closest to me," he says. "Let me watch you play with your pretty hole."

I choke on the appreciative noise that gets caught in my

throat but do exactly what he says. I relax back into the bed, knee near my chest, and let my eyes fall closed. It's easier that way. Safer. My first finger presses inside, and I relax against the intrusion. Welcome it. Hope that Keller is watching every movement as I slowly work it in and out, getting deeper with each pass.

"There we go," he rumbles. "Get yourself nice and loose, just like that. Now, add another finger for me, just like I would if it was my hand working you open."

The image floods my mind. Keller hovering over me like he is right now, large hand between my legs, thumb brushing my balls while he worked another finger in, just like I'm doing. My long fingers become his thick ones; my hoarse breathing is replaced by his. It's his hand holding my leg up, his warmth pressed against me, his cock he's getting me ready for.

And while that might not be reality, this isn't a terrible alternative. Keller and I are getting ourselves off, separate but together, which is more than I ever would have dared to hope for when I moved in, and I'm still struggling to believe he's here.

There's going to be so, so much that needs to be cleared up when we're done, but in this moment, the only thing I care about is putting on a good enough show to make him come.

"Do you want me to add a third?" I ask.

"Is your sexy little hole ready for a third?"

"It's ready for whatever you want me to do," I rasp.

Keller groans, and when I open my eyes, he gives himself a good pump. "Do it. Give yourself more. Get stretched nice and wide so you don't hurt yourself, Will. I won't be happy with you if you do."

My head arches back into my pillow as I let those words

flow over me. Did Keller reach into my brain and pluck out my deepest fantasy? I have to be dreaming—there's no way this is real. And if it's not real, then who the fuck cares how this goes down as long as it's good for us both?

Dream me is going to enjoy himself.

I let go of my leg and reach down to give my dick some relief. Just gently, loosely, not enough to make me come because that needs to happen later. Once I've given Keller what he wants. I take my time stretching my hole open, fucking myself on my fingers, rubbing my prostate, stretching gradually wide enough to take that toy to the base.

"I'm ready," I say, pulling my fingers out as my ass aches to be filled.

"Show me."

My whole face flushes as I pull back both legs and Keller leans over. His hair is a loose mess, only half of it held up in the band, and as I watch his strong hand jerk himself off, I'm reminded of an enormous, dark-haired Viking getting ready to have his way with me.

Precum leaks out onto my abs at the sight, and Keller's eyes lock onto it.

"You like me looking at you."

"I'm starting to get that impression," I joke, but it's weak.

"Your hole looks mouthwatering like that. I want to lean down and lick you. See how far I can get my tongue inside."

"Oh, fuck."

He chuckles as more precum dribbles from my slit and settles back beside me, so close I can feel his body warmth. "Show me how you fuck yourself. I want to see the way you make your body feel good."

I'm like a fucking puppet for him, ready to do any and

everything he asks. I don't even care. I have no limits when it comes to him. My hand closes over the lube, and I cover the toy in it. I'm still slightly apprehensive because I can honestly say I've never wanted to shove one of these up my ass, and for a first time, I'm really pulling out the stops, but here I go anyway.

I bite down on my lip as I position the tip at my hole.

Keller's lips brush my ear. "If you don't want to do this, I want you to stop. I'll be more than happy to watch you give that sexy cock attention."

His voice shivers down my neck, my torso, into my gut.

"Well, I need something in my ass, and since you won't give me your cock, this will have to do."

His groan is the perfect answer.

I press the toy in, my hole finally getting what it needs. The silicone feeling is different from a real cock, but Keller was right about the design. The suckers are stimulating the nerves around my hole, and I get almost half of it inside me before the toy shape thickens dramatically.

"You're doing amazing, Will," Keller says. His voice is heavy with lust, so deep I can feel it. "I've never seen anything so fucking sexy in my life."

That helps me to relax enough to stretch a bit wider, take a bit more. I alternate between fucking myself with the thin end and stroking my cock as I inch in the bigger side. It's even wider than Keller's cock, but not as thick as the monster we left in the box. I'm sweaty and panting by the time I reach the base, but I feel so mind-numbingly full. The toy is pressing on that delicious spot in my ass, and my cock is still steely and desperate.

"I have a tentacle in my ass," I say, a cross between amused and too turned on to care.

"You do, you filthy boy. All for me."

"All for you," I confirm. I pull it out, and my eyes almost roll back as I press it back in. And once I start, I can't stop. No matter what the fuck it looks like, it feels way better than I could have expected. It's warmed to my body, stimulating each inch of my hole, and the feeling of being split open and used like this is making my cock too hard to stand.

I reach for it, ready to jerk off to the end, needing to come and watch Keller watch me unload, then hopefully be treated to the same sight.

I'm in a world of mind-numbing bliss, fucking myself hard, when suddenly Keller's hand closes over mine, and he pulls the toy out completely.

My eyes snap open in time to see his thick tongue lick a wet stripe over the suction cap at the base, and then he seals it to the wall.

"On your knees and bend over," he growls. "I want a better view."

He sits with his back against the wall, holding the dildo in place as I hurry to follow his direction. I know he's watching every second as I arch my back and push onto the toy, feeling my body open up around it. Keller moves his hand before my ass can reach it, and it almost makes me sob.

I need him to touch me. Just once. Just a little bit.

But then I turn my head toward him, and his cock is *right there*. Leaking and shining, so thick and mouthwatering. I'm in heaven as I stare at him touching himself while I fuck myself on the toy. That mind-melting spot inside is lit the fuck up, and my balls are aching. I'm so goddamn close it's painful, and I need this release the way I need air.

"Look at you being railed by that thing," he growls, tugging his sac. "Just bent over and taking it. Like you were made for it. So desperate to get off, you'll do anything I say, won't you?"

"Anything," I gasp. "Fuck, I wish I could touch you. I'd make you feel good. So good."

"You're not even touching me and you're making me feel incredible. The way you're staring at my cock like you're hungry for it. Like you want to be filled from both ends."

I whimper again. The thought of him pressing to his knees and fucking my face while I'm filled by the toy is too much. The second my hand closes over my cock, it's instant relief. Like a dam bursting, my orgasm brings sweet relief, and I milk my cock of every last drop.

"*Nrg*, shit," Keller gasps. "So good, Will. You're so good. So perfect. So goddamn sexy ..."

I'm locked to the sight of him coming. Strong legs parted, toes gripping the sheets, abs flexed and shoulders tensed, head dropped back and exposing his thick neck, while his eyes never leave my body.

I'm shivering, boneless, unexpectedly crashing. When I pull off the toy, my ass aches like never before, and I flop onto my side, just trying to catch my breath.

Keller climbs off the bed and disappears out the door, but before I can panic about him regretting things, the sound of running water hits me, and he's back a moment later with a warm washcloth and a blanket over his shoulder.

"How you feeling?"

"Amazing. Sore."

His brow bristles. "You didn't hurt yourself?"

"No, it was just more than I normally take."

He nods and hands the washcloth over. While I clean myself up, Keller whips my blanket off the bed and replaces it with his. He climbs under the covers naked, and even after what we just did, nerves tickle through me.

I reach across him to toss the washcloth on my nightstand, but before I can pull back, Keller grabs my arm. He looks up at me, dark eyes soft in the warm light.

"Was that okay?"

It takes me a second to realize I'm still shivering. "I have no words for how okay that was."

He releases me with the kind of smile that makes my knees weak. "Good. Because you've left me with no words either."

Hearing that he doesn't regret it turns me to liquid, and I melt against the pillows beside him. I'm so sated yet still so wired, unable to believe that actually happened. So grateful it did, and also kind of embarrassed about how much of a show I put on, but I don't regret it for a second.

"Hey, Keller?"

"Yeah?"

"Just don't be weird in the morning, okay? It's not like we had sex." Even though we totally, one hundred percent did.

"As long as you can promise the same."

I laugh. "I'm always weird around you. But I promise not to be weirder than usual."

"Deal."

My eyes fall closed, and I forget to even be worried about the sleepwalking because nothing can bring this moment down.

23

KELLER

WILL IS SOLID AND WARM IN MY ARMS. MAYBE I SHOULD let him go before he wakes up, but I can't bring myself to do it. It's too late when a yawn stiffens his body against mine, and then he seems to catch on to where he is. His head pops up from my chest, and he looks horrified.

"I'm so sorry."

I don't let him go. "Apparently, you sleep snuggle as well as walk."

"I'm an embarrassment."

"Cute one though."

He lets loose that lopsided grin. "You think I'm cute."

"Very cute." My gaze slides to the wall. "Your friend, not so much."

Will's head snaps around to see the giant tentacle still hovering where I stuck it last night. His whole face reddens, and I change my opinion from cute to adorable. "Huh. So I didn't dream it."

"Unless we both shared the same magnificent dream, I'd guess not."

He sits up and grabs the toy, attempting to tug it from the wall. I snigger.

"Keep jerking it like that and you'll turn it on again." I reach around him and release the little tab. It falls to the bed with a heavy *thunk*.

"One day, I won't be so stupidly embarrassing around you."

"Maybe. But I hope not."

Will throws me a sly look. "You like me being embarrassed?"

"I don't want you to feel shitty, but I'd be lying if I said it doesn't turn me on when you're all flushed and shy."

"Oh, really?" That flicker of confidence lights up his face. "So you actually don't regret it?"

Now, that's a hard question. In the light of day, what we did was really, really stupid. We can pretend like it was a totally innocent thing, but the fact remains that if Molly found out, he wouldn't want to know enough to ask if we touched or didn't touch. He wouldn't care. His best friend and Dad both got off together, and that definitely would be enough to make him feel ... something.

I trust Mols to be rational about it—I think—but I also shouldn't be putting him in a situation where he has to be.

"Yes and no."

Will's face falls, and I hate it.

"Being with you, no. No regrets." I need to make sure that's clear with him. "That went beyond hot to fantasy levels, and you having a little bit of an exhibition and praise kink in you ... that does things for me. Obviously."

Will's lips pinch. "It's Molly, isn't it?"

"He's my son. He always has to be my first thought, and let's be real here, I can't see him being happy about this."

"I get it."

"Would you be willing to risk your friendship for a bit of fun with me?"

It actually impresses me that Will takes the time to think about it. He doesn't think with his dick, but he doesn't disregard my feelings either. Will loves Molly, and that only makes me like him that much more.

"No," he finally says. "I'd hate for Molly to think I was just waiting for him to leave so I could hook up with his dad. That's not what this is."

"Good. We're on the same page."

"Agreed." He props his chin on his hand from where he's sitting cross-legged. "We keep what happened between us. Again."

"I don't believe in filthy little secrets or whatever, but it's probably for the best. Neither of us wants to hurt him."

"Exactly. Plus, I sorta need this room here."

"Your staying with me has nothing to do with sex."

He lets out a long, slow exhale. "Thanks, Keller. I think I needed to hear that."

I sit up and move a bit closer, wanting to draw this moment with Will out for as long as I can. "Since we're keeping this a secret, I just want to do one more thing."

"What is it?"

I reach out and cup his chin, steering his face closer to mine. "Something I was desperate to do last night."

I give him time to pull away, but instead, Will closes the distance between us. His warm mouth closes over mine, lips soft and strong before parting and giving way to the gentle swipe of his tongue. The kiss is like everything else with

Will. Hot. Easy. Addictive. I want to sink into it, deepen it, press against him, and pin him to the bed.

But one time together is more than I want to hide, let alone two, and the last thing Will deserves is to be my secret hookup. He's so much more than that.

I pull back, leaving his eyes glazed and his lips dangerously puffy. They're calling for me to kiss them again, but instead, I force myself to get up.

"You're hard," he sighs, flopping back on the bed.

"Ehh, kissing you will do that."

"Actually, if you let me kiss your dick, I think you'll find it has the opposite effect."

There's that confidence again. "Behave yourself."

He waves a hand my way. "Can you blame me?"

I copy the motion. "Having the same issue here. But I don't like keeping things from Molly, and I don't like you being some guilty secret either. So go easy on an old man."

"Old." He scoffs. "I'm the one who was struggling to keep up with you last night."

And what a night it was. "That'll just have to be enough to tide us both over. It happened, it's done, we can jerk off—separately—over it later."

"Fine …"

"If Molly gave us his blessing, I wouldn't let you out of bed for a week."

"I've changed my mind. Tell him, tell him now."

I eye Will, worried for a second that he's serious, until he gives me a sad smile.

"I'm joking. But it's nice to pretend."

SUNDAY AFTERNOONS ARE MY MARKET DAYS. I GO DOWN, pick up all the food for the week, and take a moment to walk along the boardwalk and just hit pause on the stresses of everything else.

This week, it also gets me away from Will.

I definitely expected him to act off after last night, but nothing has changed. He cooks us breakfast, we work out, and he's just as awkward and chatty as he's ever been. In fact, if anything *has* changed, it'd be that he's more confident with me. Flirty. I like it too much. I leave the heat of the day behind and enter the cool bar that Art owns. It's large, mostly wood, and has a homely feel that few places in Kilborough give me.

There are some people eating lunch inside, but it's nowhere near as busy as the cafe out front with the view of the water, and while I don't usually stop in here before heading to the market next door, I need to talk to someone.

I climb the stairs behind the bar and stall when I reach the top and find Orson, Mack, and Ford sitting in the couches under the window, but no Art.

"Where's our lord and savior, Art de Almeida?" I ask dryly.

"You'll be as shocked as us: he has the day off."

"No way." I shake my head. "That Joey is so bad for him."

Ford laughs at my obvious sarcasm. Art's a workaholic, and it's only now that he has Joey, who won't put up with being ignored, that Art is finally taking time away from the brewery.

Which is great for him but not so much for me. Then again, his advice would be to just keep fucking around with Will and keeping it a secret. Hard pass on that.

I flop down opposite Orson. "Hey, remember when you came to me after you hooked up with Ford the first time?"

Ford fails to hide his smug expression. "You did, did you? Give him all the sordid details?"

Orson pinches his leg. "Only that you got me with your gay agenda."

"You're the one who did the grinding all over me, sweetheart."

"Oh!" Mack says suddenly, like he's only just noticed I'm here. "The, uh, roommate, huh? Very hot. You should do him."

I glance at Orson. "Do us all a favor and tell Art that next time he has shit-stirring plans to leave Mack out of it."

"Sorry," Mack moans. "What were you talking about?"

That's spacey even for Mack. I set my issues aside for a moment. "What's up with you?"

His face falls, and he glances at Orson.

"A friend of ours who's new to town wants to be set up. Mack and Davey were going to go on a double date with Luke and Brayden, but now Davey wants out."

Who's dumb i-fucking-dea was that? Of course Davey doesn't want to go on a double date with his ex-husband. I'm also surprised Mack agreed, considering he's still in love with Davey and regrets ever getting a divorce.

Like Orson can read my mind, he says, "Mack was scared and put Davey on the spot when I asked about Luke, and then it turned into a double date."

I don't know who to feel most sorry for. "Mack, I say this with love, but thank fuck Davey is pulling out."

"What? Why?"

"What would you have done if the date went well and you had to stand there and watch him kiss his guy goodbye?"

It hurts the way Mack's eyes get all big. "I was planning to get his attention. To make it like the date was between us."

"I love you, but no. You're divorced. You can't keep doing this to yourself."

He slumps back on the couch and crosses his arms. "What do I do now? I can't go on a date with both of them."

"Maybe Keller could go with you," Ford suggests. "He's been looking for someone, and these guys are great."

Mack lowers his voice. "Aren't we supposed to be getting Keller with his roommate?"

Orson pinches the bridge of his nose. "Definitely telling Art to leave you out."

"What? I'm confused!"

And while going on an actual date is the last thing I want, leaving Mack to it doesn't sit well with me either. He really does need to get over Davey before Davey moves on and leaves him even more heartbroken than he currently is.

"I'll go," I say. "But I have to tell Will first."

"Why?" Orson asks, immediately suspicious.

"Because we sort of, not actually, but totally did have sex last night."

The three of them stare back at me.

"It was hot, we didn't touch, but we also agreed that it shouldn't happen again because neither of us wants to hurt Molly."

Ford and Orson trade a glance. I know exactly what they're thinking. They want to say something, but when it comes to Molly, neither of them wants him getting hurt again either. What Molly did wasn't their fault, but I know Ford feels partially responsible.

"Out with it," I say.

Orson goes first. "I'm shocked that you went there at all, if I'm honest."

"Then why the hell were you part of the plan to get me to?"

"Because it's funny when Art gets like a dog with a bone over something. I didn't expect it to actually happen."

"Are you judging me?" I ask stiffly.

"He's a lot younger than you."

"Did I pull out the age card when your boyfriend was flirting up a storm with my son?" I snap. It's a low move, but I'm actually shocked that out of everyone, Orson is saying this shit to me. "Or judge when, after you got off with Ford, you still tried to play the straight card?"

"Nobody is judging," Ford cuts in. "Knowing how protective you are of Molly, we're just surprised."

"Have you seen Will? I love my son, but I only have so much restraint. Plus, not only am I attracted to him, I like spending time with him. We've been hanging out a lot, and Will is … he's just …"

"Maybe Molly won't care," Mack says. "You clearly like this guy."

Well, if even Mack can pick up on it, I'm being more obvious than I thought. "We agreed to last night and then not again."

"If that's the case, why do you have to run the date past him first?" Orson asks.

That's a good question. Will has no say over what I do, and he even told Molly he'd help me find a date. Well, now I have one.

But that damn feeling in my damn gut is insistent.

"Something's just telling me I should."

THE SUPREME MASTER OF THE KILLERVERSE

Keller: *Know anyone who's free for a date tonight?*
Art: *How desperate are you?*
Keller: *Very.*
Art: *Fine. I'll ask Joey.*
Keller: *Wait. What?*
Art: *You wanna be wined and dined by the best. I get it. Just know, I wouldn't ask for anyone but you, sweet cheeks.*
Keller: *Dear god, I need to hear the answer to this.*
Art: *Yeah, no go. I love you, man, but I also love my balls attached to me and not floating in a jar, so I'm out. I'd lend you Joey but if you laid a hand on him, I'd have to kill you so it's probably best not to risk it.*
Keller: *Great. Now that we have that cleared up and out of the way: know anyone who's free for a date tonight?*
Art: *I thought you were doing the online thing?*
Keller: *Nope. I'm doing the helping-Mack-on-a-double-date thing.*
Art: *So you need a date for the double date?*

Keller: *No, I already have a date. I'm looking to replace ME on the date.*

Art: *Wasn't finding a date top of your dream board?*

Keller: *Yeah, but ...*

Art: *I'm here, Kels.*

Keller: *There's something going on between me and Will and I'm worried this will make him mad.*

Art: *Ooooh ouch.*

Keller: *Yeah.*

Art: *Do you have a thing for him?*

Keller: *A very big thing for him.*

Art: *I bet you do **winky face***

Keller: *Why do I try to have a serious conversation with you?*

Art: *Sorry. I'm done. What do you want to do?*

Keller: *Date Will. But I can't. So I figure I need to try and let that go.*

Art: *It's hard to listen to the head when the heart is so loud.*

Keller: *You're telling me ...*

Art: *So let the little head lead instead.*

Keller: *Good talk.*

24

WILL

Keller's gone way longer than I'm expecting while he picks up food, and I have to hold off from messaging to check if he got lost. I won't be clingy. I won't let on that last night meant everything to me. I will be laid-back and respect his boundaries and do my best not to get all boned up tonight when he's lying beside me. In a bed that smells like him and sex.

I'm outside weeding the garden when he pulls up, gold sunglasses in place, hair out, cutoff denim jeans and band T-shirt hugging his frame.

"You know, you could look less like a goddamn model when you head out places," I joke, digging at the stubborn root in front of me. Unlike him, I'm covered in dirt, wearing running shorts, sneakers, and my hat on forward for once.

His shadow falls over me. "Says the sweaty, muscly garden boy."

I squint up at him. "No way you find this attractive."

His eyes track slowly from my hat to my ankles before he swallows. "If you say so."

"Stop." I groan. "You're gonna get me all boned up."

"Funny, that sounds like exactly the outcome I'm going for."

I flick dirt at him. "Don't be a dick."

"Then put yours away," he calls as he heads up to the house.

I stand and give the dumb root a kick before following him. Leaving my sneakers outside the front door, I brush off my shorts and welcome the cool shade inside.

"Since I've been doing all the work since last night, I figure you should cook me dinner for a change," I say, following him into the kitchen.

Keller freezes where he's unpacking a bag on the counter. "Actually ... I won't be here for dinner."

His tone tells me everything I need to know, and that happy bubble I've been surrounded by all day pops. I sink into a stool across from him.

"Oh. You're going on a date."

He doesn't answer, and I hate that. Hate that he can't even bring me words to make me feel better, but why should he? We're nothing to each other. Just because we had some fun last night doesn't mean he owes me shit. I just thought it would maybe be more than a whole day before he went after someone else.

I'm an idiot.

For the first time, I don't try to hide how it hurts me.

"Come on, Will. Don't look at me like that."

"Like what?"

He drops the pumpkin he's holding back into the bag and leaves the groceries to approach me. We don't touch—I can't even meet his eyes—but he leans against the counter right beside me, and I can feel the way his gaze is burning into my face.

"I don't even know the person. I'm doing it for Mack."

"What do you mean?"

"He got it into his head that his first date should be a double date. With his ex-husband there as well."

"What?" Even to me, that sounds downright dumb. We're nowhere near the ex-husband level of history, but trying to go on a double date with Keller seeing someone else would kill me.

"Davey rightfully canceled. So Mack was stuck, and because he needs to get over Davey, I offered to step in."

While his explanation makes sense and helps to kill some of that hardcore jealousy, it doesn't take it all the way away. Keller's still going out. Still going to charm some guy, and then what if they hit it off? What if Keller's gut decides this guy is the one?

"That was awful of nice of you" is all I can get out.

"If this fucks things up between us, just say so, and I won't go."

"You can't put that on me."

"I don't know where the lines are, Will. We crossed boundaries last night, and we agreed it won't happen again, but that leaves us both right back where we were before it. And before it, I was trying to find a partner."

I nod because he's right. Damn Keller and always having to be so logical and levelheaded. "Mack needs you," I point out.

"He'd understand."

I shake my head, not willing to be the reason Keller's friend is left on his own. "Just do me a favor and don't bring the guy back here. I ... I just don't think I can see that. Right now."

"I'm not going to hook up with anyone."

"Yeah, well, you haven't met him yet." I try for a playful smile. "He might be way hotter than me."

Only I make the mistake of meeting Keller's eyes, and the way there's so much open regret in them just makes me sad.

"No way could he be hotter than you."

"Yes or no, he won't be Molly's friend, and that's the whole point."

But knowing that Keller is as conflicted over this whole thing as I am really helps settle me. Whatever happens tonight, I'll just have to deal with it and hope for the best. Until I'm willing to risk my friend and Keller's willing to risk the relationship he has with his own kid, this is hopeless.

"I hope he's everything you're looking for," I say.

Keller shakes his head, eyes never leaving mine. "I can guarantee he's not."

"You haven't even met him yet."

"I don't need to." He reaches up to swing my hat backward. "I'm sorry."

"I know you are."

Having that talk with him, knowing he legitimately doesn't want to hurt me, feeling the way he's as lost in this thing between us as I am, it's the only thing that helps me get through the afternoon. Hearing him shower. Rummaging around in his room for clothes. The smell of his aftershave, which fills the hall. Every little reminder of him getting ready for a date hits me in the chest.

He's wearing his good watch. His hair's secure in a neat

bun. His button-up and dress pants are both tight and clean and so, so sexy.

The closer it gets to him needing to leave, the slower he moves. I try to avoid him, and I know he's doing the same. He walks into the kitchen, and I walk out. He's putting on his shoes in the living room when I go to put a show on to distract myself, and he jumps up like his ass is on fire.

There's no more talking.

No more heart-to-hearts.

Just two roommates who shared orgasms and now don't know how to behave around each other.

It's not until he's heading for the front door that I speak again. "Enjoy your date."

He pauses, and I expect him to say something, maybe that he won't be late or he's not excited—*anything*.

But Keller just rubs his face roughly and leaves, and I have to screw up my face against my stupid feelings. I always knew this was how it was going to end up. Always knew that I'd end up in this exact situation over and over the entire time I was living here. And sure, it's delayed since I vetoed all his other dates and then started sleepwalking, but —*fuck*.

The sleepwalking.

I forgot to ask him if I tried it last night because I was so distracted, and he didn't bring it up either. If he's out tonight, will he come into my bed when he gets home? Do I want that? Knowing that he's potentially gotten off with some guy, then is sleeping beside me right after?

I hate myself. Am so, so angry that I can't just let it go. We'd be sleeping. Nothing else. Keller's literally doing it for my safety, and I wouldn't want him there because what? My precious feelings are hurt?

If I love Keller, I should want him to be happy. Should be setting aside how I feel about him and hoping that this date tonight goes well. Instead, I'm sitting here hoping his date eats with his mouth open, hates Kilborough, and talks nonstop about doomsday prepping or murder mysteries or ... or ... *The Great British Bake Off.* Well, not the last one. Knowing Keller, he probably loves that show.

The point is, I'm not a good, selfless person.

Watching a dumb movie doesn't help because the whole time, I keep wanting to make a joke or point out all the stupid shit I know will make Keller laugh. So, at around ten when he still isn't home, I make my way upstairs, hoping I can fall asleep and ignore the painfully empty house.

Only when I get to my room, there's something on my bed that shouldn't be there.

Keller's pillow.

I approach and read the note he's left on top. *Sorry I'm not here, but my pillow will keep you safe until I'm home.*

I pick up the pillow and press my face into it, his clean scent both easing and increasing the ache at the same time. It's proof he was thinking of me, that he cares, and that only makes my heart ache more.

Nothing will ever be a stand-in for him, and all this does is remind me that one day, he won't be sharing my bed anymore.

He'll be sharing someone else's.

I curl up with his pillow and count down the hours while I try to fall asleep.

Eleven o'clock ... Midnight ... One ... Two ...

Every hour that passes is like a knife in my chest.

KELLER

Brayden and Luke are best friends who moved to Kilborough a few months ago. They're cool, and something about them screams big city. Maybe it's the fancy clothes they're wearing, or their style, or even the way they talk—I can't put my finger on it exactly.

"How old are you?" I ask Brayden.

"Thirty-three."

"And what made you want to move here?"

"My parents found out I'm gay and basically told me I'm embarrassing the family, and they didn't want to see me again until I got through this phase."

"Ouch. I'm sorry."

"I'm not, but I do wish they hadn't found out how they did."

Next to him, Luke snorts into his beer.

My gaze flicks between them. "How did they find out?"

"Mom's career-hopping and has been taking classes to

become a nurse. She made friends with a guy my age since they're both technically mature students, and he was scrolling through Grindr. Mom happened to look over right as a picture of me with my ass out popped up on the screen."

I choose the wrong moment to have a drink because I damn near almost spray it from my nostrils. "Holy fuck, I'm sorry."

"I told him not to have his face in the shot," Luke adds.

"It's my best feature," Brayden argues.

And he's probably right about that. Brayden is gorgeous. Luke too. But while Mack looks absolutely miserable, I'm trying to keep an open mind. I stand by what I said to Will in that no one will even come close to him, but I have to try. I have to see if there's any connection here because I'd hate for Will to move out and move on, all while I'm left wondering what the hell happened.

Will is young enough that he doesn't have to have it all worked out, and while I joke about being old, I know I'm not really. I have plenty of time to find someone to settle down with, but I'm at the point where I *want* to settle down now.

Waiting around for the perfect person to fall into my lap isn't something I'm counting on, and I don't trust myself to be able to keep resisting Will if I keep the flirting up. At least if I'm actively dating, I'll have something else to focus on that isn't how desperately I want to have sex with him again. Properly this time.

Actual touching and kissing and—

"There's so much seafood," Mack mutters, looking over the menu.

Fuck. I completely blanked out to what they're talking about.

I shake off the hold Will has on me and turn to the menu

as well. "It's a seafood restaurant," I point out. "But they've got chicken there."

"Chicken's good." But he still doesn't look any happier.

While Luke and Brayden are distracted by the server, I lean closer to Mack.

"Dude, you've got to pull it together. You look like you'd rather be anywhere else."

"I wish I was at home."

"I know that, but it's not their fault Davey canceled. I'm not saying you have to fuck the guy, but don't treat him like shit. You might actually enjoy yourself."

"I don't want to enjoy myself."

"Then stop thinking of it as a date, and think of it as some friends grabbing food."

"I ... I can do that."

"Good." I pat his back. "They don't deserve us both sitting here moping."

"You're moping?"

I think about how much to tell him. "Who I want isn't sitting across from me either, but I'm not going to sulk about it. It sucks, and I hate it, but these guys are cool. They at least deserve a chance."

Mack smiles, but it's still heavy with sadness. "You're right."

"Usually am."

"I'm going to enjoy this meeting of friends for food."

Whatever gets him through.

It seems to work though. Mack is more connected to the conversation, and I can tell Luke is interested. It's there in the way he laughs at Mack's cluelessness and the patient way he explains why Pluto is no longer a planet.

Mack pouts. "Poor Pluto. They can't just say it's a planet and then change their minds. That isn't fair."

"To who?" I ask.

"*Pluto*, obviously."

Luke gazes indulgently over at him. "Somehow, I don't think Pluto has feelings over it one way or another."

"You can't just *boot* a planet off the list, can you, Keller?"

I shrug. "They can and did."

Brayden keeps throwing glances Luke's way. Each attempt I make to drag him into a conversation is derailed by Luke or Mack. It's almost amusing that Will was worried. Mack and I aren't the only ones at the table with someone other than our dates in mind.

If I'm picking up on this right, Brayden and Luke aren't just best friends. At least not to Brayden.

Mack clears his throat beside me, but when I turn to see what's up, his attention is still on Luke.

"Think you'll stay in Kilborough for long?" I ask Brayden.

"I don't know. It's nice here, but I'm still trying to figure out what I want to do. For a career. It's super important to me to help people, and I—"

Mack clears his throat again, but this time, it's far louder and more obnoxious.

I turn to him. "You okay, man?"

"I just … need water …"

I hand his glass over and watch while he drains it. He sets it down with a thud and tugs at his collar.

"I, umm." He coughs lightly. "I think I …"

"What the hell's going on with your face?" Luke gasps.

Mack's lips and eyes are reddening and getting puffier as I watch.

"Mack ... tell me you didn't avoid the seafood because *you're allergic*."

He holds up his thumb and pointer finger, a hair's width apart. "Just a ... teensy ... bit ..."

A *teensy* bit? His face is doubling in size.

"Do you have an EpiPen?"

He shakes his head, and if he wasn't swelling up so rapidly, I'd want to fucking kill him. I pull out my phone and call 911 while I point at Luke. "See if anyone here has an EpiPen."

He almost flies out of his seat while Brayden stands there, gaping at Mack like he isn't sure what to do.

Why the hell my friend came here without an EpiPen, I'll never know. Sure, we didn't know where we were heading for dinner, but no one would have cared once we got here if he'd asked to go somewhere else.

Goddamn Mack and being too goddamn nice for his own goddamn good.

I relay what's happening to emergency, and they assure me they're getting an ambulance out. Mack's breathing is getting louder, and his face has turned splotchy.

I stoop down to haul him out of his seat. "Let's get you out the front to wait."

He stumbles along beside me, breathing uneven but still there, and it's a relief when I hear the sound of a siren building.

"I couldn't find one," Luke says, rejoining us.

"It's okay, they're not far." I rub circles into Mack's back. He's still swelling to the point where his face doesn't look like his face anymore, but as far as I can tell, he's breathing, and that's the main thing.

"Why didn't he tell us?" Brayden asks. "We could have gone anywhere."

"Mack ... he isn't like that." It's why he ended up divorced when he doesn't want to be. He's a softie, doesn't speak up, and will generally just go with the flow. I love my friend, but it's frustrating as hell sometimes.

"How are you doing?" I ask him.

"M'kay."

"They're nearly here."

And as soon as I say that, the ambulance turns into the street and pulls up out the front. The EMT smiles at me before turning her attention to Mack.

"How long since symptoms appeared?"

"About fifteen minutes," I say.

"Looks like anaphylaxis. Let's get him into the ambulance and to the hospital."

"Can I ride with him? I'll call his ex-husband on the way."

"Yeah, of course."

She takes care of Mack while her partner drives, and by the time we get to the hospital, he's still swollen but breathing normally again. They want to keep him for observation for a few hours, and while Davey wanted to come up here, the kids were both sleeping, so he couldn't get away. I'm not leaving him alone though.

"I'm an idiot," Mack mumbles.

"Little bit," I agree. "But we love you anyway. I swear though, man, put me in that situation again and we'll be having words."

"I'm sorry."

"I know you are. But you've got to start speaking up for yourself."

An exhale whooshes from between his puffy lips. "Maybe."

"Not maybe. You're a good person, Mack, but you're allowed to say when you don't like something. Maybe ..."

"What?"

"Maybe you sabotaged this date. Subconsciously. You're clearly not over Davey, and I don't think you ever will be until you get closure."

"I have closure. We're divorced."

"And when he's back in town, you both act like nothing has changed."

His bottom lip shakes. "I don't want it to change."

I think of Will and my plans to date and Molly moving to Seattle and just how much my world has upended in the last month. "Sometimes change is good."

"Yeah. Maybe."

He takes a nap after that while I doze off and on in his chair. I can't imagine what he's going through, and I don't want to. My own life is enough of a mess at the moment.

I'm woken around three by voices and look up to find Davey standing in the doorway with a nurse. The bags under his eyes are deep, and his black curls are a chaotic mess.

"Hey, Kel," he whispers, stepping into the room. "How is he?"

"Fine now."

"I can't believe he went to a seafood restaurant. He did the same thing on our first date."

"Jesus fuck. Really?"

"Yeah." Davey's looking at him with so much love in his eyes I honestly don't understand these two. And really, it makes a little anger flicker in my gut. There's no reason they shouldn't be together. Nothing is keeping them apart. When I have a sexy, fun, interesting guy at home who wants to sleep with me as much as I want to sleep with him and can't.

So I do something I'm not proud of. I pull an Art.

"Who knows, maybe that's a sign Luke is meant for Mack."

"What do you mean?"

"The guy was smitten, I swear." I force a laugh, not feeling great about the pain that crosses Davey's face, but not able to stop myself either. "Even after everything that happened, he asked me to text him to make sure Mack is okay."

Davey swallows, eyes still on his ex-husband. "I'm not surprised. Mack's kind of incredible, isn't he?"

"Sure is. I don't know how you let him go."

Davey's face falls. "Yeah. You and me both."

I pat his shoulder. "You good to stay? Where are the kids?"

"Yeah. Fine. Our neighbor came over to watch them for me. I had to be here."

Just like I have to get home. Now I know Mack is okay and I'm not leaving him on his own, I need to get home to check on Will. With any luck, my pillow will have done the trick. He didn't wake up at all last night, so I hope that's the same for tonight, but I also won't forgive myself if I get home and find him hurt.

26

WILL

SOME KINDA SUBCONSCIOUS AWARENESS MAKES ME JOLT OUT of sleep and look around my dark room. Shadows shift by my door, and as they get closer, Keller comes into view.

"You're awake." His voice is a tired croak, making my eyes fly to my phone. The display is soft, but I can very clearly see it's almost four. There's literally only one reason for him to have been out until this time.

"I *wasn't* awake," I point out, falling back onto my pillow and turning to face the wall. It doesn't help though. All it does is remind me of the last time we were in bed together. I don't want to talk to him, just want to ignore him and go back to sleep, but I can't. "What are you doing in here?"

I'm a dumbass for asking in the first place, but his answer only makes me feel worse.

"You have my pillow."

Oh.

I huff and pull it out from under me, then throw it back in his general direction. "There."

At least my voice doesn't give away how much I wanna cry. Probably. It's just not fair that the closest I ever got to him was nothing compared to what any old person gets. That a casual stranger is freely given what I've only ever dreamed about. And I've dreamed a lot.

"Did you get up at all?"

"Kinda hard to sleepwalk when you're not sleeping to begin with."

"Why weren't you …"

It must hit him because he doesn't finish that sentence. I'm both relieved that he knows I'm upset and scared that he won't react in the way I need him to. But how can he? We've talked about it, and I agreed that keeping things friendly is for the best.

So why won't my stupid head listen?

"Are you upset because of the date? Will, I tried to get home earlier, but—"

"In the nicest way I can possibly say this, I don't wanna know a single detail about your night. I just wanna sleep."

He's quiet for a long time, and I wish I knew what's going through his head, but it obviously has nothing to do with reassuring me.

"Do you need me to stay in here?" he asks.

I honest to god could not think of anything worse. "I think I'm good."

"Okay."

There's movement behind me, and I assume he must have picked up his pillow because a few seconds later, he heads for the door. My whole body sags in defeat because that was the exact opposite of how I wanted that to go. And I only have myself to blame. If I'd let him stay though, we probably would have talked, and there's no way I'd survive him confirming that he went home with that guy.

There's also apparently no way for me to fall asleep either, which sucks, considering I'm supposed to be working today. Zombie-Will it is, then.

I'm still tossing and turning when five thirty rolls around, so I climb out of bed, resigned to dealing with the measly hour or so of sleep I scraped together. I've been able to work a full shift after being out all night, so this shouldn't be any different.

Unlike those times, I'm not just tired but emotionally exhausted.

I cook Keller breakfast, but he doesn't show, so I just eat that as well. Then I work out by myself. Shower. He's still in bed, and the house that was feeling so promising the past few weeks is silent and cold and lonely.

Molly doesn't answer when I call, so I switch over to Joey's number, realizing, very fucking plainly, that they're the only two people I have. And if Molly finds out what I did with his dad, would I even have him?

Probably not.

We were right to agree to nothing else happening, so why does it feel so shit?

I set my phone down. I can't keep calling people whenever I'm stuck and expecting them to give me the answers. What the hell is Joey even gonna say? Get over it? There's no winning here. I've just gotta suck it up until I can move out next month.

Why does that feel like forever?

How many dates and all-nighters am I going to have to endure? It's not fair to ask Keller to put his whole life on hold for me, because I know he'd do it. I know he'd want to make sure I'm okay.

So we're at a shitty fucking impasse where he's trying to get on with his life while I'm just hanging around and waiting for mine to start.

And honestly, I'm worried.

Joey asked me to move in and help him out with rent and utilities back before he started dating Art. There's always that doubt in the back of my head that when Joey's sister moves out, he'll want to move in with Art. I mean, his boyfriend's a millionaire. Why the hell would he wanna stay in some tiny house with a roommate?

I don't think Joey would screw me over and change the plans, but I don't wanna be holding *him* back either.

This is why it's so important to me to be able to stand on my own and why it's so damn frustrating that I'm not at that point yet.

I sigh and switch on the coffee machine, then open a real estate app and type in Kilborough. It's something I do every now and then, to keep an eye on prices mostly, but also with the very low hope that something will magically appear that I can afford.

The best thing for everyone will be if I can get my own place, but the universe is still working against me there. Sure, I could scrape together enough for rent if I'm careful with my money, but renting still means being at someone else's mercy.

I'm looking to buy a place. Keller wouldn't take money for board here, so I'm saving a lot faster than I would have hoped, but I'm still a long, long way from a deposit. The good thing about small towns, though, is that sometimes shitty little places will hit the market for a steal, mostly because no one can be bothered doing anything with it.

All I'm after is a tiny bit of land. Just something. I don't give a shit if it has a house or not or even if the house is livable. The only requirement I have is that the price tag is where I need it to be. Everything else I can figure out later.

"Houses?"

I almost jump for my life at the voice in my ear. "Where the hell did you come from?"

Keller chuckles and reaches around me to grab a mug from the cupboard. He sets it beside mine, then hip-bumps me out of the way as he gets to work making both our coffees. Exactly the way I like mine.

"Just woke up," he says, making me feel like shit all over again.

"Lucky you." And even though I'm sulky and hurt, I want to talk to him anyway. Love's a headfuck. "No work today?"

Keller shakes his head. His hair is out, and it's a sexy, slept-in mess. An improvement to that neat bun he had last night. "I sent Valerie a message that I was taking the day off."

He hands my coffee over, and I take it, knowing I should hightail it up to my office but too pathetic to do it. "Can you afford to do that? With all the work you have on?"

"Not really, but I needed it."

I scowl, unable to avoid the topic, I guess. "It must have been good for him to wear you out like that. I'll remember to step up my game."

Keller's face falls, cup halfway to his mouth. "What are you talking about?"

"Your date. Sounded fun."

I see the exact moment it clicks. "You think I slept with that guy?"

"Didn't you?" Almost as soon as the question is out, I throw my hands up. "Don't answer that."

"Will—"

"No, seriously, I don't want to—" I turn to leave, but Keller's arm wraps around my waist, and I'm pulled back against him. Stale cologne and sleep-warmed skin surround me, and I have to remind myself that melting back into his chest is even more pathetic than I've been so far.

"I didn't sleep with anyone."

Relief floods through me, and I hate how much I needed to hear those words. "Then ... why ..."

"I was at the hospital."

Those words crack a whip in my heart, and I turn on him. "Oh, shit, are you hurt?"

"No, no, no. It was Mack."

Thank fuck for that. "What happened?"

Keller smirks, dark eyes finding mine. He's so close, arm still locked around my waist and body heat seeping through my shirt. "We went to a seafood restaurant ... and he's allergic."

"Oh no."

"Yep. Had to call an ambulance and everything. I sat with him until Davey showed up."

"And that officially makes me a selfish asshole."

He laughs, and it shakes through his chest and into mine. "Why?"

"Because here I was sulking, and you just spent the night being a good friend."

He hums, then steals my hat from my head and pulls it down over his head. "You *were* sulking, weren't you?"

"Did ... before all that happened, did you like the guy?"

"He was cool."

"Right."

But I should know by now that Keller is good at seeing through shit. "Why were you looking at houses, Will?"

"I need to buy something someday."

"So you have a deposit ready?"

"Well, no, but—"

"Let me rephrase. Why were you looking at houses *today*?"

I break his stare, mine dropping to where my hands are resting on his chest. "I think I gotta move out."

"What?" Keller stiffens under my hands. "Why?"

There's only so much I can say before I start getting into stalker territory, so I go with the truth—just not all of it. "I ... I can't see you go on dates. I don't want to. All night, I was picturing you out with some guy, and I was ... I got ..."

"Jealous?"

I swallow and, when words don't come, just nod.

He curses but thankfully keeps holding on tight.

"I knew you weren't happy about it, but I didn't realize it made you feel that bad. I told you, it was just to help Mack out. I had no intentions of going home with Brayden, even if there was something there."

Just hearing that's a possibility doesn't make me feel any better.

"Will, the other night ..."

"No, no, no. We're not having the mistake talk."

"Good, because I had no intention of calling it a mistake."

"Huh. Well, good."

"I was just going to say that it meant something to me too."

"It did?" There are no words for how rapidly my chest fills with happiness.

"Yeah, actually. I can't lie and say it didn't catch me off guard, but I definitely wouldn't be okay with you turning around and sleeping with someone the next night. I'd never do that to you."

"Thank you. But also, maybe if you were more of an asshole, I wouldn't get so jealous."

Keller bursts into laughter before letting me go. I miss his arms, but the sad bitterness has completely gone. Like he absorbed it from my body. "I'll get to work on that, then," he says, lifting his mug to take a drink. He watches me for a moment, smiling. "Don't move out, Will."

"Got nowhere to go until August, anyway."

"Even then."

I frown, wondering if he's been following the conversation. "I can't stay. Even if nothing happened last night, it will at some point, and I can't keep dealing with that jealousy. I don't like it."

"I don't like it either."

"Okay. So August."

His eyes bore into mine. "*Stay.*"

"Do you know what you're saying? I can't be here while you date. I can't do it to myself. Which means that unless you get off on actually hurting me, you wouldn't be able to date the whole time I'm here."

"I know what I'm saying." Keller steps forward, fingers under my chin, and tilts my face toward him. "And I'm asking you to stay anyway."

27

KELLER

I'M FULL OF CONFIDENCE ASKING WILL TO STAY, BUT I HAVE no idea what I'm doing. He doesn't give me an answer, just smiles in a way that my gut approves of and then disappears upstairs to work. Even though I'm tired, Will's right in that my workload is huge, so I grab my laptop, a stress ball, and a pillow, then join him in his office.

He's talking into his headset, long, slim fingers moving faster over his keyboard than I'd ever be able to accomplish in my lifetime. He's not even looking at the keys, just typing away, and he glances between screens and relays something to the person on the other end of the call.

Will is ... he's something else. Something that makes me feel all big and warm inside. We agreed nothing would happen, but after he admitted he can't watch me date, I get the feeling he's in the same place as I am. A place we really shouldn't do anything about, but I can't stop myself from gravitating toward him. Wanting him.

I'm quiet as I drop my pillow, then sprawl over the floor with my laptop beside me before rolling onto my back and tossing the stress ball into the air.

Will throws a millisecond glance over his shoulder at me before getting back to work.

I eavesdrop, purely because I like the sound of his voice. He's got a professional tone on that smothers his Southern accent more than anything I've heard so far.

When he hangs up, I ask something that's been bugging me for a while. "Why don't you like your accent?"

Will shrugs those gorgeous shoulders, not turning to look at me. "People don't take me too seriously with it. Lots of people at college said it made me sound stupid, so I practiced getting rid of it. The only thing that made me *feel* stupid was trying to speak differently, but here we are."

"They're the dumb ones. I like the way you talk."

"Well, bless your heart, but I'm busier than a cat on a hot tin roof over here. You gonna make me madder than a wet hen if you keep yammering on now."

It's so unexpected, my laugh slips from me before I can stop it, and I miss the stress ball, which hits my nose and flies off to the side. "*Argh.*" I rub my face. "See? Adorable."

Will throws a sheepish grin back over his shoulder. "At least someone thinks so."

"Anyone who thinks you're an idiot needs a head check." I wave a hand toward where he's working. "I didn't understand half of what you were talking about."

"Just basic remote access to walk her through a step."

"Nothing about that sounds basic."

He swings around in his chair, looking proud of himself. "I'm young enough to have grown up with the internet, old man."

"Fuck you, so am I."

"Tell me, how did that dial-up work for you?"

"Surprised you know what that is," I grumble.

"I know what a *land line* is too." He taps his computer. "You'd be surprised what you can find on one of these things. It's not just MSN chat anymore."

"I don't think I like this game."

"Hmm ... you're getting cranky. Makes sense since it's almost three. Time for your afternoon nap?"

I hate the fact that I actually wouldn't pass up a nap now he's mentioned it, but I'm sure as shit not going to admit to that. I had a late night, sue me; it has nothing to do with my age.

"Does someone's diaper need changing?" I throw back.

"Kinda creepy comeback when you got off to me being fucked by a tentacle the other night."

"Fine, you win." I start throwing the ball again. "But I'd challenge anyone not to get off on that sight."

Will smiles, and I beg myself to keep my trap shut, but instead, I meet his eyes.

"You were so good. Took that thing perfectly."

His whole face flushes, and he hurries to turn back to face his desk. "Don't you dare."

"What? I'm just pointing out you were a very good boy."

Will flips me the bird over his shoulder, and I crack up laughing. He ignores me as he should, and eventually, I turn my laptop on and get into it.

The floor isn't comfortable, and there's no reason I shouldn't be working from my dining room table, but I like the idea of hanging out in here. Even though we aren't talking, I get the sense Will needs it after last night. And if I'm wrong, he can tell me, but even when he's on calls and I'm typing away, he doesn't ask me to leave. It's nice having someone to work with. Sure, at the office I have Valerie, but it isn't the same thing. Or maybe I want to claim it isn't the same thing, purely because I'm enjoying Will's company so much and don't want to look too deeply into it.

The way I don't want to look too deeply into asking him to stay with me, permanently, even if it means I have to put an end to my dating.

It's worth it to get Will to myself.

Then again, would it be to myself? Last night was hard on him, but how would I take it if it was him out on a date? Easy answer: not well. If Will stays here and *he* starts dating, I'd have to assume he'd be okay with me doing the same.

Which means ...

Neither of us will be dating.

Both of us will be living here.

Hanging out.

Watching movies.

Cooking.

Preventing sleepwalking and ...

I'm trying not to imagine hooking up with him again, but it's a huge fail. I want it, badly, and I know the reason why we shouldn't, but Will's jealousy can't have just been over sex. And if it wasn't, would I be willing to risk everything to explore that?

I'm terrified my answer might be yes.

"You're distracting me."

His fake annoyance is sexy as hell. I'm up and leaning against his desk before I'm aware of moving closer, and to stop myself from doing something stupid like touching him, I take off his hat that I stole earlier and return it to his head.

"You have hat hair," he says.

I drag my hands through it. "No one here to see it but you."

"Good point. Though I think you look hot always."

"Why do I get the feeling that in living here, you're going to be teasing me like that a lot?"

"Maybe because you're a very smart person. And also, I wasn't teasing." He clicks to answer a call before I can respond. Instead of returning to work, I lean against his desk and watch him, more than a little turned on by how good he is at his job. There's no nervousness here. No hesitation. His work looks as easy to him as breathing, the keyboard and computers like an extension of him.

He's wearing gym shorts and a T-shirt, and I've never found something so casual so sexy.

Fuck, I'm a mess.

I'm an idiot for asking him to stay. I'm an idiot for letting things get out of hand the other night, even if Will did initiate it. And now, I'm an idiot for continuing to build on how much I like him and for wanting to do all that again.

The idea of sex with him is a massive turn-on, obviously, but that's not all I'm picturing when I think about getting intimate. I'm picturing kissing, taking our time, having fun while we play with each other. I'm picturing my arms around him naked, and his around me, and those deep, stuttered breaths panting by my ear.

I don't realize Will has hung up until my gaze returns to his face.

The bright gray eyes, his strong jaw, the thick, light brown eyebrows taking up the space right under his cap.

"That's a dangerous look," he says at last.

"Maybe."

"No, it definitely is. Because if you keep looking at me like that, I might have to log off and do something about it."

My smile only grows, and I wipe at my mouth to try to hide it. "That's a bold promise."

"Right. We said we wouldn't. Again."

"We did."

"But what if I really, really want to?"

That overbearingly strong lust is back, infecting my veins with the thought of getting Will naked. "I don't want things to get mixed up between us."

"No, I don't either. But ... would one more time hurt anything? We didn't tell anyone about the other times."

"I did."

"What?"

"I told my friends. I'm not ashamed of you, Will. It has nothing to do with that."

"I'm glad, but aren't you worried about it getting back to Molly?"

"Nope. They'd never tell. It's good to have friends like that."

"My best friend is the one person I can't talk about it with."

I cringe at the thought of that awkward conversation. *Mols, you'll never guess what! Your dad said he wanted to fuck me with his tongue.*

That's definitely not something I need my kid to hear about.

But if we kept this a secret, like Will said, then he never would hear about anything. It goes against my comfort levels; I don't want to think of Will as a secret. I don't want to come between anyone.

But what I'm feeling for him has grown to a point where I don't think I can fight it anymore.

At what point do I reach the stage where I consider my own happiness? My whole life, I've put Molly first, and I wouldn't want it any other way. It's my job as his dad.

"I don't know the right move here," I say.

Will logs out of his computer and stands. "Come with me."

28

WILL

I don't feel bad ditching out on work early. They have my cell if there's anything urgent that pops up, but the afternoons are usually quiet. Besides, there's no way in the world I'm going to pass up the opportunity of a round two with Keller.

After how I felt last night, I'm done pushing my feelings to the side. He might not know how deep they go or for how long I've had them, but he knows they're there. He knows, and he's still willing to do this, which makes me think he's feeling something too.

I'd never purposely hurt my best friend, but my relationship also has nothing to do with him. Love goes both ways. I've done everything I could to ignore and resist for *him*, but now Molly is going to have to meet me halfway. If this gets out or it turns into something, I have to trust that he's going to understand.

Molly and Keller are both amazing, and I'd never want

to have to choose between them. I have to hope that Molly would never ask me to.

"Where are we going?" Keller asks.

"I want to play a game."

"Like what?"

"Well, we didn't have sex the other night, and I thought we could not have sex again today."

His dark eyes narrow. "I'm listening."

Fuck, even his voice turns me on. So deep and laid-back, a slow rumble that gives me an eargasm.

"Well, the other night, we didn't touch. That's the key, right? No touching. And the way I see it, we have plenty more toys that we can not touch with."

"See? You're a fucking genius."

I lead him to the box we stashed away in one of the kitchen cupboards and pull it out. "Lucky dip?"

"How would that work?"

"Whatever you touch, we use."

"And if it's the monster schlong?"

I think of the giant double dildo. "Okay, anything but that." I stand up and give the box a shake before tilting it toward him.

Keller's eyes hook mine as he reaches inside and withdraws his hand with—

"Oh, thank god."

A Fleshlight. One meant to look like an asshole instead of the creepy animal snouts.

Keller takes the box and sets it on the dark countertop before stepping closer. "You gonna use this for me?"

My cock stiffens at the way his gaze slides over my face. That delicious approval is shining in his eyes, and I want nothing more than to be upstairs naked with him.

"You'd do anything for me, wouldn't you?" he asks, reaching up to drag his thumb over my bottom lip.

"Embarrassingly, yes. Want me to sit on both ends of that dildo? I'll do it."

He chuckles. "Luckily for you, your pain wouldn't turn me on. Seeing you feel good does. Seeing someone as easily embarrassed as you just forget about everything but how you feel?" Keller's eyes flutter closed. "Goddamn beautiful sight."

"We're doing this?" I check. "Because I'd never want you to do something you don't want."

"It has nothing to do with want, Will." He leans in until his lips are so close to my ear that his breath sends ripples down my throat. "If I took what I want, you'd be bent over the counter with my cock inside you already."

Nerves dance through me. "I wouldn't stop you."

"I know you wouldn't. You'd take my cock so good, wouldn't you?"

"The best." I turn my head to look him right in the eye. "No one could ever take your cock the way I would."

White teeth dig into his lower lip. "You're going to get me into trouble."

I wrap my hand around the Fleshlight and take it from him. "I'm not forcing you into anything. You can either watch me fuck this, or you can not. Your choice."

Then I break away from him and head into the living room.

I'm already naked by the time Keller appears. He's unbuttoning his shirt, slowly revealing my favorite view, and I thank the fucking universe that this is actually happening again. Because now it is, I'm going to get Keller like this as often as I goddamn can. Maybe I'll even do what Joey said and brave up enough to tell Keller how I really feel. How I've always felt. How I'm a selfish bastard and want more.

He drops his shirt to the ground, then pops the top button on his jeans. It's a tease, waiting, wanting, but the way his eyes move slowly over me as he lowers his fly is something that will keep me going for a while.

"Where do you want me?" I ask.

"Lying along the couch."

I kick my legs up onto the leather cushion beside me, just like he wanted, as he shucks off his jeans and moves to sit on the shiny, black coffee table. He's completely naked, showing off his cut arms, his broad chest, the way his torso funnels down to the most amazing cock I've ever seen. My mouth waters for it. If I reached out, I could touch him. Feel the hairs on those strong legs, trace the muscle with my fingertips. Hell, if I leaned over far enough, I could slide his cock into my mouth.

"Grabbed this for you," he says, dropping a lube packet onto my chest.

I grab it and tear it open with my teeth. "Tell me what you want."

"Slick that mouthwatering cock up until it's good and shiny. Then fuck the life out of that little hole."

I don't know how Keller can say so many right things all in a row, but the man manages it. A moan slips from me as I stroke my length, loving the smooth glide of the lube and gentle friction of my palm. Then I turn for the toy and pick it up.

Like last time, the silicone is an obviously different sensation, but it doesn't take long to warm up. It's never going to feel like a real ass, but as I push inside, the toy opening to hug my cock, I'm definitely not complaining.

Joey was right to feel sorry for my sex life. How the hell have I never tried one of these things before?

My eyes flutter open to find Keller's focus glued to me, and I have my answer. This wouldn't be even one percent as hot as it is without him here to watch.

I start out slow, jacking myself with the Fleshlight, enjoying the sensations. I'm turned on, but not wildly so, and the more confidence I gain, the more comfortable I am to face him. To watch his face as he touches himself. To get off on how I'm getting him off. And as amazing as it is, Keller is too far away. My dick is in heaven, but the rest of me is restless. I can't complain, not when this loophole allows us to steal these moments together, but at facing the very real possibility that he might never touch me? It almost makes me call this thing off right now. I need his hands. His mouth. His murmured reassurances in my ear. I want to hear him tell me how well I'm doing up close. I want him to hold me and want to hold me and not feel any regret between us.

I grit my teeth and move the Fleshlight faster, trying to match the pace Keller is stroking himself with. Trying to picture it's his hand holding me.

He abruptly stops. "You're not enjoying this."

"No. I definitely, definitely am."

"Then why are you frowning?"

"I … I'm …"

"What do you want, Will?"

I sigh, eyes clashing with his. "You."

29

KELLER

Loopholes be damned. There is no way for me to watch Will, spread out on the couch, cock buried inside a silicone hole, as he begs for me and deny him a damn thing. My arms are dying to gather him up and crush him to my body, to hold him and stroke him through his orgasm until he's gasping my name.

I can't make big decisions like this when I'm horny, though, because giving in to my urges will always win.

So I do the next best thing.

I close the yawning space between us.

There's room between his spread legs for me to climb onto the couch and kneel, and then I lean forward and set my forearm on the couch beside his head. We're barely touching, just a whisper of thigh and my elbow by his shoulder, but when he tilts his head back and I look down into his eyes, our faces are lined up perfectly.

"How's this?" My voice is lower than usual, like I've never used it before, and I'm surprised I can manage words at all with how scrambled up Will makes my brain.

"So good." His hand hasn't stopped moving with the Fleshlight, so I reach down and cover it.

"I'll take over this."

His pupils blow out. "Please."

He doesn't need to beg. Doesn't Will know that he's already got me in the palm of his hand? That I'd never do this with anyone but him? I don't take chances, I don't make my life complicated, and yet Will's the biggest complication I've faced, and I'm lying here wanting to face it head-on.

His raspy groan is a sound I want to swallow, but I'm still not far gone enough to go there. Kissing is dangerous. More than this even. Our one and only might have been mere seconds, but it was a kiss that spun my brain.

So I put all my focus into my grip on the toy, trying to imagine I have my hand wrapped around him instead. His perfectly straight, veiny cock. I picture how smooth his skin would be. How heated. Imagine rubbing my thumb into that spot under his crown that sends me wild with need.

Will's lips part, each inhale and exhale labored. He hasn't looked away from me, and I'm holding his eyes right back, because when a man like Will is under you, nothing else matters.

It's a struggle to stop my eyes from slipping to his mouth, from tracing the defined line around his lips, from following the track down his throat that I'd like to take with my tongue.

Would it be so bad if I touched him? Kissed him?

No one is going to know about this. If we're keeping

hooking up a secret, does it matter if he or I use the Fleshlight? Does it matter if I replace the Fleshlight with my hand? My mouth? Or the dildo with my cock?

I shiver as I imagine pushing into his body, and if his hole was prepped at the moment, I probably wouldn't hold back. I'd hook his strong leg over my shoulder and press my way inside. My blood heats at how tight and hot his body would feel wrapped around me.

"Tell me what you want," he pants.

"I want to fuck you. I want you to come on my cock while you're screaming my name. Shit, Will, I've never wanted anything more."

He gasps and grabs my shoulders, nails digging into my skin. Right as I think he's about to tell me to just do it, he bows off the couch and lets out the most perfect grunt I've ever heard.

"*Ugh.* Kel ..."

A possessive wave rolls over me at the sound, and I watch every flicker of his face as he comes with a satisfaction so deep it makes my balls ache.

When he falls back panting, I slide the Fleshlight from his softening cock and shove my own inside.

"So wet and tight," I rumble. "Love the feel of your cum on my cock. Love filling this hole you got ready for me."

"Holy shit, you're gonna get me hard again."

Like he can talk. My balls are in agony, thanks to him.

"Wrap your legs around me."

He does it immediately, and my whole body hums at the contact. As much as I want to, I still don't bring our bodies together, but that has less to do with loopholes and more that I won't be able to use the toy if I do.

I dip my lips near his ear.

"Know what I'm picturing?"

"What?"

"That I'm fucking your hole. That it's your ass milking my cock."

"Is it doing good?"

"So good. I've never had an ass suck on me like yours does."

Will trembles, then surprises the hell out of me by reaching up, wrapping my hair around his hand, and pulling tight. "Fuck me harder."

I pick up the pace, thrusting into the toy like my life depends on it. It almost does. Will and I are going to have a lot to talk about when we're done, but for this very moment, everything is perfect. All the nerves around my cock are alive, my balls are full and tight, and there's a zapping at the base of my spine that's urging me on, pushing me faster, harder, just needing that little bit more.

"I'm gonna come inside you," I growl.

Will whimpers, and the sound is my fucking kryptonite. "Do it. Show me how good I get you off." His teeth sink into my ear, and it's all over. The pain mixed with the deep pleasure building in my gut makes me unleash.

My cock twitches with every spurt, cum joining Will's to fill the toy, and while it might not have been his ass I was really using, sharing this with him is hot as fuck.

And apparently, he feels the same because the second I pull the toy off and set it aside, Will flips us and slams his mouth down on mine.

It isn't a gentle kiss like last time. Nothing sweet or appreciative. This is hunger, pure and simple, and as his tongue fills my mouth, I kiss him back just as deeply. Our chests meet, legs tangle, and even though I got off three seconds ago and probably won't have it in me again today, it doesn't matter. I want him now just as much as I did before we got naked.

"I always knew you'd taste good," he says, tugging my bottom lip between his teeth. "But this is ridiculous. I'm already obsessed with you. Why are you making it worse?"

I laugh and knock his hat off his head, burying one hand in his hair as my mouth finds his neck. "You think this is bad," I tell his skin. "I haven't even touched you yet."

"Yet?"

I groan, hands tightening on him as I press my forehead to his shoulder. "I think ... Well, our loophole talk is out the window now."

"If you want me to be sorry about that, I'm not."

"Honestly ... neither am I, but ..."

"You feel guilty."

"Of course I do. Wanting you like this makes me feel some things about myself that aren't the nicest."

Will pulls back so he can see me. "Like what?"

"Like the fact that maybe I'm a shitty dad after all." Even saying those words hurts. "All my life, I've fought to make people see that I could do it. From the first day I held Molly, people assumed I'd fail. I guess no one realized it would take me twenty-six years to do that."

"No." Will cups my face, and there's nothing uncertain in his tone. "Molly's an adult, and what's happening between us has nothing to do with him."

"He introduced us."

"And? People get introduced all the time. Madden's

setting Molly up on dates with men he knows. Does that give Madden a right to Molly's relationship?"

I haven't thought of it like that.

Sadness fills Will's eyes. "I love him too. He's been my best friend for years, and I hate the thought of hurting him. It makes me sick, actually. And then I look at you and ..." I wait for Will to finish that sentence, but he changes his mind. "I want to see where this thing could go."

The heaviness in that statement makes me nervous. There's too much weight to my answer, too much riding on this moment. Walk away and be the dad I've always been, or lean in and hope I've raised my son right?

I'd been looking for someone, hoping to find someone that I felt that connection to, who I could see myself sharing a life with.

Could I see myself doing that with *Will*?

Holy fuck, I think I can.

Everything in my gut is telling me this feels right.

It's never steered me wrong before.

"I'm terrified," I admit.

"Me too."

"But I want to try anyway."

Will's eyes widen like it's the last response he'd been expecting. I'm not surprised. I can hardly believe I'm doing this either. Not only because it's Will, not only because he's friends with my son, but the age difference isn't far from my mind, and I'm not sure I'll ever completely trust that this is happening because it was meant to and not just because we're both here, we're both horny, and him living here has given him some kind of Stockholm syndrome probably.

The only thing I can do at this point is put trust into whatever is growing between us and see what happens. Who knows? It might fizzle out, and then we don't have to tell Molly a thing.

But then I look at Will, and I take in his caring eyes and messy hair and soft smile, and I just *know* that whatever we have is going to ruin me. Whether that's for better or worse, I guess I'll find out.

30

WILL

I haven't worked out if we're calling this a relationship, or situationship, or a seven-day trial, but I'm just going to go ahead and call it amazing. After working for so long on keeping my hands to myself and my feelings under wraps, being able to just go up and touch Keller whenever I want takes me the rest of the day to get used to.

We cook dinner together, we shower together. I watch another of his dumb movies, and he holds me while we laugh until we hurt, and when he takes me up to bed after it, he touches me for the first time, and I get the hand job of all hand jobs.

There's nothing like the sight of Keller between my thighs.

Everything is just *nice,* and I fucking love it. I don't want a life filled with adrenaline and high stakes. I don't want high ambitions or to be constantly trying to level up. I just want to be happy, and sometimes I worry that getting this chance with Keller is giving me more than my share. It's been a long time since I felt like I could relax and just be, and it's that feeling that keeps throwing me off and making me wait for the other boot to drop.

We agreed to see if this is anything before we tell Molly, but it'll be a lot easier without that constant tension over my head.

Keller throws himself onto the couch beside me, grabs my leg, and drags me into his lap, where he can reach my mouth with a soft, drawn-out kiss.

"You're an easy man to date, you know," I say.

"Is that what we're doing? Dating?"

"What else would you call it?"

"Eating ass every night."

"*Every* night? It's been one so far, and that definitely didn't happen."

He hooks a dark eyebrow upward. "Is that a complaint I hear?"

"Not at all. The spooning was fantastic."

Keller brushes a kiss over my cheek this time. "You know how badly I want you. There's just a lot going on in my head."

"I know."

"When I fuck you, I want to be able to enjoy every second."

I pull back, bunching his hair in my fist and pulling it tight in the way that makes his eyes all dark. "When you fuck me, you won't have another option but to enjoy every second."

That gets one of his sexy, wicked grins. "Tell me more about this incredible ass."

"Nope. I'm not giving away all my secrets. You're just going to have to wait and find out for yourself."

Keller's hands drop to my ass, and he gives it a solid squeeze. Blood shoots straight to my cock, and I wish like hell I didn't have to start work in five minutes, or I'd be taking him out and sitting on him, full head be damned.

"Tonight," I whisper. "Please let me feel you."

His grip on me tightens. "You sure?"

"I'm sure," I hurry to tell him. "I promise I'll tell you if anything changes for me, but I just don't see how it could. I've wanted you for a while now." Total understatement. "I'm aching for this."

Instead of the heat I'm expecting to fill his gaze, Keller's eyes soften instead. He pulls me in for a slow, deep kiss that travels all the way to my heart.

I pull away sooner than I want to. "I've gotta get to work."

"Me too."

"Will you be late?"

"Nope." He nips my jaw. "Because I'm going to take you out on a date."

"Like ... a real one?"

He laughs. "Yes, a real one."

"Where people see us together and everything?"

"No idea yet—I decided about a second ago. But if we go somewhere and it's just us, don't think it's because I don't want to be seen with you. I do."

"You're not ... umm ..."

He tilts his head while he waits for me to finish.

"It's gonna sound so dumb, but you're not worried about people seeing you with someone who's ..."

"My son's age?"

I screw up my face but nod anyway.

"I'm not excited about being judged, but I don't care all that much. If people want to obsess over our relationship, they're going to do it no matter how I feel. The age thing, well, it's a big one. We have hugely different life experience for a start, and being significantly older means—"

"If you start talking about dying or something, I'm going to hit you."

"I'm *just* saying—"

I pinch him. "Well, don't. You're getting way ahead of yourself. And frankly, if we work out, I will take having whatever number of years with you over ending things now because of what-ifs. Besides, there's nothing to say I won't die first."

"Wise. Which of us is the older one again?"

"Not you." I shrug. "You're behaving like a big baby."

He slaps my ass, and *oh*, I like that. "Watch yourself. Our date could be very good or very bad depending on how much of a shit you are to me."

I give him my most innocent look. "And our sex could be very good or very nonexistent if you don't pull out all the stops and make me feel special."

Keller groans, but I catch his smile before he rests his forehead on my shoulder. "I'm never going to win against you, am I?"

"Depends. If you think having a great dinner and great sex isn't winning, then I might need to rethink who I'm dating."

"Good point. And there you go being wise again."

I cup his face as he kisses me again, and while we might not have had all the sex I'd like, I meant it when I said I had no complaints at all. I could kiss Keller forever and be happy.

When Molly's name lights up my phone, I let the support chat know I'm taking my lunch break, then log out and hurry to answer him.

"Mols! What are you doing?"

"Taking a break."

"Me too. I was gonna call you tonight. You beat me to it." That's a total, total lie. I was gonna go on a date tonight that ended with his dad's dick in my ass.

Fuck.

I hate secrets.

I'm beating myself up the whole way down to the kitchen.

"What's new with you?" I ask before Molly can get in first.

"Well ... I have news."

That makes me perk up. "News?"

"I'm dating someone."

"What?" I'm torn on whether to be excited or not. My default is to cheer him on, but I have to make sure this is the real deal first. "Like, an actual boyfriend?"

He chuckles. "Officially. All mine. And ... I'm not going overboard like I normally would."

I switch my phone to the other ear and hold it with my shoulder as I pull open the fridge to find something to eat. "You sure about that?"

"Yeah." And to his credit, he sounds less intense about

this guy. Which is a good thing. "He's helped ground me in a way no one ever has before."

"Tell me about him."

"Nope. It's very new, so I'm keeping him to myself. For now. I want to see how things play out without all the pressure I normally put on my relationships. He's, uh ... he's already told me I'm it for him though. No one else."

I laugh. "No pressure. Right."

"Shut up, you know what I mean. Normally, I'm the one wanting all the attention and needing to be smothered and super intense about everything. Seven doesn't let me get like that. He's ... everything I didn't know I needed."

Hearing the love in Molly's voice makes me want to cry. I'm so fucking relieved for him that it sounds like he's finally found his person. And I've found mine. But I can't fucking tell him that.

"You're happy."

"Will, I ... I know I've only been gone a few months, but these guys here, they've helped me a lot. Definitely helped me pull my head out of my ass, and ... I'm sorry. I'm so sorry for being an asshole for a while there."

Relief sweeps through me. Molly sounds like Molly again. Like that resentfulness has left him, and maybe, *maybe*, Keller and I can tell him our news too. Maybe he'll be happy for us.

"I understand. You know I do. I'm just glad the move has done what you wanted it to."

"Yeah ... the only shit part is being away from you and Dad, but it's also good in a way."

"Independence?"

"That, and ... I hate seeing you guys together."

"What?"

Molly huffs. "I know, I know. It's dumb. But I think that was playing into my resentfulness. I hated how close you were getting, and, like, he's *my* dad, you know. You're *my* friend. It killed me to even suggest you move in there, but even though I didn't want you around each other, I couldn't let you go back to your family."

The more he talks, the more it's like a knife in my chest.

"I love you. I could never let that happen."

Molly put me first. He set aside how he felt and made sure I was safe. Happy. Did what was best for me. And how have I repaid him? I've put *myself* first.

If he hated me and Keller being close, what the hell is he going to think about our relationship?

I think I've fucked this whole thing up.

31

KELLER

I LIKE TEASING WILL, LIKE KEEPING HIM GUESSING, AND THE whole drive out to the farm, I do exactly that. It isn't until I hit the long dirt road running between perfectly straight hedges, tires crunching over gravel, that it clicks.

"Are we going apple picking?"

I mime locking my lips. It's late afternoon, but there are still a fair few cars left in the parking lot, and with summer in full force, the farm doesn't close for hours.

When I pull up, Will climbs out of the passenger side, gray eyes bright and blond tuft of hair sticking out from under his cap, catching the sun.

"This is cool. I don't think I've done something like that."

"Not even when you were little?"

Will shakes his head. "Nah, my weekends were spent taking swimming lessons on a Saturday and doing the Lord's work on a Sunday. Then the rest of the week was all about school and homework."

"What about summer break?"

"Mom and Dad still worked, so I'd mostly ride my bike around town with my friends. Go swimming in the creek. And there was this abandoned shack we made our home base, so we spent a lot of time there, fixing it up and making it nice."

"That sounds pretty awesome."

"Yeah, wasn't bad." His sigh is so heavy it makes me reach over and take his hand. "Hurts sometimes, you know? To remember how good it was and that I had no idea how everything would change. Just for being me."

"I'm really sorry."

"Ahh." He squeezes his eyes until they're not glassy anymore. "Can't say all that change has been a bad thing."

"I agree. Especially in the last month or so." I tug him to fall into step with me, and he walks so close his shoulder keeps bumping mine.

"What happened in the last month?" His innocent tone doesn't fool me.

"I got close with my incredibly sexy roommate who doesn't wear nearly enough clothes most of the time and even less the rest of the time."

Will laughs, throaty and addictive. Given the brief sadness that took over him before, I'm proud to pull that sound from him. "I can wear a full snowsuit if that's more to your taste?"

"Hard pass. That said, a gimp suit might be fun."

He stares at me as we walk up to the farm's entrance. "I'm not sure I want to know."

"Probably not, but there's a very high chance you'll find out."

"I had no idea how freaky people could get with sex stuff."

Tentacles and gimp suits are only scratching the surface, but I'm not about to tell him that. I don't think his mind could handle it. "It's all about keeping an open mind. If it feels good, I don't judge, and I'm always up for trying new things even if they turn out not to be for me."

"I'm going to have to be up for anything with you, aren't I?"

That makes me snort. "Not at all. I don't need toys. But if we're both into it, why not?"

Will leans toward my ear so he's not overheard. "Let me rephrase. I'm *going* to be up for anything with you. I'll enjoy anything if you compliment me enough."

"Well, I love giving you compliments, so that suits us both." I hook my arm around his neck and kiss his temple, then step up to the desk.

Will tries to pay for himself, but I wave his money away and hand over cash for our basket. He takes it from me as I lead him away from the desk and into the farm.

"Whatever we fill this with, we can take home," I explain. "There is still an hour or two of daylight left. I figured we could fill it up, grab some food, and hang out listening to the band."

"That sounds good." He takes a step to get to it, but I grab his T-shirt and pull him back against me.

"One thing. Whatever you put in the basket, I'll be eating off your body later." I press my lips against the shell of his ear. "Thought you might like to know how much I love the *juicy* strawberries."

Will presses back against me, and his voice is breathless as he says, "That could get messy."

"I'm planning on it."

When I'd scrolled through the internet earlier, trying to find date inspiration, I had no idea how Will would take it. He'd seemed excited by the thought of us going out on a public date, and I was worried that he might be picturing dinner in a restaurant. I have nothing against that, but we eat together all the time, and I'm not the kind of guy who will do something just to prove a point.

Besides, while I might not care who in town knows we're dating, I do care if Molly finds out from someone who isn't me. It means having to be cautious about who's around while making sure I don't hide Will away either. It's a tricky line to walk, but I don't plan on doing it for long.

I'll know quickly whether or not Will and I are something, and if I think this is going to be serious, I'll be telling Molly straightaway. No matter how worried I am over how he might react.

I watch Will move from plant to plant, and the man's radiating happiness. It's not that he's smiling much, just this overall feeling I get from him.

"So this date was a good one?" I check.

Will finishes stripping the strawberries from one plant and moves on to the next. "Are you kidding? This is hands down perfect. I love food, I love to eat, and even more than that, I love sex. You're combining my two favorite things, so I've gotta tell you, if you're ever planning to try and beat this, you won't be able to."

"You sound too confident about that."

"Just know it's the truth."

I move things around in the basket to make way for the

peaches he snagged. "What if I surprised you with plane tickets somewhere? Or took you on a cruise?"

"I don't need things like that. I don't want them. The rest of the world is pretty and all, but Kilborough's pretty enough in itself."

"You really don't want to travel?"

He shrugs, turning a peach over in his hands. "I know it's top of most people's dream boards, but I never had that bug. Maybe there's something missing in me, but I'm happy with where I am. It's the people that make a place—not some fancy statuses or buildings—and I've gotta say"—Will nudges me with his elbow—"Kilborough's got the best people I ever met."

It isn't something I've given a lot of thought before. Traveling is something I've assumed I'd do at some point in my life, but not necessarily because I'm excited about going somewhere. Whenever people mention dreams and their future, there's always somewhere or something they want to see. Like it's a marker of success when they can cross it off the bucket list.

But what's wrong with right where I am? My house, my job, the community. They're all things I love, and Kilborough gives them to me. All of my friends are here, and they're some of the best and strangest people I could imagine. Leaving them has no appeal. Leaving Molly's childhood home, the place where we built our lives, has no appeal. And leaving Will?

He's definitely one of the things that makes living in Kilborough a dream.

I joked about him being wise earlier, but it's true. I think I have a black-and-white perspective on things, but it's got nothing on Will. He seems to have one question he asks himself when he makes a decision: will it make me happy? If more people lived their lives that way, the world would be a friendlier place.

And probably more dysfunctional, but I'm not going to think too deeply about it.

"Favorite color," Will asks out of nowhere.

"The exact shade you go when you're blushing."

"That is such a fucking cop-out."

"Why? It's adorable."

"It's not a real color though."

"Tell that to your face."

He huffs. "My favorite is blue, not that you care."

"Of course I don't care. Favorite colors change. They're also dependent on the thing you're talking about. I like red, but I wouldn't buy a bright red car. Tell me something real. Like do you eat pineapple on pizza?"

"Of course."

I pretend to shudder. "I can't believe I kiss that mouth."

"Let me guess, you think that viral dress that went round a while back is white and gold, don't you?"

"Well, duh."

Will snarls. "It's clearly black and blue."

"How can you think that?"

"Because I learned my colors in kindergarten. You obviously didn't do the same."

"I can't believe this," I moan. "How am I attracted to someone who's just so wrong about everything?"

He cocks an eyebrow my way. "I think *you're* hot?"

"And I stand corrected. You're the smartest guy I've ever met."

He eyes the basket. "Tell me, if I grab a pumpkin to fill the basket, would that mean it's time to go?"

"No. I told you, we're having a proper date first. Besides …" I shudder. "Raw pumpkin. Not something I'm interested in trying."

"Wouldn't you cook it first?"

"That would require time we don't have. When I get you home, you'll be naked the second we walk through the front door."

Will hangs his head back. "Worst. Edging. Ever."

32

WILL

No matter how much I try to rush through the date, Keller is a smirking asshole who smirks, and he doesn't give in to the pressure to hurry things along. I'd almost say that he doesn't want to have sex, but there's nothing hesitant in the way he keeps looking me over. That man melts me. All the way through.

It's why I haven't mentioned the call with Molly. I will. Soon. I just wanted us to have this moment together because once Keller knows how much Molly is against the idea of us, he'll have no choice but to walk away.

I haven't laid my feelings on him fully because this whole thing is newer than new, and the last thing I wanna do is put Keller under the pressure of eight years' worth of building feelings. Especially because I'm feeling the pressure myself.

I want to touch his cock. I want to taste his skin. I want that world-changing crackle of need to be so unforgettable neither of us can deny that our chemistry is endgame. Then, I want to talk and cuddle and hold each other for the rest of the night. Before I have to face the conversation I'm dreading.

It's dark by the time we leave, bag full of fruit on the back seat of Keller's car, earmarked for my body. My body, which is currently humming at the thought of all the things Keller might do to it.

The streetlights flash over his features as we drive. His dark, scruffy jaw, the way the corners of his lips always point upward, his hair that's half pulled up, messy strands hanging around his face.

I glance down as he changes gears. The veins running along the back of his strong hands make my mouth water. I've met a lot of people, some from back home, some from other football clubs I'd play when I was younger, the guys and professors in my college, and not a single one of them turned me on the way Keller does. It's not even all about his looks. Those tick my boxes for sure, but you add them to the confident way he moves, his patience, his sense of humor, and the way he cares about people. He's the full package.

Keller pulls into the driveway back home, and he hasn't even got the engine off before I'm grabbing the bag from the back seat and climbing out of the car.

He isn't far behind me. I don't bother to watch and see if he follows because I can feel the tension building between us. This is so far past overdue my hand shakes as I try to get the door unlocked. Keller reaches me before I can.

His large body presses against my back. "You have three seconds to get this door open, or I'm going to strip you down and fuck you on this front porch."

"You can't say something like that and expect me to brain. You're setting me up to fail."

His filthy chuckle hits my ear as he slides one hand up the front of my shirt to touch my abs, and the other takes the key from me and slots it into the lock.

As soon as the door's open, he shoves me through it.

"Get naked."

I'm already fighting with my pants before he says that though, and as I struggle to get them off, Keller steps inside, kicks the door closed, and pulls his T-shirt over his head in one go.

My cock is rock-hard at the sight of him. I'll never get used to this. And I know he said his head was all full, but tonight, I plan to make it go silent.

He tugs open the button on his shorts, then steps forward and takes the bag from my grip. Now I have two hands, I can get my jeans off without it looking like a circus act, and then my shirt and boxer briefs are quick to follow.

I give my cock a quick pump while Keller's eyes roam over me.

"You really do have a mouthwatering body," he says.

"And if I didn't?"

"Impossible."

"Why?"

Keller's hungry gaze meets mine. "Because no matter what your body looked like, I'd want to devour you whole."

Appreciation zings through me. I feel exactly the same way about him. For me, it's not about how Keller looks on the outside. He's rough, not traditionally good-looking, but the more I see of him, the more time we spend together, the more we get to know each other on a deeper level, the more I fall for him.

It's everything inside that I'm attracted to, and my attraction to the outside stems from that.

He cups the bulge at the front of his shorts and creeps closer. "I want you upstairs, spread across my bed."

"Aye, aye, captain." I give him a two-finger mock salute and take off for the stairs. He follows me slowly, and I love the feeling of him stalking me as much as I love the anticipation of what comes next. I'm finally gonna get his hands on me, and I'm finally gonna be able to have my way with him right back.

I crawl onto his bed, fling my hat across the room, and then flop down on my back. He appears in the doorway a moment later.

It's dark, and he's turned the hall light on, so he's lit from behind, and I can't make out much of his features. He creeps closer and sets the bag on the bed beside me, then slowly pushes his shorts down and off his legs.

His hard cock juts upward, thick and dark, surrounded by a halo of dark curls.

"Can I taste you?" I ask, lust building deep in my gut.

He doesn't say anything, just kneels on the bed and shifts until he's beside my head. "Lick."

I tremble and shift up onto my elbow so I can lean forward, closer, the smell of his skin filling my nose. Then I reach out my tongue and flick it over his slit.

He exhales heavily. "The whole head this time."

I run my tongue from the notch on the underside and slowly around the smooth, glossy tip. His salty precum hits my tongue and shoots desire straight to my balls.

"Suck."

Finally.

My eyes drift closed as my mouth surrounds him, and I

suck him in. I move up and down his shaft, taking him deeper with each pass, and the way he fills my mouth so perfectly has me floating. Then his hand rests on the back of my head, and he pushes in deep and hard.

I gag, and he pulls out immediately.

"Had your taste now?"

"I want more."

"Greedy little cocksucker." Keller's lips skim mine. "You are so fucking good at that."

The praise makes my insides light up.

Keller reaches over for the bag and upends the fruit we bought all over the bed.

"You're gonna make a mess," I point out.

"Planning on it." He leans down and kisses my shoulder. "Lucky we have your bed to sleep in."

I'm not gonna argue about spending the night together again. I don't think I ever would.

Keller's thick fingers close over an enormous strawberry, and he lifts it to my lips. "Bite."

I do as I'm told, juices bursting in my mouth, and Keller immediately pulls it away again. Then he slides the bitten end down my neck and follows it with his tongue.

I sigh at the contact. "So good."

His chuckle is dark and hot. "I've barely even started, baby."

He slides the strawberry over my collarbone, tongue chasing the path as the scruff on his jaw scrapes my skin. He moves over my pec, my nipple, my abs. He drips the strawberry into my belly button, and his tongue dives in after it.

Then he pulls off the stalk and rests it right above my cock.

Keller does the same with three more before he moves

on to the blackberries, then the raspberries. My skin is sticky and tight but burning under his touch. There isn't an inch of my torso he leaves unexplored, and my cock is so hard and ready for his mouth that it's a fight not to push his head down toward it.

I shiver as his tongue traces one of my abs, and he scoops a berry up into his mouth.

Keller chews slowly, mouth on my skin, and then his eyes flick open, and he hooks mine. Even in the dim light, his eyes look black. He doesn't look away as he holds my sides, kneeling between my legs, and licks every last thing from my skin. It's a frustrating tease to have his mouth so close to where I want it, with him making no move to put me out of my misery.

"Keller, please."

And now I'm begging. Well, I never said I was cool.

I get his sexy, filthy grin. "Forgive me if I skip the peaches you picked," he says. "Because you already have one I'm dying to taste."

Then he grabs my legs, pulls them over his shoulder, and sinks to his front on the bed. His breath ghosts over my balls, and they're so tight and ready for him, but he goes on ignoring how badly I need to be touched.

Instead, he smears a blackberry over my taint before taking his time to lick it clean.

"Why are you torturing me?" I whine.

Keller's sexy smile widens, and he nips at my thigh. "I'm not. I'm tasting. Torturing you would be putting you in a cock ring and shoving a vibrator up your ass while I sucked you off for hours and didn't let you come."

My dick jumps at the image, and Keller's eyes lock onto the movement.

"You like that."

"I ... I think so."

Keller hums, filthy and low, before biting another strawberry in half and dragging it over my balls.

Yes.

The flat of his tongue runs over my sensitive skin, and I'm almost vibrating out of my body. The way he's worshiping my balls is beyond any fantasies I've ever had of him. They're wet with spit, his breath cooling my heated skin, and every time he sucks one into his mouth, his scruffy jaw scrapes my thighs. It's sensory overload.

"We're going to try it," he says, sounding as lust drunk as I am. "I want to see how thick and swollen your pretty cock can get before you cry. Before you beg. And then I'll keep going."

My thighs twitch tighter around his head. "And when you let me come?"

"You'll be riding my cock." He sucks two fingers into his mouth. "Just like you're about to do tonight."

"Thank god. I've been waiting so long."

"Shh ..." He kisses a line of soft kisses along my thigh as he presses his fingers against my hole. "You'll be wrapped around me soon, Will." Keller presses one finger inside. The stretch keeps me needy, but not on the edge, and when I glance down at his intense dark eyes and messy hair, my knees fold back to my chest. He looks every bit the Viking god I've always envisioned him as, and when he slowly drags his tongue along my length, I almost sob.

There's no way I'll survive him edging me for hours when I can hardly get through this.

"I don't know which tastes better. The sweet fruit or your salty skin."

"M-maybe you should have another try." *Please, please put me out of my misery.*

Keller only smirks and strokes his finger slowly before pressing a second one to my opening. I bear down to make it easier, his spit helping them push inside. Even though it's a little more painful this time, my cock doesn't flag. I'm so hard and needy just from the sight of him between my legs that when he fucks me, I doubt I'm going to last long. I've been dreaming about this for years, aching for it, never believing it could one day be reality.

But if I'm dreaming, I'll stay right where I am, thanks.

"That's it, open up for me."

His encouragement warms my whole body, but I'm still needy as fuck. I grope around for more of the fruit, and my hand closes over a peach. Fuck it.

I tear a side away with my teeth, then press it to my aching shaft. It's slick and soft, feels incredible as I jerk off with it, and Keller's attention locking onto the movement almost makes me blow. Then his fingers disappear from my ass as he takes it from my grip and swallows my cock in one go.

The sudden change from the cool juice to his hot mouth makes me ache. Makes me grip the blankets tight in an effort not to explode. Keller hums around my cock, taking me deeply before pulling back again, over and over, while I sink into total, mind-numbing bliss.

He licks his way over my tight balls, then my taint, all the way to my ass. His thick tongue gathers up the stickiness, leaving nothing behind. I'm barely more than a bundle of buzzing nerves as he hums and moans his way closer to my hole.

The first flick of his tongue over my rim is torture. He

circles it, slips inside, then pulls back before it can get me going. Over and over, he teases me. Over and over, I squirm and beg him to fuck me. Over and over, I'm treated to the deep groans rumbling in his chest.

His large hands close over my ass cheeks, and he pulls them apart. "That's such a pretty hole, Will. It needs to be filled, doesn't it?"

I whimper. "Please."

"On one condition."

"Anything."

"I'll fuck you with my tongue, but you're not allowed to play with yourself, got it?"

I nod before I even know what I'm agreeing to.

"Good. Because your cock is my new favorite toy, and I'm *very* possessive of my things."

How the hell am I supposed to survive this?

Keller's face disappears between my legs, and the scrape of his facial hair drives me crazy. He knows exactly what he's doing to get me to the edge, and by the time his large tongue presses inside, I'm not so sure I can take it. It's wet and thick and feels phenomenal fucking into my ass.

His teeth tease the nerves around my hole, fingers pushing in beside his tongue until I'm stretched wide. Keller eats me like he's starving for it, and I might have promised not to touch myself, but I'm not sure how much longer I can keep my word.

"You ready for me?"

"Shit, yes."

His chuckle is throaty and deep, and I try not to whine while he rolls a condom down his shaft and positions himself between my legs. "Is like this okay?"

"Perfect."

Keller dips his head to kiss me softly. "Good. I want to see how you look as you come."

"Then hurry up and make me do it."

"Who knew you were so bossy?"

"Bossy? Nope. This is needy. And it's completely your fault."

Keller wraps a hand around his shaft and presses the smooth tip to my hole. "Let me in, gorgeous."

My body sings with the compliment. I relax as he pushes forward, giving myself over to the stretch as I open around him. No matter how much Keller might have prepped me, it's nothing to the width of his cock, and I love the feel of him splitting me open.

Not only because it's sex and sex feels good.

But this is Keller Gibson.

Inside me.

Hovering over my body, intense gaze taking in every expression.

"You're taking me so well," he praises. "Your hole was made for me."

I shudder and spread my legs wider, wanting to take all of him. He slips in further, burying himself as deep as humanly possible until his balls press to my ass.

Keller leans forward and gathers me up in his arms. "You feel amazing."

"You can talk." My voice comes out gravelly. "I needed this so badly."

He rolls his hips, grinding his cock deeper, sending it over that little bundle of nerves that makes every other sensation come to a standstill.

"*Nrgh*," I choke out.

He chuckles, nosing along my jaw until his lips find the soft spot behind my ear. "Want me to do that again?"

"Yes, please."

"I love a man with manners," he mutters and rewards me with the most delicious hip flexes in history. His cock is grinding deep, but his abs have my needy dick trapped, and the dual sensations are a lot to take in.

"You're leaking everywhere," he says, one hand reaching between us to drag over the precum at my slit.

My thighs try to twitch together, but he's lying between them, stopping it from happening. "You send me into overdrive."

"What do you think you do to me? Christ, this body. I don't think I've ever seen something so sexy. Your sweet eyes, delicious cock, hungry hole."

"You just want me for my body," I joke, suddenly self-conscious.

Keller shakes his head, hair curtaining around me on one side. "I don't do relationships with just anyone. You've stolen all my good sense and made me break all my rules for you. I don't do complicated. I don't let anything get between me and my son. But walking away from you is fucking impossible, and it has nothing to do with your body." His thrusts pick up as he takes my hand and presses it to his chest. "You're in here. And nothing I do will ever get you out again."

I arch up to kiss him as he fucks me stupid. Keller kisses like he does with anything in life. So passionate and in control, so sure of exactly what he wants.

It's those things and more that fill my heart to the fullest.

He leans on one forearm while the other explores my body. From my neck to my shoulder, along my side and over my ass, then up and down my thigh. The way he's stroking every inch of skin sends warmth snaking through my chest. Keller sure knows how to make a guy feel special, and I've never felt as special as I do when he's touching me, murmuring encouragement, while absolutely wrecking my hole.

I hold him tighter. "Harder," I beg.

He gives it to me, presses my leg up to my chest and focuses all his efforts into his cock pistoning in and out of my ass. He pounds against me, numbing my ass cheeks and drawing a tingling sensation from my prostate that crawls over my skin.

My cock is pulsing hard and trapped between us, but I can't hold out from touching myself much longer.

"Please," I pant. "I need to jack off."

"You want to touch my things?" he growls against my ear.

"Yes. I need to."

"Will you take such good care of it?"

"I promise."

"Good. Because that cock's precious to me."

I tremble. "I'll be gentle."

"Will." He catches my eyes. "Don't be."

Keller pulls away slightly, giving me blessed relief as I wrap my hand around my desperate length. My cock pulses with the touch, balls already tight and needy. My whole body shifts with every one of Keller's thrusts, and I jerk off with purpose.

I'm rocked toward the edge, trying to hold off and come at the same time as him while knowing it's a losing battle. This orgasm is going to hit when it hits, and I'll be glad to welcome it when it does.

The burning under my skin increases. The pressure in my ass, my balls, my cock. I fucking *whimper* I'm so cross-eyed with lust.

"Come for me," Keller orders. "I know you want to."

I so, so do. Anything. I'll give him anything. I'd claim I'm just selfless like that, but the way I feel is anything but.

My pleasure grows, balloons out until I'm not able to focus on anything else. My cock thickens in my hand, and just when I think I can't take any more, I let go. Thick spurts, one after another, black out my brain and send me offline.

"Ah. Fuck. So tight." Keller grunts. Then he slams against my ass, slower, harder, milking out his orgasm.

He finally stills, pushing up onto his knees, chest heaving with each breath. His gaze catches on the cum drying against my skin. "You are so fucking beautiful."

"Come here and say it like you mean it."

33

KELLER

I'M STICKY ALL OVER AND FEEL INCREDIBLE. WE'RE BOTH covered in fruit, it's caked through my hair, there's cum drying between us, and the scent of sweat is heavy on the air.

But fuck, that was worth the wait.

Will's fingers dip into my hair before coming to a sudden stop. "It's all knotty," he complains.

"Yeah, it's a pain in the ass." My hair is thick and has a slight curl to it, so it doesn't take much for it to go wild. "I think I need to cut it off and be done with it."

"*What?*"

I chuckle into his neck. "It's long overdue. I like it, but it makes me look feral when I don't take the time to keep it under control."

"But then what will I hold on to when you're fucking my brains out?"

I shrug. "The bed? The counter? A swing?"

"Swing?"

"Whatever I'm fucking you on will work."

He chuckles and wraps a chunk of hair around his finger. "I love your hair."

"You do?"

He looks relaxed as hell. "What can I say? Feral does it for me. Reminds me that you fuck like a wild man."

"Oh, really?"

"Makes me feel like you want everything about me. I love how claimed you make me feel."

I run a hand from his chest to his abs before resting it over his soft dick. "Who the fuck wouldn't want all of this? It short-circuits my brain that you're giving it to play with whenever I want."

"Right back at you. But I really don't want you to cut your hair."

Considering I don't actually want to do it either, I'm not going to argue with him. "Deal. But I'm going to have to get up and wash it before something starts growing in there."

Will's eyes light up with amusement. "Can I?"

"Wash it?"

"Yeah."

I process the request for a moment. "I've never had anyone ask that before. But sure. If you want to."

"I want to. And we both need a shower anyway, so …"

I lift his hand and kiss it before standing and helping him up off the bed. "Let's do it."

There's nothing better than a good fuck. My body's relaxed, my mind is clear. There's a happiness in my gut that only increases every time I look at Will.

He leads the way into the bathroom, reaching into my shower to turn on the water, impressive back muscles flexing with each movement. His perky ass is marked with my fingerprints, and I've never seen a sexier sight.

"God, I'm so sticky," he complains, stepping in, head immediately tipping back under the spray. And while I want to step in after him, press against his back and map out his body with my hands, I give myself a moment to look. To admire.

His head tilts toward me, and his bright gray eyes flick open. He doesn't say anything, just looks at me with all the happiness bottled up inside him, and something happens that catches me completely off guard.

I look at Will and just see ... him.

His straight nose and square jaw. The deep eyes and soft lips. Quiet uncertainty and hidden confidence. I step into the shower and pull him to me.

Our lips brush softly, his chest close to mine, heart against heart, steely abs against my less defined ones.

Everything about this feels right.

Will's strong hands find my waist, squeeze, fingers splaying out over my skin, and I wonder what it would be like to have this always. It's been a question in my mind, a what-if, the barest possibility, but as we stand here and kiss in the shower, I know deep down this is more than that.

All those years between us. They started slow. Just a guy hanging around, bugging me, flirting with me. I'd assumed it was all innocent and fun, less interest and more of a tease. And maybe it was. But all those moments, all those years, they were building toward this.

Us.

We had to simmer then so we could burn now.

My mouth breaks from his, and I pull back to look at him. His stare is steady as he gazes back.

"You know how I'm always saying that I listen to my gut?"

Will swallows thickly. "What's it telling you about me?"

"That you're the man I've been looking for."

One side of his lips pulls up, a quiet version of his lopsided grin. "I've been dying to hear those words since we first met."

My eyebrows flex into a frown. "Since we first met?"

He doesn't seem at all embarrassed. "I didn't know whether to say anything. To let on what this means for me, but I can't hold it in. And I don't think you'd want me to."

"You can tell me anything."

"I know." He rests a hand on my chest. "I've had feelings for you for years. It started as a crush and has only gotten stronger, deeper, the longer I've known you. It's why I wasn't sure about moving in here with you at first, because I didn't know how to be around you one-on-one. At least when Molly was there, I didn't feel the pressure as much, you know?"

"Maybe if we'd had one-on-one time sooner, this would have happened sooner."

"Maybe." He smiles. "Probably not though. You had to get your slut era out of the way first."

My laugh bounces off the tiles. "You telling me you haven't had your fair share of fun?"

"Sure, I've had hookups, but ... none of them did it for me like you. I just stopped trying."

I hate that he had to wait so long for me, and it's blowing my mind to think that all the time I've known him, he's seen me that way, and I didn't know.

I know now though, and it only makes me more determined for this to work out.

"Now." Will pulls back and grabs my shampoo. "I've got a job to do. Turn around."

"Yes, sir."

"That's my line."

I close my eyes and feel the cool liquid pool on my head. "We might need to give that a test drive."

"I'll add it to our ever-growing list. Sir."

Will's fingers follow the shampoo into my hair, and he takes his time with it. His fingers dig slowly into my scalp, massaging it through my hair, kneading down my neck to my shoulders, and then back up again. He combs his fingers all the way to the ends, making my head prickle pleasantly. When he rinses it out again, I'm so relaxed and floaty my eyes fall closed.

Will kisses my exposed neck. "Conditioner next."

He repeats the whole process. And as I stand there, surrounded by the smell of vanilla, soothed by the warm water and Will's hard body brushing mine, I realize it's the first time ever that someone has taken care of me.

That's always been my job.

I've handled everything, raised Molly, supported us both. Proved everyone wrong.

And all it's taken is Will wanting to wash my hair to show me I don't have to do everything alone again.

As soon as he's finished washing the conditioner down the drain, I grab him, spinning us both and pressing him up against the tile. I kiss him until our lips are numb and the water's cold. Until I never want to remember a time before we started.

The heat is thick between us, but my cock isn't ready to rally again. Will's is though. It's trapped between my hip and his abs, trying to make its presence known.

So when I'm done kissing him—for now—I drop to my knees and kiss him in other places. With one finger up his ass and his cock in my throat, he shoots hard, and I swallow him down.

There's nothing like getting him off.

Nothing.

And the more certain I get about Will being serious, special, the more worried I become that Molly is going to freak out. A few weeks ago, if I'd had to choose between them, my son always would have been first. That's the way it's supposed to be for a parent.

But now?

How the hell do I choose between the son who means everything and the man who *could* mean the world? Will's the key to my happiness. He's everything I was looking for and kept failing to find because I subconsciously already knew. I'd already found him.

Molly makes me a dad, but Will makes me feel *human*.

Now I just have to hope like hell that Molly understands, because if he doesn't ...

I really don't want it to come down to a choice between my son and my happiness. I've made that choice too many times, and he's always come out on top. I don't know how to choose differently.

For the first time, that doesn't make me feel like a good father.

I hate keeping this from Molly, but I'm not ready to risk it ending so soon.

34

WILL

Keller and I fall into a rhythm. I'm hardly ever in my own bed anymore, and I can't say I hate it. Whether it's him fucking me or me fucking him or sharing some incredible blow jobs, our nights are a goddamn dream. Then we sleep all twisted up in each other and wake up to morning breath and knotted hair, and I never felt so damn lucky.

I'm just *happy*.

I can see this for me. For my life.

Living here with him and working from the office and catching up with his friends on the weekend. There's some kinda divorced guy thing happening that Keller is taking me to, and he said we're not gonna hide our relationship there. It means so much that he isn't trying to make me some dirty secret, that our relationship might mean to him what it already means to me.

The problem is, we still haven't told Molly, and I'm terrified he's going to find out before it can come from us. I don't want to push Keller, but I care about Molly too, and every day I'm with his dad behind his back fills me with nauseating betrayal.

The other thing playing on my mind is Joey. I'm supposed to be moving out with him in just under a month, and I'm not sure where I stand on all that. Keller wants me to stay, and if I'm totally honest, I want that too. But I gave my word to Joey, and having that conversation with him makes me nervous, especially because it doesn't seem smart to stay here. Between the relationship being new and Molly not knowing about us, officially living together full-time seems like a disaster waiting to happen.

I need to talk to Keller about all my worries, I know that, but things have been so fucking perfect I'm worried about screwing it all up.

"Nearly ready?" Keller yells up the stairs.

I jump, not realizing that I'd completely zoned out, and hurry to pull on my sneakers. "Coming!"

"You will be later!"

Aww, he says the sweetest things.

"You sure it's okay that you're bringing me?" I double-check as I jog down the stairs. "I don't want to crash some super-secret cool kids' club thing."

"Do me a favor and call it that in front of Art. I'm begging you."

I pull a face. "Do you want him to hate me?"

"Makes no difference to me, but his face would be priceless."

Well, at least I know there's no pressure to impress Keller's friends. I might have met them all before, but it wasn't as his boyfriend, and I know Keller doesn't give a shit about people judging our relationship, but I do.

Not because it will change my mind about anything but because I don't want the guy I love to have to deal with any of that."

I reach out and take his hand before he can move away. "What if someone sees us and tells Molly? This isn't like the farm. Killer Brew is right in the middle of town."

"It'll be okay."

I sigh, knowing I can't put it off any longer. "I spoke to Molly."

"And?" He's immediately on his guard.

"I didn't tell him," I hurry to clarify. "But we were talking, and he sounds good. Apologized for being so down."

"Well ... that's good."

"Yeah, except he said that *we* were part of the resentment."

Keller looks like I've slapped him. "What?"

"He said he hated that we were close. That you're his dad and I'm his friend and ..."

There's a lot going on behind Keller's eyes that I can't make out. His hand turns, grips tight to mine. "What else did he say?"

"About us?" I wish I could reassure him, but I've got nothing. "That was it."

"He *hates* it?"

I swallow thickly and nod, not trusting myself to talk.

"Fuck."

"I'm sorry."

My whisper catches his attention because those racing thoughts cut off as he makes eye contact. Slowly, he leans forward and presses his lips to mine. "This doesn't change anything."

"W-what?"

He pinches the bridge of his nose with his free hand. "We knew this wasn't going to be easy. But I have to believe Molly will come around. If I didn't believe that, I wouldn't have started this to begin with."

"Okay ..."

"So we keep doing what we're doing. Making sure this works. That it's what we want. If you're still in."

"Of course I am."

"Good." Keller kisses me again, and even though he doesn't seem like himself, the word is genuine. "Let's get moving."

Killer Brew is an imposing building right in the middle of town, and there isn't a single person who lives in town who doesn't hang out there often.

My worry over Molly might be low-key on the back burner, but my worry about going out as Keller's *boyfriend* isn't.

Even though I kinda know everyone who'll be here, and I'll have Joey for support, it doesn't stop me from being nervous as high hell when we climb the stairs behind the bar to where the sound of talking and music is. Unlike last time, it's not a casual meet-up. It looks like their entire group is here, and at least with thirty or so others occupying the space, no one's looking too closely at me.

Keller reaches over and takes my hand, setting loose the butterflies in my gut.

"Want a drink?"

"Nah, I'm so hyped up I might pee myself."

He laughs, lines by his eyes deepening. "Why am I picturing an excitable puppy?"

"Let me guess, you wanna add that to the list of things to try?"

"I'm game if you are."

At least that's one thing I know: we're never gonna get bored in the sex department. Last night, he ate the edible underwear off me, taking his time to nibble and suck my cock as much as the candies. The night before, I used the alien flower-looking Fleshlight on him while he rode me.

"Uh-oh," Keller mutters, turning me toward Art.

He's spotted us from across the room, and with his eyes trained on our joined hands, he makes a beeline our way.

"I did it!" he declares. "I'm a genius. All hail Art de Almeida!"

Joey appears from nowhere and elbows him in the ribs. "*You* did it? This was all me."

"I almost have to agree with you," I say. "The sex toys got him hooked."

Keller glances from me to Joey. "That was a setup?"

Joey shrugs. "Why do you think they were addressed to you and not him."

"Huh." He rubs his scruffy jaw. "I didn't even think about it."

"Too busy reaping the rewards," I tease.

"You know ... it actually wasn't totally the sex toys, so I don't know that Joey can take credit."

"Say what now?" Joey gasps.

Keller smirks at him. "Sorry to say that I was attracted to Will before that, but they gave us the excuse to cross those lines."

"I dunno," Art says. "It sort of sounds like it was all Joey. And if it was Joey, it was also me. Because we're partners, so basically, we're back on my original point. I'm a genius."

"Way to steal my thunder."

I scoff at Joey. "Way for both of you to steal mine. You heard Keller—he was already into me. The nervous stammering and idiotic blushing did the trick. I knew what I was doing all along."

"So we shouldn't mention the time you called, freaking out because Keller had arranged to hook up with someone?"

"You what?" Keller turns to me, and I quickly grab his arm, pulling him toward the bar.

"Suddenly thirsty. Wanna get me that drink now?"

"Will ..." The look Keller's pinning me with makes it very clear he's not about to take my avoidance.

"Yes?"

"You were upset?"

I sigh, resigned to get it out there. "Yeah. Obviously. I wanted it to be me."

"Shit, I'm sorry. You know that isn't something I ever would have done intentionally, right?"

"I know." I give him a sad smile, just needing to get it all out. "You had no clue how I felt."

"If it helps, I only wanted to plan that hookup because I was feeling awkward about all these new feelings I was having for you."

"Surprisingly, that does." A lot. "None of this is new to *me* except for you apparently feeling the same way. So yeah, I was upset, but I also don't blame you for it. My feelings are mine. I wouldn't be with you if I thought you'd ever hurt someone on purpose."

Keller pinches the bridge of his nose. "I am though."

"What do you mean?"

"Hurting someone on purpose. Two someones. The two someones who mean the most to me."

I tilt my head, waiting for him to clarify.

"You and Molly."

His words steal the breath from me. "I'm one of your most important people?"

"Yeah, is that really a surprise?"

"Kinda."

"Then you're underestimating my feelings for you. It might have taken me a minute to catch up, but I have. I want to tell Mols. I can't stop thinking about what he said, and you only just told me. I can't imagine how it's been for you."

I'm both excited that he's open to it and scared as hell. "How? Over the phone is—"

"Not happening. I can't. Maybe ... want to take a trip to Seattle?"

"Oh ... Ah, yeah. I guess. We could do that."

Keller's smile is small but genuine. "We have to trust him."

"We do. And I think it's less about not trusting Molly and more about the fact I have everything I ever wanted, and I can't see me getting to keep all this good."

"I'm not going anywhere."

"Not even if Molly makes you?"

Keller swallows, and I immediately wish I could take my question back. It's not fair on him. So, before he can answer one way or the other, I press my fingers to his mouth.

"I don't want you to answer that because I'd never ask you to choose me over him. But you're right, we need to trust him."

Keller kisses my fingertips, and it warms my doubt. "I don't want to brag, but he was raised by an awesome guy."

"You're right. We've got nothing to worry about."

I'm obviously talking out of my ass, and so is he, but there's nothing else we can do right now.

"Are you going to be okay if I head over and chat to Payne? He keeps throwing me looks."

"Yeah, of course."

Keller leans forward and kisses me softly. "Such a great boyfriend," he praises, making it hard to breathe. "So good for me."

Aaaand now my cock is trying to get hard. Just perfect.

Keller leaves, and Joey almost immediately takes his place.

"So how is living in heaven?"

"Constant orgasms, snuggles, and food? It's the worst."

"Total shit show." He cocks his head while I order a soda. "You know ... your agreed rent doesn't cover those things at my place."

His probing tone makes me stop. "How much extra would I have to pay for the full service?"

"More than you could afford. And I'm not talking about money. Art would kill you."

Considering the ridiculous display he put on when he thought I was flirting with Joey, I don't doubt it. "What are you saying?"

Joey crosses his arms over the countertop. "You're always welcome to move in. That hasn't changed, and it doesn't have to happen in August either. I'm only saying that we're both in different places compared to when we had that chat, and you don't need to be all Will about it. I don't want you overthinking and worried about hurting my feelings."

Apart from my name being used as an adjective, the rest floods me with relief. I reach over and pull Joey into a hug. "You're the best."

"Not new information."

Of course that's his response. I pull back. "I was right in making friends with you."

"Dude, I'm the one who high-school friended you, okay? Yet another example of me being the greatest."

"As long as you think so."

Joey orders a beer and turns back to me. "You know what you want to do yet?"

"Nope. Is that okay? If you need an answer—"

"I don't. The room's either yours or it's no one's. Take your time. I mean, it might be too soon for you guys to be living together, but then you might find out you like it as well."

"So far, I really do."

"Good. Go with that, then, and let me know if anything changes."

Well, that's one problem down, one more to go.

Joey was the easy part though. We don't have a deep history, and he's always been a relaxed guy. Molly is another story completely.

I'm so excited to see him again. I only hope when he hears the news that he feels the same.

DMC GROUP CHAT

Keller: **Mack added to group chat**
Keller: **sends photo**
Keller: *On our way to see Molly. Wish us luck!*
Orson: *Good luck!*
Griff: **crossed fingers**
Payne: *It's going to be great!*
Mack: *It's fiiiiine. Planes take this trip all the time. Nothing to worry about.*
Keller: *Well, I wasn't worried about THAT, but I am now.*
Art: *Don't listen to him. You're mere hours away from letting go of the secret, embracing your new life, and getting celebration sex that comes with your son's seal of approval.*
Keller: *Oh no, we have to turn ours phones off now, I can't read all your replies byeeeee ...*

35

KELLER

I WHITE-KNUCKLE THE ARMREST AS THE PLANE STARTS ITS descent. This is unnatural. So high. All I can picture is us nosediving into the ground and my son having to see this shit go up in flames.

Will's hand covers mine. "I can't believe you've never been on a plane before."

"Never needed to."

"You're okay."

"I'll be okay when my damn feet are on the damn ground," I get out through my clenched teeth.

Will's big eyes turn sympathetic. "Just think, we'll have three whole days before we have to do this all again."

I groan and cover my face with my free hand. I've already bought the tickets, and we both need to be back at work on Monday, but we could drive back, right? If we leave tomorrow and drive nonstop, surely we could make it? I can't even math right; my brain is up too high to function.

"Just remember that Molly's waiting for us. Half an hour and we'll get to see him again."

"If my kid doesn't have to watch us plummet to our death."

To Will's credit, he doesn't laugh. It's just as well because I don't think I could take it at the moment. My gut is in knots, anxiety thrumming over my skin, and I'm not so sure I won't be sick all over our shoes.

"You're doing amazing. And luckily for you, I'm not someone who's all that interested in traveling. The furthest we'll ever need to fly is right here. Seattle, then home. That's it."

That's if Molly's planning to talk to us again after this visit. The standoffishness since he left doesn't give me a lot of hope, but I raised him the best I could, and I just have to cross my fingers that's enough.

Will's hand tightens around mine. "Hey."

I glance up, and like always, he takes my damn breath. The earnest gray eyes, the serious set to his square jaw, the way he blinks a couple of times faster the second we make eye contact.

"Umm ... I've suddenly forgotten what I was going to say." His voice deepens, thumb brushing back and forth over the side of my hand.

"Molly needs to be okay with this." I don't mean to say it, but the way he makes my chest warm feels too right to ignore. The feeling is almost panicky, desperate, that all it would take is Molly saying he isn't okay and then I lose what Will and I have for good.

There's no way I'll be able to move on after him.

I might have been able to fool myself into going on dates, thinking I could find this with just anyone, but now I've had it with Will, I know how high the bar really is. What I feel for him can't be replaced, and I don't think I'd ever want it to be.

"I'm scared," he says, almost echoing my thoughts.

"Yeah, me too."

"He'll be okay, right? He has to be."

I chuckle, but there's nothing funny about it. "I'm about to tell my son I'm dating his best friend. I don't think there's any set way for this to go down."

"I can't lose him," Will whispers. "But there's no way I can walk away from you either."

"You won't," I say with confidence I don't feel. "And Molly loves us both. That has to mean something. Maybe it'll catch him by surprise, but he wants us to be happy as much as we want that for him."

Will nods like he's trying to convince himself, turning back to the front of the plane. And when I'm jolted and thrown back into my seat, I realize we've landed. It might not have been the happiest conversation, but it took my mind off it, and we're finally, *finally*, back on land.

For now.

The whole time we're waiting to deboard and walking through the terminal, Will and I don't talk much. We don't touch either, and considering I could use his comfort, that's the part I hate the most.

I throw him a quick smile before we head out into arrivals. "We got this."

His answering smile makes my heart do fucking cartwheels. "We do."

And even though I can't take his hand like I want to, it makes it easier to keep moving. We're in this together, and if we can get through this, it means no more hiding. No more discounting what we have or feeling like I'm letting Molly down by keeping this from him.

The second we step into arrivals, I scan the crowd for a head of messy brown hair. My heart is in my throat, and the second I lock eyes with Molly and his whole face lights up, all my worry leaves me.

He runs our way, and I open my arms, prepared for the impact. Molly doesn't disappoint. His thin frame hits me with enough force to jolt the air from my lungs, and my arms immediately close around him. His head tucks perfectly under my chin, and I pull him in tight, missing this. As much as I feel for Will, Molly's my son. Nothing is ever going to change that.

"You've been gone too long, bub."

Molly pulls away. "I was at college for way longer."

"Yeah, but it wasn't on the other side of the country."

"Okay, Dad." Molly rolls his eyes, but he's smiling. And when he turns and hugs Will, they grip tight to each other. The good mood that hit me when I saw Molly ebbs. If he's upset, it's not just our relationship it'll affect, and I'm coming at it from the position of his dad. Our relationship will take a lot to destroy, but him and Will?

Guilt trickles into me.

"Let's get our bags," I say, breaking up their hug. I can't stand around doing nothing anymore. I need to move. Need to get this nervous energy out.

"In a hurry?" Molly asks, trying to keep up.

"Hungry. I want to get out of here and get some food."

"Ooh, can we go out for lunch? It's been forever since I went to a restaurant."

"You're not dating?" I ask.

I'm not sure I need to know the answer to that question, given Molly's history, but I would have assumed he was.

Molly gives me a sly look. "I'm not, because ..."

"Because ..."

"It's new, so we'll see."

Well, that's a big jump from the phone call I got from him a few weeks ago. He was crying so hard I couldn't understand what he said.

"Everything okay with you?" I ask, spotting my bag and getting ready to grab it.

"Yep. I'm actually doing well. This move was good for me."

Well, that's a point in our favor. And after I grab Will's and my bags, I take a second to look him over. Molly *does* look good. Happy. Like he used to. There's none of that guardedness in his eyes that was getting more and more common before he left.

"You *look* good," Will says. "Whoever this guy is, I like him already."

Molly laughs. "I haven't told you anything about him."

"Doesn't matter. He makes you happy, and that's enough for me."

They're the same words I hope Molly throws back at us later, but I know Will. He's being sincere. I'm not sure I have the same requirements—Molly's ex made him happy initially, and look how that turned out—but if Molly can give us this, I'm going to have to bite my tongue and welcome any future boyfriends Molly has with open arms.

"So ..." Molly shoots a sly look my way. "How's dating going?"

I grunt. "Couldn't even let me get out of the airport, could you?"

"I'm curious!"

I make the mistake of glancing over at Will, who looks like he might be sick. Instead of answering, I shake my head, completely clueless about how we're going to get through this. "Food first. Talking later."

But avoiding anything with Molly doesn't work. He gasps. "You've found someone."

"Did I say that?"

"You didn't have to." He clutches his hands to his chest. "Quick, Will, where's a cafe? A taco truck? A McDonald's—anything! We need the tea."

Will shuffles his feet. "Let the man eat, Mols."

Molly huffs. "Fine. But the second you're fed, I'm getting it out of you."

That's exactly what I'm worried about.

36

WILL

KELLER IS EATING SO. DAMN. SLOWLY. MY BURGER WAS gone ten minutes ago, and Molly's fries were gone not long after.

But my man is eating every damn thing in his salad piece by piece, and I'm *twitching*.

Molly scowls his way and turns to me. "What's new with you?"

"Ah, nothing much." My gaze darts toward Keller. "Just ... saving money. Working." Sleeping with your dad. Hot damn, I really, really need this over and done with.

"No men in your life?"

Well, it's not like I can outright lie, can I? I'm on edge trying to think of how the hell I answer that when Keller speaks up.

"Actually, he's been too busy helping me."

Molly's attention snaps back toward his dad so fast it's

like it was on a timer. "Helping? Find you a boyfriend? My plan worked?"

I snort a laugh into my drink that they both ignore, but I'm so goddamn nervous. The only thing I *can* do is try to shake off the tension infecting my bones. "Let's all remember this was your plan," I mutter.

That gets Molly's attention. He glances between us both. "What's going on?"

Keller sighs, trying for a smile as he reaches for Molly's hand. "You know you're everything to me, right?"

Molly's eyebrows fall, which doesn't seem like a good sign.

"Your opinion means the world."

"Dad, you're scaring me."

"Nothing like that," I jump in. "Nothing's ... wrong." At least not to me.

Molly might have a totally different idea about what we're about to tell him.

"Will's right." I watch Keller's hand twitch tighter around Molly's. "I'm actually feeling better than I have in a long time."

"So ..."

Keller takes a deep breath. "So ..." His dark eyes flick up and meet mine, setting my nerves to a thousand. I can't lose him. I can't lose Molly either though. I've never been in the kind of position where I'm so goddamn torn every shred of my happiness hinges on this moment.

A moment that stretches on ... and on ... and—

"We're dating!" The words burst from me before I can stop them, and the second they're out, sheer relief and terror hit me at once. That was not at all the gentle way we were planning to break the news to him, but hey, at least I didn't shout *your dad's cock was in my mouth last night!* Small mercies.

Molly tugs his hand back from Keller's. "W ... hat?"

"Oh my god." I drop my face into my hands. "Oh my fucking god."

"*Will.*"

I glance up at Keller's voice, and something powerful passes between us. Something that helps calm my panic by the most tiny, little baby amount.

Keller sets his jaw and turns to my best friend, who still hasn't said anything. He's glancing between me and his dad with those big eyes of his, and all it does is make me wanna climb under the table and hide.

"Yes, we're dating," Keller says. "It's very, very new, but I've never felt for someone what I feel for Will. He's an amazing man."

"You think I don't know that?" Molly whispers, and at least he sounds dazed rather than outright angry.

"He makes me happy, bub. And I'm sorry if that's uncomfortable for you—trust me when I say we both tried to stay away from each other out of respect for you, but ..."

I force myself to pick up where Keller left off and speak from the ache in my chest. "I've loved Keller for a really, really long time. Years, Mols. And I hated myself for it because I felt like I was betraying you, but I kept it under wraps. I pushed it down. Tried to date other guys, but it never felt right. Just made me sad. Even now, if you tell me to walk away, I will. I'd never want to come between you two, but my dumb heart won't listen to my head, and now I'm in this mess where I'm terrified I'm gonna lose you both."

"Us both?" he parrots.

"You're my best friend. I love you. And I hate this. But after years of trying, Keller's the only man I could ever see myself wanting more with, and I'd really like to try."

"We know we're hitting you with a lot," Keller says. "And I know you came here to work on yourself, but we couldn't go on without talking to you, and this isn't the type of conversation you have over the phone. If you need time, it's yours. Just please don't be angry. Will's right that we'll walk away if you ask us to—I always have and always will put you first—but I'm going to be real here for a moment because I think you need to hear it: leaving him will destroy me. There hasn't been a single person in my life I've felt strongly enough about to risk our relationship, so please understand that I'm not doing this lightly."

Then Keller's big hand crosses the table and closes around mine this time. I grip him back just as tightly, barely breathing, while I wait for Molly to stop gaping at us and just *say* something.

Life slowly comes back into Molly's features. "You two are ... together?"

"Yes."

"Like ... romantically?"

And a whole lot more than that I'm not going to elaborate on. I just stare at him, too sick to say anything.

Then Molly does the last thing I'm expecting: he throws his head back and laughs.

Keller and I exchange a glance while Molly breaks into full, body-shaking giggles. "You ... together. You're together."

"Mols ..."

"Holy fucking *shit* was I off base."

Keller frowns. "What do you mean?"

"I thought ... I thought ..." He can't get the words out. And I have no clue what the hell is so goddamn funny, but he's not yelling, so ... maybe this is better? I'm too confused to be sure though. "I thought that ... I was jealous because ... because ... I thought you wanted Will to be your *son*."

What.

The.

Unholy.

Fuck?

"Excuse me?" Keller asks as the hysteria seeps from Molly.

He slumps, smiling, staring at us like he's concerned for our sanity. "I've been jealous of you guys for about a year now because you're so close. I thought ..." He hiccups a laugh. "I literally thought you saw Will as a better son than me. I hated all the time you spent together because I felt like I was being replaced."

Keller's as stunned as I am. "Better ... son?"

"Replaced?"

Molly shrugs, and Keller leans right over until Molly has to look at him.

"That's fucking impossible. There will never, *ever* be a better son than you."

Molly's bottom lip shakes, and he throws himself into Keller's arms. Seeing how quickly Molly's swung from uncontrollable amusement to sobbing makes me want to join them. To hug him tight and apologize over and over. I knew he was having a rough year, but I didn't realize that I was actively making it worse.

"I'm *so* sorry."

He pulls back, drying under both his eyes, and offers me a watery smile. "Actually, I'm sorry. For thinking the worst.

I got it into my head that because your parents are so shitty that you were trying to steal mine."

"Never."

"Well, I know that *now*." He lets out a long exhale. "Gotta say, it's a relief to know that Dad didn't want to adopt you. He wanted to bone you."

I scrunch up my face. "Maybe that's one side of our friendship that we don't talk about." Even though I mean to sound confident, it doesn't come out that way. It's obvious to all of us what I'm asking: are we still friends after this?

Molly grins. "Deal."

Keller relaxes back into his chair, long legs stretching out. "Not that I'm not thrilled with this turn of events, but that went a lot easier than I thought it would."

Molly snags a stray slice of pepper off Keller's plate and nibbles on the end. "I've been doing good here. And I actually learned that if I have to chase people to be in my life, they probably aren't supposed to be in it. I've never had to chase either of you. And I'm sorry for being so moody—I guess you both made me feel safe, and I took advantage of that."

"We can deal with the moody," I assure him. Because we can. I'd never expect him to be perfect all of the time, so long as he gives me the same right back.

Molly shoots me a look. "Already talking like a *we*? Damn, am I going to have to start calling you Daddy, Will?"

My face floods hot. "No. Hell no."

"Stepdaddy, then?"

Keller tsks. "Stop embarrassing him."

"But it's what he'll be if you two get married."

"Why don't you let us give this relationship thing a go before you start trying to marry us off."

"But it would be so beautiful! Only ... whose side would I stand on? I'd have to keep jumping back and forth. Best man for both of you, obviously, and—"

Keller whacks him over the back of the head. "You're *my* son. I'll chain you to my side if I have to."

I splutter. "He's *my* best friend. Are you gonna deny me my best friend on my wedding day?"

"But you can steal my son from me?"

Molly clutches his chest. "The planning has already started."

"Fuck me." Keller runs his fingers through his thick hair. "Can we go back to the point before we told you?"

"Nope," I answer before Molly can. "I like knowing my entire world isn't going to crash and burn, thanks."

His eyes soften as Molly laughs and kisses me on the cheek.

"You really thought I'd be mad?"

"Like you said, you've been a grump lately, so I didn't know how it would go. I get it now"—unfortunately, *yikes*—"but I had a lot riding on this."

"Well, other than having to deal with the grossness of knowing you've seen my dad naked, I'm excited. You're both my favorite people, and knowing you're each other's favorite people, too, makes me happy. It also helps me feel less guilty about the move."

"A minute ago, you were jealous of how close we were, and now you're okay with us dating?"

Molly nods enthusiastically. "My roommates have been good for me. I'm not going to lie, if this had happened before I moved, I don't think I would have been okay. I was lonely then, and it was like you both didn't even care if I was there or not. I know that wasn't the case, but I was feeding into the negativity. I'm really close with two of my roommates, and they have a ... *unique* relationship that's taught me a lot about sharing. That just because a person in your life needs someone else, it doesn't mean they need you any less." Molly looks up, brown eyes pinning me. "If I have to share my dad with anyone, I'm glad it's you."

It's my turn to hug him, and the relief is making my eyes a bit wet. Him being in Seattle will never not make me sad and miss him, but knowing how good it's been helps.

Molly needed this.

And I needed him to be okay with how I feel about Keller.

"After that," Keller says, "we all need a drink."

I couldn't agree more.

And when they're brought over to our table, we catch up just like old times. Molly is the Molly I first became friends with, and that guardedness is gone.

I can't believe how lucky I've gotten.

37

KELLER

Will's crying. Full cheek-staining tears that make my already hard cock throb. I lean down so I can lick the salty taste from his skin, and he bucks under me. His hands are handcuffed above his head, and every time he struggles, it makes his impressive biceps bulge.

"Babe, please," he whines. "Please, please, please."

There's no sweeter sound than his begging. It gets me every time. Pulls up a need I never knew I had to give Will everything.

His poor dick and balls are a beautiful red color and sexily swollen. I run my hand over his shaft again, slippery with precum and lube, before pulling away. The sound he lets out is hardly human.

"I hate you."

"No, you don't," I rasp, dragging my teeth over his nipple. "You love me. That's why you're being so perfect. So good. Damn, Will, you know just how to turn me on. I've never seen a prettier cock than yours before."

He moans deep, and I know how much the compliments turn him on. About as much as seeing how painfully hard he is turns me on. I'm not a sadist by any means, but torturing him with pleasure is something I'll never get enough of. All I ever want is to make Will feel good.

Even if he has to work for it.

"I'm in so much pain," he says, more tears slipping from beneath his tightly squeezed eyes.

"One word and it's all over."

He grits his teeth. "I'd say it if I thought you'd actually let me orgasm."

"Yeah, but that's cheating." I duck my head lower to flick my tongue over his slit.

Will hisses but still doesn't say the word.

Fine by me. Besides, I don't know how much more I can take either. I reach back and tug out the butt plug I shoved up my ass before we got started, and Will tracks the movement.

"What's all that?"

"Who knew my boyfriend was so impatient," I sigh.

Then I crawl up the bed, snag the ball cap from his head, and tug it on backward. "You ready for this?"

"Yes. *Fuck*. Come on. Please, baby, do it."

"Such good manners."

Will chuckles, but it sounds painful, and so I finally put him out of his misery.

I straddle his hips, grab the base of his swollen cock, and slowly sink down onto him.

"Yes," he cries, thrusting up into me. "Yes, yes. I'm not gonna last long, Kels."

Just as well because I don't plan on it either.

I ride him hard, buzzing with the force of his cock pegging my prostate. His body beneath me is all hard muscle and narrow waist and broad, round shoulders that I want to sink my teeth into. Will is so incredibly sexy, but knowing what a sweetheart he is inside only makes him ten times hotter.

My hard cock bobs between us, wanting to get in on the action. I'm so close already though, balls aching with the delicious thrumming filling every one of my limbs, barely able to hold out for the moment I cover him in my cum.

"So close." He grunts. "Almost there."

His movements stutter beneath me, and I take that as the marker to jerk off like my life depends on it. With each *slap* as my ass meets his hips, I barrel closer to the edge. I'm close, aching, getting a taste of what Will has been going through as I edged him. Only my hole is wonderfully full, giving my ass something to hold on to while I take Will's pummeling.

"Right now," he growls, almost bowing off the bed.

My orgasm crashes into me, balls tight and throbbing with glorious release as my cum coats his chest and abs. Will's eyes roll back as his body locks up and his cock twitches inside me. It's a floaty, addictive, mind-spinning moment as I collapse onto him, and his softening cock slips out of my ass.

I gather him into my arms, my legs twisting with his. "Gimme a second to catch my breath and I'll free you."

"My arms or my cock?"

"Both. I'm considerate like that."

He chuckles and nudges my head until I look up at him, and he draws me into a long, deep kiss. The kind of kiss that's slow and all tongue and exactly what I need from him.

I might take control while we're fucking, but there's no question about who's in control the rest of our damn lives. I'm whipped for him.

I have to force myself to break away and unlock his wrists. As soon as they're free, I press a line of soft kisses to the red marks on one and then the other. His cock and balls are next. The condom goes first. He's soft, but I add a tiny bit of lube to make removing the ring easier, and then I give it the same treatment as his wrists.

Will relaxes into the bed as I press featherlight kisses over his length and sac.

"Wanna shower?" he asks, pulling me against him.

"Always."

"Can I wash your hair?"

I smirk. "*Always*."

A cheeky glint hits his eyes. "Will we be like this forever?"

I surprise him by shaking my head. "I expect it'll only keep getting better from here."

38

FOUR MONTHS LATER

WILL

"We're going to a teddy bear's picnic?" I ask.

"Yup."

"For ..."

"Art's niblings. It's not my thing either, but he low-key threatened us all to be there to fundraise for the school, and Orson pointed out that it must be important since Art usually keeps us as far as possible from his family."

"Art doesn't seem like the kind of man who knows what private is though."

"When it comes to his niblings, he does."

Considering all the DMC events I've been to as Keller's boyfriend, I've gotten to know him pretty well. Not to mention all the double dates he and Joey drag us on. If Art wasn't so possessive, I'd think they were gearing up for a partner swap situation.

And as much as I joke around with them that they only want to see Keller naked, the close friendship the four of us have developed means a lot to me. Even if something did come between our relationship, I know the DMC guys enough to have friends on the other side of it.

Thankfully, we're stronger than ever with no signs of slowing down.

I'd been nervous about staying with him instead of moving in with Joey. It was a lot of pressure to put on a new relationship, but everything with Keller is easy. He's laid-back, no bullshit, and actually talks to me if there's an issue so we can both work through it.

The last six months haven't been perfect ... they've been even better. With every new blip we've faced, we've ended up stronger than ever.

I wrap an arm around his shoulders and pull his large, warm frame against me. "What will you give me if I'm on my best behavior today?"

Keller throws me a look. "My cock."

"Excellent."

"With that demonic schlong right alongside it."

I shiver, both scared and excited. Our sex life is everything I never thought it could be. And sure, we're only six months in, and things will probably slow down at some point, but I don't care either way. Sex with him blows my fucking mind, but so does just being with him. I'll take Keller in whatever way he wants.

Even if that way includes a demonic DP.

"And just like that, I have the sudden urge to be a goddamn preacher boy."

"Amen."

We grin at each other, and before I can stop him, Keller snags my cap and pulls it down over his hair.

"Got to be sun safe."

"What about me?"

"Your young skin will be fine."

I pretend to pout, but we both know I love him wearing my cap. There's absolutely nothing to stop him from wearing his own, but the WHU is all me. And I'm oddly primal about people knowing it.

Plus, he just looks really fucking hot in a hat.

"That look you're giving me isn't very good."

"You're exploiting my weakness."

We get to the large field where the festival is being held and arch our necks around the little booths and kids' activities set up to see if we can spot anyone.

Joey's the first person I see, right in the middle of a sea of picnic blankets full of club members and their partners. We approach them and say hi to a few people I know.

Mack waves us over to where he's kneeling next to a cooler. "Want a drink?"

"Yeah, Coke. Thanks," I say while Keller opts for a water.

My eyes land on another guy not too far away. He has black curly hair and a lot of freckles.

"Why does he look familiar?" I ask Keller.

Keller chuckles. "You might have tried to set me up with him at some point."

"I *did*?"

"Yeah, when we were looking at that dating app."

The memory comes back to me, but it's kinda murky. I'm so glad that whole thing never worked out, but I'd go through all that pain again to end up here.

Mack interrupts us. "Davey's on a dating app?"

Keller's face pales. "This was a while ago. It might not even have been him."

Mack nods, doing that thing where he's trying to smile and failing. He slowly closes the lid of the cooler and stands up. "Good. Great. Nice day for it. All the ... sun. Might go see Art and, uh, the teddy bears ..."

He wanders away before I can work out what the hell that was.

"Why did you lie to him?" I ask Keller, who's staring off the way Mack left.

"He's still in love with Davey. And I'm ninety percent sure Davey is still in love with him."

"Then—"

"Don't know. Not our business." He tugs me closer by the belt loops. "I just know that if anything happened between us and I found out you were on a dating app, I wouldn't be okay either."

"Seems like an easy solution to me, then."

"Oh, yeah?"

I give him a quick kiss. "Don't leave me and I won't need to make you jealous like that."

He chuckles. "Deal."

And as I stare into his face, a chunk of hair unsettled by the breeze, deep eyes looking so deep inside me they take my breath away, I couldn't imagine ever losing this. Keller and I are just *right*. Destined. The fact everything's worked out is more than I ever would have dared to dream about a year ago.

But here we are.

Him.

Me.

So fucking happy my heart could explode.

Keller has overloaded every part of my life, and I wouldn't have it any other way.

"I love you so much," I say.

He smiles softly, thumb lightly brushing my jaw. "Fine," he says, dropping his voice. "You know just what cards to play to get some demon dick."

I laugh, but he cuts me off with a swift kiss.

"I love you too, Willy-boy. Now. Always. Forever."

EPILOGUE
EIGHT MONTHS LATER

KELLER

I SIP MY COFFEE, WATCHING MY MAN CART A HEAVY wheelbarrow of soil across the yard to the garden. He's shirtless, body glistening with sweat and covered in dirt, and all it does is make me think of all the things I'd like to be doing to that body ... if we didn't have a flight to catch in a couple of hours.

As always when we head to Seattle, I'm too useless with nerves to do anything. Will, on the other hand, just takes it like any other day. He's so relaxed over everything, and it makes us fit. Usually. Right now though, I'm trying not to rattle out of my skin.

The coffee isn't helping.

"I can hear your panic from here," he calls.

"No panic. Don't know what you're talking about."

"You're sweating worse than me." He sets down the wheelbarrow and pumps his eyebrows in my direction.

"Shouldn't have bothered to get dressed at all. I could have used the view while I worked."

Well, then. I reach for the back of my shirt, pulling it off in one swift movement. Then I flex my muscles, just a little.

Will takes off his cap and fans himself with it. "Damn, babe, I'm trying to work here."

"You asked for it."

"Yeah, but apparently, I forgot about how you short-circuit my brain. Where am I? What was I doing?"

"I've been asking the same questions since you got up at stupid o'clock."

Will jogs over the yard and up the stairs to pull me into a kiss. He presses his sun-warmed skin against mine, and I pull him closer, running my hands under his gym shorts to palm his sexy ass. I'll never get tired of this. The sexual attraction between us has only gotten stronger the more we learn each other's bodies. The more we grow as a couple. The more I get to know who he is inside as well as out.

Will fills my chest with a happiness that goes so deep it's bonded to me. Keller and Will. Will and Keller. I don't want to even try and picture my life without him in it.

"Maybe I can call it a day and leave everything where it is while we can take a shower together?"

I groan because I know what he's doing. "Fine. I'll help."

His grin is immediate. "If you insist."

We spend the next hour turning over soil and filling the garden beds, and once we're done, I drop down onto the grass. It's hot for so early, but I actually love it. Especially when Will flops down beside me and props his head on my shoulder.

It's not until I'm looking at the sky that I remember our flight to see Molly and meet his boyfriend. Officially.

"You distracted me." I laugh because, somehow, he always does.

Will rolls onto his side and reaches up to run his knuckles down my cheek. "You know I hate to see you stress."

"I don't know how you do it so easily."

"I'd joke it's because you're obsessed with me, but"—he shrugs—"I just know you, Kel. You're mine. It's my job to pick up on these things and fix them."

"Fix them?"

"Yeah, because it's something you can't fix yourself. You need that extra help. Like you fix it when I get all in my head about my parents."

"I hate them." I've only spoken to them once, over the phone, and after telling them exactly how much their bigoted views have made them miss out on with him, I'm willing to bet that feeling is returned.

"I know, but you love me and always remind me you do, and that's the part that's important."

"That fixes you, huh?"

"Yes. When I start getting bummed out that I don't have any family, I remember you and Mols. I remember that I have a whole lot of friends. And I remember Molly's boyfriend, Seven, who's joining our family too."

My lips pinch at Seven's name. I think, deep down, no one is ever going to be good enough for my son. Him being cheated on didn't only affect him, and it makes it hard for me to trust that Molly won't be taken advantage of, especially considering Seven's had a hard life.

But Molly supported my relationship, so I'm going to set aside everything and support his. He's a grown man who can make his own decisions.

I'll do it for him.

And I'll do it for Will.

I'll do anything for Will—which is why all the tabs on my laptop are open to the same thing right now.

How to adopt.

The thought fills me with nervous anticipation, but raising Molly was the best thing I ever did with my life until Will. I want to give that to him. I want to give him more avenues for all that love he's got. I *want* to have another kid. With him.

I already know he's going to say yes, because I know Will. It's like he said. He's mine. But it's still a conversation I have to build myself up for, and if he surprises me and isn't interested, that's okay too. He gets to be the one to make that call.

All that matters is I have him.

THANK YOU SO MUCH FOR READING!

Want to find out what's up with Molly?
You can grab his book here:
https://geni.us/notmaterial

And to read my next book before it's released, see awesome character art, and get bonus content, check out my Patreon:
https://geni.us/saxonpatreon

Look out for Mack's book, coming 2024.

AUTHOR'S NOTE

Thanks so much for reading these gorgeous guys!

The fact you keep showing up for me, release after release, means the absolute world! My dream has always been to have a career as an author and it's mind-blowing to me that I get to live it.

If you're a lover of signed paperbacks, special editions, audiobooks or merch, don't forget to check out my store.

You can find it through the link or QR code: www.saxonjamesauthor.com

MY FREEBIES

Do you love friends to lovers?
Second chances or fake relationships?
I have two bonus freebies available!

Friends with Benefits
Total Fabrication
Making Him Mine

This short story is only available to my reader list so follow the below and join the gang!

https://www.subscribepage.com/saxonjames

OTHER BOOKS BY SAXON JAMES

ACCIDENTAL LOVE SERIES:

The Husband Hoax

Not Dating Material

The Revenge Agenda

FRAT WARS SERIES:

Frat Wars: King of Thieves

Frat Wars: Master of Mayhem

Frat Wars: Presidential Chaos

DIVORCED MEN'S CLUB SERIES:

Roommate Arrangement

Platonic Rulebook

Budding Attraction

Employing Patience

System Overload

NEVER JUST FRIENDS SERIES:

Just Friends

Fake Friends

Getting Friendly

Friendly Fire

Bonus Short: Friends with Benefits

RECKLESS LOVE SERIES:

Denial

Risky

Tempting

CU HOCKEY SERIES WITH EDEN FINLEY:

Power Plays & Straight A's

Face Offs & Cheap Shots

Goal Lines & First Times

Line Mates & Study Dates

Puck Drills & Quick Thrills

PUCKBOYS SERIES WITH EDEN FINLEY:

Egotistical Puckboy

Irresponsible Puckboy

Shameless Puckboy

Foolish Puckboy

Clueless Puckboy

STAND ALONES WITH EDEN FINLEY:

Up in Flames

FRANKLIN U SERIES (VARIOUS AUTHORS):

The Dating Disaster

And if you're after something a little sweeter, don't forget my YA pen name

S. M. James.

These books are chock full of adorable, flawed characters with big hearts.

https://geni.us/smjames

WANT MORE FROM ME?

Follow Saxon James on any of the platforms below.
www.saxonjamesauthor.com
www.facebook.com/thesaxonjames/
www.amazon.com/Saxon-James/e/B082TP7BR7
www.bookbub.com/profile/saxon-james
www.instagram.com/saxonjameswrites/

ACKNOWLEDGMENTS

As with any book, this one took a hell of a lot of people to make happen.

The cover was created by the talented Rebecca at Story Styling Cover Designs with a gorgeous image by Wander Aguiar, and edits were done by Sandra Dee at One Love Editing, with Lori Parks proofreading the bejeebus out of it.

Thanks to @caravaggia13 on IG for once again creating amazing artwork and to Charity VanHuss for being the most amazing PA I could have ever dreamed up. Without you I'd be even more of a chaotic disaster and there isn't enough space to list the many hats you wear for me.

Eden Finley, thank you for being there for all the doubt spirals and hand-holding. Whether you wanted to be or not. AM Johnson, Becca Jackson, Louisa Masters and Riley Hart thank you so much for taking the time to read. Your support is incredible and I really appreciate it!

And of course, thanks to my fam bam. To my husband who constantly frees up time for me to write, and to my kids whose neediness reminds me the real word exists.

Printed in the USA
CPSIA information can be obtained
at www.ICGtesting.com
JSHW020744160224
57396JS00001B/1

9 781922 741349